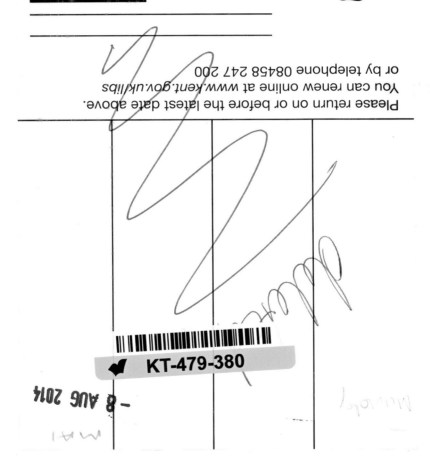

And then there was *him*.

The young man with hair like a Viking. The moment Anna had seen him the most ridiculous idea had jumped into her head—a most ridiculous, yet dangerously compelling idea…

That man is desperate. A man like that would surely do anything to regain his freedom. Marry him.

Marry a slave?

Yes! Marriage with a man such as this, a desperate man, will be your means of escaping marriage with Lord Romanos. Once it is done, you can give the slave his freedom. You will never have to see him again and Lord Romanos will not touch you when he learns you have married a slave.

I cannot marry a complete stranger! And yet…

The idea would not leave her.

AUTHOR NOTE

For me, the word *Byzantium* conjures images of an exotic medieval empire. It carries with it an aura of magic. Byzantium… I loved learning about it at university, and enthusiastic teachers ensured that Byzantium lost none of its shimmer.

These books bring Byzantium alive:

Byzantium, the Surprising Life of a Medieval Empire by Judith Herrin (Penguin, 2008)

Byzantium by Robin Cormack and Maria Vassilaki (Royal Academy of Arts, 2008)

Fourteen Byzantine Rulers by Michael Psellus (Penguin, 1966)

The Alexiad of Anna Komnene translated by E.R.A. Sewter (Penguin, 1969)

Names can be tricky. Without being too rigid, I have used Greek versions of names where possible, and in a couple of cases I have shortened the names of real people.

CHAINED TO
THE BARBARIAN

Carol Townend

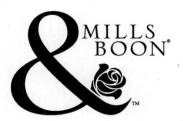

MILLS
BOON®
™

First published in Great Britain 2012
by Mills & Boon, an imprint of Harlequin (UK) Limited.
Large Print edition 2012
Harlequin (UK) Limited, Eton House, 18-24 Paradise Road,
Richmond, Surrey TW9 1SR

© Carol Townend 2012

ISBN: 978 0 263 22533 4

Harlequin (UK) policy is to use papers that are natural, renewable and recyclable products and made from wood grown in sustainable forests. The logging and manufacturing process conform to the legal environmental regulations of the country of origin.

Printed and bound in Great Britain
by CPI Antony Rowe, Chippenham, Wiltshire

Carol Townend has been making up stories since she was a child. Whenever she comes across a tumbledown building, be it castle or cottage, she can't help conjuring up the lives of the people who once lived there. Her Yorkshire forebears were friendly with the Brontë sisters. Perhaps their influence lingers…

Carol's love of ancient and medieval history took her to London University, where she read History, and her first novel (published by Mills & Boon) won the Romantic Novelists' Association's New Writers' Award. Currently she lives near Kew Gardens, with her husband and daughter. Visit her website at www.caroltownend.co.uk

Previous novels by the same author:

THE NOVICE BRIDE
AN HONOURABLE ROGUE
HIS CAPTIVE LADY
RUNAWAY LADY, CONQUERING LORD
HER BANISHED LORD
BOUND TO THE BARBARIAN*
*Part of *Palace Brides* trilogy

Look for the final instalment in
Carol Townend's
Palace Brides
mini-series
BETROTHED TO THE BARBARIAN

**Did you know that some of these novels
are also available as eBooks?
Visit www.millsandboon.co.uk**

With love to my sister, Jillie.

And many thanks to my editor, Megan.
Her many creative suggestions and insights
make her a pleasure to work with.

Chapter One

William gritted his teeth—he would *not* lose consciousness. Dark waves threatened to block his vision, his head was pounding from the beating they had given him, but he was *not* going to lose consciousness.

The children were huddled at his feet. Thus far, neither Daphne nor Paula had been put up for sale. Nor had he. Not that anyone was likely to buy him in his current battered state. William was not generally a praying man, but he was praying now. *God grant that we are not separated.* If he and the girls were kept together, he could protect them for a little longer. Lord. Two tiny girls, and they only had him, an enslaved knight, to watch over them. William knew first-hand what it was like to feel abandoned at an early age. And these mites were even younger than he had been when...no matter, what had happened to him was nothing compared with what these children were suffering. They were too young to fend for themselves.

William could not bring their mother back to life but, if humanly possible, he would help them.

Something thudded into William's back. The butt of a spear. As he stumbled on to the auction block, more darkness swept over him. His chains rattled, hobbling him at the ankles, weighing heavy at his wrists. The darkness was all but impenetrable, he could hardly see. It looked as though twilight was gathering, but surely evening could not have come so soon? He would have sworn it was not yet noon…

William fought to stay on his feet as he fought to keep his wits about him. This was combat, a combat that was as challenging as any he had faced and he must not fail. *The children need me.*

There was buzzing in his ears. A number of black splotches were flying about the auction hall, like crows in a cornfield. William knew what that meant—any moment he could topple like a felled poplar. His limbs were heavy as lead and his movements, as he mounted the dais, were slow. His head throbbed. His vision cleared a little to reveal Paula and Daphne in front of him on the platform, clutching each other. Paula's eyes were huge, her face white. Both girls were half-starved, that went without saying, but William had learned that in the diminished world of the slave, lack of food was one of the lesser evils. His lip curled. The miscreant who was trying to sell them considered that half-starving a slave was merely one way of controlling him. Or her. He concentrated on the children, praying to be sold alongside them. Paula must be what—about two years of age? And Daphne was only a babe. He blinked to rid himself of the black splotches, bile was bitter at the back of his throat. And to think he had thought his early life harsh. Lord.

A lock of blond hair fell into his eyes. When he shook it aside, pain shot to his temples, there was rushing in his ears. Meanwhile, fury sat like acid in his stomach, burning, burning. *I should not be here. This is the slave market at Constantinople and I am up for sale. A knight on an auction block. Jesu, what has the world come to?*

Grimly, William forced himself to take stock of his surroundings.

The auction block was a raised dais in the centre of a covered market that was packed with people. Stone pillars held up the roof. With something of a lurch, William realised why the torches had not been lit. It wasn't twilight, far from it. Sunlight was streaming through Romanesque arches, bright shafts jabbed like hot knives into his brain. The darkness had been conjured by his exhausted mind, by his beaten body. The citizens of Constantinople were jostling each other, talking and laughing as they pressed up to the dais. They were narrowing their eyes as they stared at the children. At him. As William understood it, slavery was common here at the heart of the Empire.

This was the second time William had been put up on a slave block. He didn't recall anything about the first time—then they had drugged him into oblivion, rather than beating him. Drugging had been most effective. William had known nothing until he had woken in chains to find that he, Sir William Bradfer, had been enslaved.

Fury at his fate, at the sheer injustice, had his guts writhing. *I am a knight, I should not be here!*

Resolutely, he set fury behind him, there would be time for fury tomorrow. Today, the girls needed him.

The black patches, the crows—William's mind was fumbling over the distinction between reality and imaginings—were swooping towards a slash of sunlight as though they were attacking it. He blinked and the auction space swam back into focus. Columns. Two small girls. Strangers staring. Assessing eyes.

He must stay conscious, he must ensure the children were not bought by a cruel wretch like the last one, the darkness could not take him until he knew they were safe…

The auction house wavered, the crows swooped and soared, light knifed the back of his eyes. Biting down on his tongue, William tasted blood. Scraps of black flickered at the edge of his sight, but he did not faint.

A movement at the front of the crowd drew William's gaze. Two young women were gazing intently at the children. William shook his hair out of his eyes again and felt himself freeze.

Hope.

He prayed he wasn't imagining it, but both women's eyes were full of what looked like compassion. And shock. Emotions that were surely alien to a cruel soul, emotions that William had not thought to encounter in the Constantinople slave market.

'You must buy those two, you must!' The taller of the two women caught her companion's arm as she looked at the children. She had smoky grey eyes that were luminous with tears.

William held his breath as her gaze turned in his direction. A single teardrop caught the light as it fell from her lashes and everything seemed to slow. Despite the shufflings and mutterings of the crowd, despite the pain throbbing in his head and shoulder, William caught the hiss of her indrawn breath. He saw the whitening of her fingers on her friend's arm.

Hope.

'Buy him! You must buy him!' Her voice was clear. Urgent.

If William had strength he would frown—the woman wanted to buy him, bruised and battered as he was? She must be mad. But those smoky grey eyes were kind.

The auction hall rippled, his sight was definitely going, it was like peering through a heat haze.

Stay conscious. If these women buy the children, they will be safe.

How he knew this, William had no idea, but he knew it, no question. If these women bought the children, he need have no more worries on their behalf. It wouldn't matter then who bought him, he was no slave, he had no intention of remaining in the City, not once the girls were safe. He had plans—he had only delayed putting them into action because of little Daphne and Paula.

William fixed his gaze on those luminous grey eyes and the rest of the market faded from his awareness. Dimly, he heard her friend make some objection. 'He looks like a troublemaker.' She was talking about him.

The grey eyes never left his face, the young woman's veil trembled. Like her gown, the veil was brown and plain. 'Buy him as well as the children,' she said. 'Please, my lady, I...I don't have money of my own, but I will pay you somehow. You can have my gold bangle and the rest of my jewellery. You can sell the lot and buy more slaves.'

The buzzing in William's ears was louder, the crows had flocked back, their ragged wings fluttering between him and the two young women. The floor rocked.

'My lady,' said the girl in brown. 'I will give you Zephyr, you can sell her, too...'

William must have blacked out for a few moments, because when he came back to himself, the bidding was underway. His stomach cramped. The young women did not look wealthy enough to be buying slaves, indeed, the one who was bidding had a gown that one might expect to see on a maidservant. They were being outbid by a man with the air of a prosperous merchant and a woman in a cherry-coloured gown whose face was wearing so much paint it looked enamelled. The words 'whore of Babylon' leaped into William's mind.

He grimaced—he must be fevered. His right arm

throbbed like the devil. Chains clinking, he struggled to ease it by cradling it in his other arm and fought down a wave of nausea. He wasn't going to contemplate the thought that nausea was often sign of a break.

At the foot of the dais, the young women were muttering. Comparing them to the other bidders, William's heart sank. The fabric of their gowns was far too plain, the weave too simple. Brown homespun. Their clothing was simply no match for the merchant's luxurious green brocade or the painted lady's cherry-coloured silk. It was a dream to imagine those women would have enough money for both William and the girls.

Buy the children. Forget about me, but for God's sake, buy the girls.

He was peering past a swirling, sickening grey mist, trying to decide whether the women had any chance of winning the bidding contest when there was a disturbance in the crowd.

A man was pushing his way to the front—his hair was dark as night, his face intense and angry. When he reached the side of the smaller of the young women, the one who was placing the bids, he attempted to take her arm. Something about the way the man held himself told William that he was a soldier.

Despite William's efforts to stay on his feet, the grey mist drifted inexorably nearer. First it swallowed the pillars of the auction house, then the young women started to fade.

No! Stay awake!

The platform shifted.

Lady Anna of Heraklea dug her nails into her palms. Her pulse was shaky and uneven. It was only her second day back at the capital and the last place she wanted to be was the slave market. Who would be here, if they could avoid it? At best it was a brutish place where the most squalid of deals were made. Here, they traded in human flesh.

She did not like to think about it, particularly when she ought to be thinking about what she was going to say to her father when she met him tomorrow. *Two years—I have not seen Father since I went to Rascia two years ago. Will he still insist that I marry Lord Romanos?*

The thought made her ill. Anna had to work out the best way of convincing her father that marriage with Lord Romanos was impossible, but instead, here she was at the slave market.

Katerina had been determined to come, and Anna had realised that if she did not accompany her, Katerina would have come on her own.

Which would not have been safe. It is bad enough that we left the Palace with only a Varangian sergeant and a handful of off-duty Guards, but for Katerina to even have considered coming here on her own—such foolishness! Katerina should be keeping up appearances, she is meant to be playing the part of Princess Theodora.

Katerina should be queening about in the Princess's apartments with a vast entourage, she should be convincing everyone in the Great Palace that she is the Princess. Katerina should not be in the slave market, she should not be buying slaves!

Thank God Commander Ashfirth has found us. He believes her to be the Princess and he has the sense to be discreet...

Anna listened with half an ear while the Commander tried to dissuade Katerina from buying the slaves.

'Those children are far too young to be freed,' Commander Ashfirth was saying. 'You will have to look after them until they are grown. And if you have a mind to train them as servants, it will be years before they are of use...'

Anna's throat tightened as she looked at the children huddled on the auction block. *Poor souls. Poor little souls. Their clothes are in tatters, their faces are filthy and, what is worse, they look as though they haven't eaten in a week. If Katerina does buy them, she will have done a good deed. It will have been worth coming to this terrible place.*

And then there was *him*. The young man with hair like a Viking. The moment Anna had seen him the most ridiculous idea had jumped into her head—a most ridiculous, yet dangerously compelling idea…

That man is desperate. A man like that would surely do anything to regain his freedom. Marry him.

Marry a slave?

Yes! Marriage with a man such as this, a desperate man, will be your means of escaping marriage with Lord Romanos. Once it is done, you can give the slave his freedom. You will never have to see him again and Lord Romanos will not touch you when he learns you have married a slave.

I cannot marry a complete stranger!

Better that than marry Lord Romanos…

Holy Virgin, I cannot do this! And yet…

The idea would not leave her.

Commander Ashfirth was frowning at the young man. 'And as for that male slave,' he said, 'he looks to be in a very bad way. I doubt that he will take instruction.'

Tipping back her head, pulse racing, Anna studied the young man who, despite his chains, stood so protectively over the children. The resemblance to Erling was uncanny. The slave was unusually large, with long, strong thighs and wide shoulders. So would Erling have been, had he lived. Locks of tangled blond hair were falling into his eyes, he had vivid green eyes that had, for one unsettling moment, tugged at her heartstrings. Those green eyes had reminded Anna of Erling. They had taken her back to another time and another place.

It was an ugly memory, she shoved it to the back of her mind. *Not my fault, what happened to Erling was not my fault. In any case, this man is not Erling. Erling is dead. There is no way I can know whether this man can be relied upon.*

The slave will obey you, he does not look as biddable as Erling, but he will surely obey you. Look into his eyes—that man wants freedom more than he wants his next breath. Offer him that and he will surely obey you.

And Father? What will he do if I delay our meeting until I have married the slave? How would Father react?

As Anna stared up at the dais, her guts knotted. The slave had been beaten. His cheekbones were bruised and there was a rust-coloured stain on the ripped fabric of his tunic. When he shifted, his chains clanked.

Are those chains necessary? He looks half-conscious. Might Commander Ashfirth be right, though? Might he be a troublemaker?

No matter if he is. He looks perfect for my purposes, just perfect. He should be more than capable of keeping my father at bay. This man will make him realise that marrying me to Lord Romanos is no longer possible.

Anna shot Commander Ashfirth a sideways glance, the Commander was scowling. Anna received the impression that he was weakening over Katerina buying the two children, but he certainly did not want her to buy the male slave.

But she must buy him, he needs our help! I may have failed Erling, but I will not fail this man.

Provided he does exactly as I wish. Provided he marries me.

As a means of evading an unwanted marriage it was sheer madness, Anna knew that. Marrying one man to avoid another was not something she had considered before today. But the moment she had looked at the blond slave, the instant she had seen the resemblance to Erling, the idea had jumped fully formed into her head.

Madness. I wonder who is the more desperate, me or that slave?

Anna needed time to think this through, but first they had to buy the man. Conscious that the auctioneer was looking at Katerina and an expectant silence had fallen, Anna nudged her. 'Bid again, or you will lose them!'

Commander Ashfirth's scowl deepened, but since he believed Katerina to be the Princess, he would not gainsay her. When Katerina's chin came up, Anna saw that she would have her way.

'Sir, I will make my purchase,' Katerina said. She raised her hand, nodded at the auctioneer and the bidding resumed.

The merchant across the other side of the platform looked as though he had a roomy purse. *Have we brought enough money? Will we be outbid?* Tension tightening every muscle, Anna's nails gouged into her palms.

There was more bidding but, finally, Katerina raised her hand, and a gong rang.

'Sold!'

Anna released her breath in a rush. *Blessed Virgin, we have done it, the slaves are ours!*

* * *

William came back to himself as he was prodded off the dais and into a pen at the side. A black head-ache had descended on him, and since he could barely see through it, let alone stand, he slumped against a pillar and watched bemused as the auc-tion house floor began to float towards him.

And then *she* was there, the woman with misty grey eyes. A burly young man with a martial look to him stood at her side, but William was not in-terested in the burly young man. Those grey eyes held his and a feminine hand reached towards him. Spring flowers—he could smell spring flowers.

'Let us help you.'

Her voice was soft and smoky, like her eyes. Between them, she and the burly young man low-ered William to the ground.

'The children...Daphne...Paula?' William forced the words through his teeth with difficulty. His Greek was somewhat rusty. Of course, he under-stood more than any other Apulian knight of his acquaintance, but today it was a battle to express himself clearly.

'They are safe, they will be cared for,' the girl said softly. 'As will you.'

'Where...where...?' And then, before William

could marshal the strength to ask where they were being taken, the grey mist came for him, swirling through his sight, stealing his voice. As his head lolled, the only answer he received was the clatter of chains.

Back in the Boukoleon Palace, in the reception chamber in Princess Theodora's apartments, Anna knelt on the marble floor by the slave's pallet. She studied his unconscious features—just before they had found him a litter, the slave master had revealed that he was a Frank, one of many Normans who had found their way into the Empire.

He is Frank, he is not all Viking, not like Erling. He is a Frank who has likely inherited his colouring from some distant Viking forebear. But, had Erling lived, he would certainly have resembled this man. The flaxen hair and green eyes—now closed—were the most obvious similarities, the general resemblance was undeniable. Erling was there in the large build, in the protective way the young man had stood over the children. Despite his chains and his injuries, he had been ready to fight the world on their behalf. Erling had been just as protective. Of her.

Anna had failed Erling and guilt had haunted her

for years. *I will not fail this man. I may not have decided whether I have a use for him or not, but whatever happens, he will be freed.*

The Frankish slave groaned, the fair head shifted on the pillow, but his eyelids barely fluttered.

Anna clapped her hands to summon one of the serving girls. 'Send for more water, if you please, Maria. And clean linens. And…' she grimaced at the bloodied tunic '…fetch some scissors. I will have this man clean and comfortable.'

'Yes, my lady. Those tiles will be hard on your knees—would you like a cushion?'

'Please.'

Anna glanced across the wide floor towards the two children. Her heart twisted. *Poor mites.* At her command, a bevy of serving girls had taken them into their care. A large copper basin had appeared, with steaming jugs of water, sponges…

'They will need food first, I think,' Anna said gently. 'I doubt they have been fed in some days. Let the older girl have some bread and milk. As for the infant—is there a wet-nurse in the Palace?'

'I shall enquire, my lady.'

One of the girls curtsied and ran past the guard at the doors, another came in with an armful of white linen. Anna's attention returned to the Frankish slave.

His hair needed cutting. Matted and dirty, it had not seen a comb in some time. Carefully, wary of waking him, Anna smoothed it from his face. His face had stopped her breath the moment she'd seen it, and not simply because of the resemblance to Erling. The slave's features were attractive, regular and even, his mouth was most beautifully formed. He had a strong jaw that was shadowed with several days' growth of beard, he was overpoweringly male. But the bruises beneath the beard! Anna frowned. His cheekbones were far too prominent, not to mention that they were bruised and bloodied. Overall, the Frank had a gaunt look that was at odds with the powerful build.

Half-starved.

'Juliana?'

'My lady?'

'Send to the kitchens for meat and wine.'

'Meat, my lady? It is still Lent.'

'Meat,' Anna repeated firmly. 'Preferably beef. Tell them it is needed in the Princess's apartment, no one will gainsay you.'

'Yes, my lady.'

Taking hold of the Frank's ragged tunic, Anna began easing it from him.

'Here, my lady.' Shears were thrust into her

hand, a tasselled cushion was placed on the floor next to her.

'My thanks.'

Anna pulled at the fabric of the slave's tunic. Like his face, his chest was black and blue. Grimacing, Anna exchanged glances with one of the serving girls. 'Some people do not deserve to own slaves.'

'No, my lady.'

The double doors at the entrance to the apartment were flung back and Commander Ashfirth stalked in, his expression was thunderous. He had Katerina by the arm and was towing her behind him.

Anna caught her breath. Heart cold, she pushed to her knees. She was afraid, very much afraid, that the moment she had dreaded was upon them.

Has the Commander found us out? Has he realised that the woman he believes to be the Princess is, in fact, just a serving girl?

She swallowed. 'Princess Theodor—'

'Later,' the Commander snapped, marching towards the Princess's bedchamber. His face was closed, his shoulders were rigid with anger.

A white-faced Katerina shot Anna a desperate look, but with the Commander hauling her along, she had no choice but to follow.

He knows! Yes, there is no doubt, Commander

Ashfirth knows that Katerina is an impostor. Merciful heavens, if this becomes common knowledge, Katerina and I will be in deep, deep trouble...

Commander Ashfirth poked his head through the bedchamber door and signalled to the guard. 'Kari?'

'Sir?'

'The Princess and I do not wish to be disturbed.'

The guard's eyes widened. 'I see.'

'I hope that you do. No one...' pointedly, Commander Ashfirth jerked his head towards Anna '...and I mean *no one* is to enter this bedchamber.'

'No exceptions, sir?'

'None except Captain Sigurd. Do you understand?'

'Yes, sir.'

The bedchamber door slammed and the bolts shot home.

Juliana let her breath out in a rush. 'Holy Virgin, what is that all about? The Commander will not hurt the Princess, will he?'

Anna blinked uncertainly at the closed bedchamber door, painfully conscious of the need to guard her tongue. 'I do not think so.' Her mind raced. Like everyone else in the Palace, with the possible exception of Commander Ashfirth, Juliana believed Katerina to be Princess Theodora. 'Commander Ashfirth has a strong respect for the Princess,' she added carefully. 'Remember, the Emperor has commanded him to protect her.'

Juliana's eyes were round as she gaped at that closed bedchamber door. 'But surely he should not enter the Princess's bedchamber! What are they doing in there?'

What indeed?

'Come, Juliana—' Anna made her voice brisk '—help me shift this man to one side so we may bathe him.'

Juliana turned a disapproving face towards her. 'You will bathe him yourself, my lady? A *slave*? A *male* slave?'

'It is…' Anna hesitated, unwilling to reveal too much to a woman she did not know well '…it is a penance I have set myself for past sins.' *For Erling's sake.*

Pointedly, Juliana raised a brow at such an un-orthodox penance—a lady, bathing a slave!—but after a moment, she grudgingly bent to assist. Anna hoped that the shock of witnessing Lady Anna of Heraklea bathing a Frankish slave would distract Juliana from whatever was going on in the Princess's bedchamber.

Chapter Two

Head thumping, William woke with a start and grabbed for his sword. Then he remembered—his sword was lost, he was a slave. Mind fogged with pain, he heaved himself into a sitting position. Out of the tangle in his head one question emerged. *Are the girls safe?*

He had been put on a clean pallet in an airy room that was busy with activity. He caught a brief impression of a wide tiled floor; of a line of tall windows billowing with drapery of some kind; of women rushing to and fro, long skirts swishing as they skimmed over polished marble. There was so much marble, so much light and air, he could not imagine where he might be.

He could not see the children.

A feminine hand pushed him back against the pillows, it belonged to the woman from the slave market, the one with smoky grey eyes. He wondered who she was. The brown gown and veil were so plain, she might be a servant. Yet her companion's clothing had been equally plain, and that had not prevented her from finding money for three slaves…

'Paula?' His voice was creaky. He struggled back onto an elbow. 'Daphne?'

The woman settled on a cushion at his side, a glass goblet in hand. The goblet caught William's eye—the glass looked Venetian, it must have cost a fortune to have shipped it here. A Venetian glass goblet?

Where am I?

The woman smiled. It occurred to William that she was observing him most carefully, and had been for some time. 'I take it that Daphne and Paula are the girls in your…party,' she said, pointing to the other end of the chamber. 'They are being well cared for. See?'

And there, in the centre of a circle of women, were the girls. Paula, in a fresh tunic, was holding the hand of one of the women. She was smiling. William's throat tightened, he could not recall the last time he had seen Paula smile. Daphne, closely wrapped in what looked like silk, was safely in the lap of a motherly-looking wet-nurse on a gilded stool.

A gilded stool? Lord.

What is this place?

Daphne was being fed. The wet-nurse glanced William's way without embarrassment and nodded at him.

'As you see, the children are safe.'

William swallowed, but his throat was so parched it was well nigh impossible. Grimacing, he massaged his throat.

The woman leaned towards him, offering the goblet. 'Wine?'

Clumsily, for his hand did not seem to be obeying him the way it ought to, William grasped the goblet and sipped.

'I hope it is to your taste, it is watered,' she said, lowering her voice and leaning towards him. Beneath her veil, he caught a glimpse of wavy brown hair. 'I thought perhaps, you have not taken…refreshment for some time.'

Giving a jerky nod, William drank. He drank deep. The wine might be watered, but the flavour was richer and smoother than any he had tasted in his entire life. When he had emptied the glass, he sank back against his pillows and peered in amazement at the few remaining drops. *Excellent wine served in a Venetian glass, a pillow softer than thistledown, a chamber that is the size of a knight's hall, huge windows fluttering with silk draperies...*

He cleared his throat. 'Where? Where am I?' His voice sounded like an unoiled hinge.

She gave him another of those tentative smiles. 'In Princess Theodora's apartments in the Boukoleon Palace.'

'The Palace! This is the Great Palace?' His head throbbed, the glass wavered in his grasp. A rush of emotion ran through him, confusing in its intensity.

Here, almost a quarter of a century ago or thereabouts, his reclusive mother had met his father. His irresponsible, careless father, the unknown Norman lord who had refused to marry his mother and had never acknowledged William's existence. Having spent most of his life outside the Empire, William had never thought to set foot in its capital Constantinople, never mind the Great Palace.

'Yes, you are in the Great Palace.'

Bile stung the back of William's throat. Holy Heaven, finally, he had come to his mother's birthplace. As a slave. 'And the other woman, the one who was with you in the…market—she is Princess Theodora?'

The woman gave a jerky nod and the precious goblet was plucked from his fingers.

William glanced down the length of the chamber, the girls looked happier than he had ever seen them. Paula was still smiling, Daphne still feeding. Relaxing into the pillows with a sigh, he closed his eyes and willed his head to stop throbbing. He needed to think, but not about his mother, not yet. First, he had to get out of the Palace.

'You are hungry?'

He opened his eyes. Hungry? His stomach growled.

The smoky grey eyes were anxious. 'I have ordered beef. Would you like some?'

Briefly it crossed William's mind that this might be a new torment his previous owner had devised for him. Beef. His mouth watered. He levered himself into a sitting position, almost choking on a sudden rush of saliva. Bruised muscles screamed in protest. Another pillow was thrust behind him and a bowl was handed over, smelling fragrantly of meat and herbs. When William reached for the spoon, he was shamed to see his hand was shaking, he was practically drooling.

She, bless her, pretended not to notice.

Beef. Lord. And bread.

William forced himself to eat slowly, but he did not pause until the bowl was empty, even going as far as to mop up the gravy with a chunk of bread.

She gave him a measure of privacy while he ate, flinging the odd remark to the other women in the chamber. 'The baby feeds well, Sylvia?'

'She is fine, my lady.'

My lady. She was no maidservant then, but why was she wearing such plain clothes? In the auction hall, Princess Theodora had been dressed equally simply. Had they been trying to conceal their status? But why should they want to do that? Were Imperial princesses forbidden to leave the Palace? Were they hedged about by rules? Certainly they had not gone to the slave market unaccompanied— dimly, William remembered a small escort. There had been that burly young man who might have been a bodyguard, as well as a couple of other men with a military look to them.

'More beef?'

'Please.'

The meat was tender and melted in his mouth, it was a struggle not to moan with delight.

Outside the tall windows, the mew of gulls told him that this part of the Great Palace was close to the sea. William racked his mind to recall what he knew of the Imperial Palace, but for the most part, his mind remained unhelpfully blank. His mother had not wished to speak about her time here and he suspected that what he had learned later in his life was closer to myth than reality.

The Norsemen had their own name for Constantinople—to them it was Miklagard. The greatest City in Christendom, the Imperial vaults— hidden somewhere beneath the Palace—were said to be crammed with the wealth of several hundred years of Imperial rule.

Smoky grey eyes were watching him.

Why was this woman, this *lady*, helping him? Why was she being so kind? It made no sense. *She wants something from me.*

'Lady Anna?' The wet-nurse spoke from across the room. She had finished feeding Daphne and was setting her down in a willow basket, cocooning her in wrappings.

William marked her name. *Anna.*

'Yes, Sylvia?'

'Do you wish me to remain in the apartment, my lady? Or shall I return to the servants' quarters?'

Rising, Lady Anna left William's side, moving with quiet grace across the marble floor. Lady Anna was tall and shapely, the brown veil fluttered with the sway of her hips. Joining the wet-nurse by the gilded stool, she smiled tenderly down at the sleeping baby. 'The Princess would like you to remain here,' she said. 'Your duty is to care for these children.'

Sylvia wrinkled her brow. 'Even though they are slaves?'

'Yes, even so.' Lady Anna's voice was firm. 'I do not believe they will be slaves for long.'

The wet-nurse's jaw dropped. 'The Princess is thinking to adopt them?'

Lady Anna's gaze shifted and came to rest on a closed door, a slight frown formed on her brow. William wondered what lay behind that door, it seemed to unsettle her.

'I believe so,' she said. 'When the Princess joins us, I am sure she will make her wishes plain.'

'Yes, my lady.'

'In the meantime, Sylvia, do your best for the children, you are in charge.'

Sylvia curtsied. 'Yes, my lady. It is an honour to be serving the Princess. I shall not let her down.'

Giving the wet-nurse a look that William was unable to interpret, Lady Anna returned to stand by his pallet. Her expression was troubled, something in her exchange with the nurse had wiped the smile from her face. William could not imagine what might upset one of the Princess's ladies, and he wasn't going to dwell on it. The key point was that, finally, Daphne and Paula had come to a safe harbour. At last he could leave them, freedom was within his grasp.

William had a vague recollection of the Princess murmuring in his ear at the slave market, he was uncertain whether it had really happened. He might have dreamed it, but a chilling echo was sounding in his mind...

'I have bought you for Lady Anna,' the Princess had said. 'It is she who owns you.'

Did he dream it? Did a mind fevered with exhaustion and ill treatment put words in Princess Theodora's mouth? Did Lady Anna own him? He rubbed his temple. He was a knight—he should never have been enslaved in the first place! If only he could think straight...

'Lady Anna?'

'Yes?' As she stood over him, the breeze from the windows pressed her gown against her body, briefly presenting him with a glimpse of a remarkably alluring body. Outside the seagulls screamed like lost souls.

William asked the important question, the *only* question. 'My lady, am I a free man?'

Lady Anna nudged a cushion closer and, sinking on to it, folded her hands in her lap. 'Are you a free man? It is true that the Princess bought you at my behest, but—'

'Why?' Months of suppressed fury made his voice curt. 'Why did you ask her to buy me?'

She caught her breath and startled grey eyes looked warily at him. 'Why? Because...because...'

'What do you want of me?' It was not this woman's fault that he had been enslaved. She was not his enemy, indeed, she appeared to be helping him. Yet she had insisted that the Princess should buy him. Why? He gestured at the maidservants, the marble tables, the silken hangings. 'You are not short of slaves here. What do you want of me?'

She recoiled. 'I have not decided.'

Her back was straight as a poker and her eyes had lost their warmth. William hadn't really noticed that warmth earlier, but now that it was gone... His heart clenched. The contrast with the confiding way she had taken her place at his side and this cold grey gaze could not be more marked. However, he had to know—Lady Anna must want something from him. Why waste money on a slave, if all she was going to do was free him? 'What do you want me to do?'

'Do? At present you do not have to do anything... except recover. I do not intend to keep you, if that is what you mean. Of course, I cannot free you officially until the Princess has signed the document of ownership over to me. You will have to wait for

that. I may have a simple task or two for you, but
as I said, I am undecided as to whether you are…
suitable. However, as soon as I can, I shall give
you your document of manumission.'

'You expect me to believe that you are going
to free me?' It was hard to keep the scorn from
his voice. In William's experience, people who offered favours always expected a sizeable return.
Always. The price for a favour as large as this—
his freedom!—was bound to be high. Not that he
intended to be around to pay it. He was curious
though, about what use a gently bred court lady
might have for a Frankish slave.

She shrugged. 'As you rightly observe, I have
no need of you in the long term. I shall free you
once the Princess has signed you over to me.' She
frowned in the direction of the closed door. 'You
must bear in mind that she must sign your documents before you may be freed.'

Lady Anna's expression was earnest, she sounded
convincing. It was tempting to believe her, tempting to think that he had at last met someone who
was capable of putting others before herself. He
shook his head. Much as he might wish it, life had
taught him that only a saint would behave in such
a way. 'Slaves are generally bought for the long

term. This simple task you have in mind must be of some importance.'

She flushed, her lips pursed. It was obvious she was not prepared to divulge the nature of the task she had in mind. It might be dangerous. And though Lady Anna did not strike him as anything but law abiding, it might be against the law.

Grey eyes searched his and after a moment she reached forwards, cool fingers feathered across his forehead. 'Are you feeling stronger?'

William nodded, he took no notice of the pounding in his head.

'Your skin was burning earlier, thankfully you seem cooler. Would you care for more wine?'

'Please.'

Recognising the change of subject as meaning he would get nothing more from her, William sipped fine wine from the Venetian goblet and willed his anger away. For the moment he was content simply to watch her. His brain didn't seem to be working for much else and watching her was preferable to snapping at her.

This woman was not his enemy. He must direct his anger at his real enemy, at whoever arranged for his capture in Apulia. Lady Anna had nothing to do with that. She may well want something from him, but she was going to be disappointed—

he was going home to search out his enemy and take his revenge. In the meantime...

Watching Lady Anna was as pleasant a way of passing the time as any. William couldn't say what it was about her, but she intrigued him. The simplicity of the dull brown gown and veil suggested someone whose rank was unremarkable, yet she was, apparently, lady-in-waiting to Princess Theodora.

And her Imperial mistress, as he recalled from what he had seen at the slave market, had worn equally unremarkable clothes. Why? And why had the Princess ventured outside the Palace with only a handful of men as her escort? Surely an Imperial princess should have a great entourage? The customs of the Great Palace were as much a mystery to William as the subtleties of female attire, but one thing he had learned from what had happened to his mother—there was a rigid hierarchy in the Imperial Palace.

Here, rank meant everything. As in any great palace, courtiers must fight and jostle for power. Reputation and prestige would be guarded most jealously. So the quiet foray that Lady Anna and her princess had made to the slave market had been unorthodox, to say the least of it.

It was on the tip of William's tongue to inform

her that he was no slave, that he was a knight from the Duchy of Apulia and Calabria, but the old instincts were strong. Until he knew more about the Palace, until he knew more about this woman and what she wanted him to do, he would tread warily. Life had taught him not to give his trust too easily, it was a lesson which was hard to set aside.

Her gaze was downcast, giving him leisure to study her. Her eyelashes were long and dark, and her eyes had been lightly outlined with some cosmetic. Other than that her face was clear of paint. His mouth went up at a corner. *No whore of Babylon here.* Her nose was straight and beneath her veil her hair looked to be wavy, dark tendrils were curling about her forehead. Her complexion was clear, her skin was a golden olive in tone.

Why should a lady-in-waiting be nursing a slave? It made no sense, unless she was studying him to see if he was fit for this secret purpose of hers.

That hazy memory stirred and he was back at the slave market with the Princess murmuring in his ear. 'I have bought you for Lady Anna, it is she who owns you.'

What can Lady Anna want of me?

Draining the goblet, he handed it back. 'My thanks.'

Mon Dieu, he was weary, from head to foot everything ached. Yawning, William let his eyelids droop.

With the children safe, there was nothing more to delay him. He would rest awhile…and then, whether or not Lady Anna freed him, he would take his leave of this place. He must find the man who betrayed him in Apulia—he would have justice!

William dragged up the covers and found himself at the receiving end of a gentle smile. The warmth was back in her eyes, Lady Anna had forgiven him his curtness. He had responded with a smile of his own before he had time to check it. Whatever she might want of him, she seemed to be a good woman, she was certainly a beautiful one. But it would take more than a gentle smile to make him put his faith in anyone but himself.

'Before you rest, please…what is your name?'

'William.'

'William of…? Where are you from? You were born outside the Empire, I think.'

Her voice was quietly persistent. It was likely she was trying to lull him into lowering his guard and believing he could trust her. She would not succeed. And even though William would be leaving shortly, he was reluctant to confess that he was in truth a knight. His pride was not ready for the public admission that he, Sir William Bradfer, had been enslaved.

'The slave master said that you were a Frank,' she added.

William grunted. Her presence at his side was oddly comforting, which proved nothing except that his months as a slave had weakened him. Hunching his shoulder on her, William closed his eyes. Now that the children were safe, he must give his body a chance to regain its strength.

And then, regardless of Lady Anna's intentions, he would make his escape. Apulia, and revenge on his unknown enemy, awaited.

Anna stood frowning outside the Princess's bedchamber. She exchanged glances with the guard at the door, a new recruit called Kari.

What is going on? Katerina and the Commander have been in there for an age! Surely they are not...are not...?

With a click, the bedchamber door swung open and the Commander came out, buckling on his belt.

He is buckling on his belt? No!

Jaw agape, Anna watched him leave the apartment. She hurtled into the bedchamber, slamming the door behind her.

'*Princess!*' she cried, remembering even in her dismay, to use the title that Katerina had assumed. 'Are you mad?'

She could scarcely believe what she was seeing. *Katerina is naked under that sheet! Naked.* 'What in heaven is going on?'

Katerina shrugged. 'I would have thought that was obvious.'

'The Commander and you...?'

'Yes, Anna, the Commander and I.'

This was terrible. *Everything* was going wrong. In her role as Princess Theodora, Katerina had returned to the Palace only yesterday, everyone believed she was preparing to meet her betrothed. As Anna bent to retrieve Katerina's gown and veil from the floor, her thoughts whirled. When Princess Theodora, the *real* Princess Theodora, had asked for Anna's help in this masquerade, Anna had feared it was doomed from the start. It was true that Katerina bore a striking resemblance to Princess Theodora, it was also true that the Princess had not returned to the Palace for at least ten years, so few here would recognise her, but the pitfalls were many. Anna had known there would be...difficulties. But never once did she suspect that Katerina might put the entire scheme at risk by bedding the Commander...!

'It must be the strain,' she muttered. 'I told the Princess that you were not suitable to take her place. She should have sent someone who understood the protocols.'

'Someone with more breeding, you mean,' Katerina said.

Conscious of those in the reception chamber— the servants, the Frank, the guard—Anna kept her voice low. 'Since you care to put it like that, yes. Someone with a little more breeding would have had some idea what is, and what is not, acceptable behaviour.' She shook her head. 'Princess Theodora would never have invited Commander Ashfirth into her bedchamber. Or into her bed.'

What a disaster!

It might have been better if Anna had refused to help the Princess. She had not wanted to come home. The thought of finally facing her father and the ghastly marriage he had planned for her had made her feel quite ill. *I should have refused to help.* But no, she could not have done that. The Princess had been good to her, she had been so kind and understanding when Anna had joined her at the Rascian court. To have refused Princess Theodora's request would have been churlish in the extreme.

Except that now... Anna bit her lip. This indiscretion of Katerina's put them in something of an awkward position, and that was putting it mildly.

The scandal this will cause!

It was not only the scandal of an affair between the supposed Princess and the Commander that concerned her, though Anna could say nothing of this to Katerina. What will my father say? *He was furious when I joined the Princess in Rascia without his permission—this will give him an apoplexy. He must not hear of it. And it is particularly important he does not hear of it before my meeting with him tomorrow...*

Anna had been determined that her return to Constantinople should mark a new beginning in her relationship with her father. She wanted to prove that she had grown into a woman who was capable of making her own decisions. This was why yesterday, as soon as she had disembarked at the Palace harbour, she had sent a message to her father arranging to meet him. She had intended to quietly persuade him that marriage with Romanos Angelos was not for her. *That would still be my best course of action. If I can bring Father round to my way of thinking, there will be no need to involve the Frankish slave.*

Unfortunately, Lord Isaac, the Governor of Heraklea, was so conventional that any scandal would wreck Anna's chances of reclaiming his good will. Inevitably she would be drawn into it, and that being so, what chance did she have of ever pleasing her father?

Ahead, she could see only scandal—scandal, disgrace and her father's undying displeasure in a daughter who could never do anything right.

'Pass me that robe, please, Anna,' Katerina said.

Anna handed Katerina the robe and watched as she climbed out of bed. 'Really, Katerina, you should not have done it. And so blatantly! You are quite without shame. The Princess should have sent a lady in her stead…'

While Katerina dressed, Anna let her displeasure be known, even though there was nothing she could do to change what had happened. Katerina might have been foolish to give herself to the Commander, but the attraction between them had been obvious and it had grown every day that they had spent together. Perhaps it had been inevitable. If only Katerina had waited until the real Princess had returned…

Nursing his throbbing arm and shoulder—William had felt someone gently probing and strapping it while he had lain in a half-sleep—he

sat up and stared at the closed door. It must lead
to Princess Theodora's bedchamber.

Listening to the low murmur of voices—he
could not make out the words—William felt his
lips curve. It would seem that Lady Anna was
somewhat strait-laced. Her face when that man had
emerged fastening his belt...it had been priceless,
absolutely priceless. Lady Anna did not approve
of the affair that Princess Theodora was conduct-
ing with that man.

Who is he? The face was familiar, but William
could not think why that should be—he could not
place him. He had the bearing of an officer, whoever he was, and he had shocked Lady Anna.

A guard was standing by the double doors at
the entrance to the apartment. William's senses
snapped awake. *A Varangian!* His heart jumped.
He had never actually seen a Varangian in person before, but the man's unit was betrayed by his
weaponry. He had one of the infamous Varangian
battleaxes firmly in his grasp, and his sword
was slung on a shoulder belt. The battleaxe held
William's gaze. A Varangian, and no mistake. This
was one of the Emperor's personal bodyguard.

Mon Dieu, the ladies here could call on men
in the Varangian Guard! It was a wonder that he
had not noticed this earlier—he must have been

more dazed than he realised. It made sense that the Emperor's personal guard should be assigned to Princess Theodora, but it was something of a setback. *Hell.* William reached for the Venetian glass Lady Anna had thoughtfully left nearby and sipped. He must plan his escape with care. No rash moves.

He stared at the door of the Princess's bedchamber. Lady Anna had looked so shocked when she had rushed in. If it were not for William's ignominious position here, if it were not for his plans to return to Apulia—plans that had been thrown into disarray by him finding himself so unexpectedly at the heart of the Great Palace—it might be amusing to pursue her acquaintance.

His headache had eased and his mind was working better than it had done earlier, he was once again capable of setting out opposing points in an argument.

Should he remain in Constantinople for a time, or should he leave? He might not wish to be in the Great Palace, but Lady Anna had hinted that freedom was soon to be his. He was not sure he could trust her, but if her promise was not an empty one, he could stay and learn something of his mother's family. He might meet them...

On the other hand, if he did not return to the

Duchy soon, the trail leading to his enemy would be stone cold.

He frowned at the wine in his glass. For years he had wanted to discover the secrets in his mother's past, such a chance might never come again…

And so it went on, the argument swaying from one side to the other, like the ebb and flow of two armies on the field of conflict.

He gazed at the closed door to the bedchamber. Lady Anna was apparently utterly without malice, she had yet to show him anything other than compassion, but it would not be wise for him to make a saint of her. She might be unreliable. After all, she had her reasons for persuading the Princess to buy him. She might never free him.

He must leave at the first opportunity.

It was a pity he was not going to stay long enough to discover Lady Anna's reasons for buying him— he had to admit he was curious. His lips twitched. The way she had scurried into that bedchamber, shocked out of her calm by the Princess's behaviour… Strangely, there was comfort in that.

The bedchamber door rattled and Lady Anna stood on the threshold.

Her huge grey eyes went straight to him. 'You're awake!' Face lighting, she closed the door and came across, skirts sweeping the marble tiles.

William nodded. Truth to tell, he had only dozed earlier, much of the time he had feigned sleep to ward off questions.

'Are you hungry?' She glanced through the window at a darkening sky, evening was almost on them. 'They will be bringing food shortly, but if you cannot wait, I can order more for you.'

'I can wait,' William said, as that light fragrance reached him. *Spring, I can smell spring. Jasmine, spices...*

Her smile was so open, it was in danger of dazzling. Lady Anna wasn't to know that William was wise to smiles like that. Lady Felisa had smiled at him in just such a way when she had led him to believe that, despite his lack of lands, she was prepared to consider his suit. William no longer believed in such smiles. It had only been a few months since Lady Felisa had smiled at him, then a few days later she had rejected him. Lady Felisa had betrothed herself to a lord with lands that William could only dream of, and this lord, naturally, was a far more attractive proposition than William could ever be.

'I am so glad your mind was not damaged,' Lady Anna said.

'Damaged?'

As Lady Anna talked, artlessly confessing that

the Princess had suggested he might have suffered lasting injury as a result of the beatings inflicted upon him, William found himself re-examining her intentions towards him.

Harmless. The woman appeared to be harmless. She had seen that the children were clean and fed, and she had assured him that she intended to free him.

However, how likely was it that she would spend good money on a slave only to free him after performing a simple task? They were not short of servants here, the Palace was bursting with them. Had she bought him out of charity? Why? Why had she bought him?

Thus far, William had to concede that Lady Anna gave every appearance of having both his interests and those of the children at heart.

'Does your arm pain you?' she was asking. Her huge grey eyes were cloudy with anxiety, an anxiety that appeared genuine. William might be turning into a cynic, but some doubt remained. *Can I trust her?*

Chapter Three

The strapping on his shoulder wasn't tight, William flexed his arm for her and opened and closed his fingers. She followed the movement. With a jolt, William saw bright colour flood her cheeks as she observed the play of the muscles in his biceps. He repeated the movement, conscious of a pleasant tightening in his belly as she jerked her gaze away.

Keeping his face straight, for this prim lady-in-waiting amused him, he cleared his throat. 'I do feel a little weak yet, I shall have to follow an exercise regime to build up my muscles.'

'Oh, yes.' Her voice was faint. Crimson-cheeked, she stared fixedly at a brazier at the other end of the room. 'Strengthening exercises.'

To draw her gaze, he touched her sleeve and instantly her eyes locked with his—the contact had startled her. *I may not touch her, I am yet a slave in her mind.* Carefully, William removed his fingers from her sleeve, but the urge to tease remained.

'My lady, I have...' he ran his hand over his cheeks and grimaced '...a favour to ask.' With effort, he kept his face straight, fully aware that what he was about to ask bordered on insolence. She was so prim, though, he simply could not help himself.

'Yes?'

'I need to shave. I must look like a wild man.'

Her eyes widened, she examined him closely and, Lord, now it was he whose cheeks were burning. Not that she would be able to see, his beard would hide it. Thankfully.

'You want to shave?'

'If you do not...' William groped for the right word '...trust me with a knife *you* could shave me.'

She drew her head back, the movement expressed outrage.

William waited. Laughter was a breath away, he could see, he could actually see her struggle to decide whether to chastise him for being deliberately insolent or whether to let it pass because he might really want to shave. In her eyes his motives would likely be mysterious, he was a Frank, a barbarian from beyond the boundaries of the Empire.

It was when she nibbled her bottom lip, that full bottom lip, and William could not take his eyes off it, that he realised that somehow the boot had got on to the wrong foot. Suddenly, most inappropriately, he was aching to feel those gentle fingers on his cheeks, he wanted them caressing him under the guise of rubbing soap into his skin.

In a heartbeat, the idea of being shaved by Lady Anna had transformed. It was no longer a suggestion designed to wring an interesting reaction from her, it was a suggestion that had sent the hot blood rushing to his loins. Lord. Shifting on his pallet, William watched and waited to see whether she was prepared to give him the benefit of the doubt.

She swallowed. 'It is customary for Frankish men to shave off their beards?'

For a second time, William was forced to clear his throat. 'It is customary. I feel unkempt.'

'How long have you been in our Empire, William?'

'Not long.' In truth, William could not give her a full answer. What with the drugs the slavers had given him and the subsequent beatings, he had no clear idea how long it had been since he had been taken from Apulia.

'Here in our Empire, *men...*' careful emphasis

was placed on the last word, those tantalising lips pursed '...wear beards. You will look like a eunuch.'

'A eunuch!' God have mercy! William had forgotten that here in the Imperial Palace eunuchs were commonplace. They were chosen for high office because it was thought that men who were unable to found a dynasty were more likely to be loyal. 'Do I look like a eunuch?'

And then he saw it. A tiny smile trembled at the corners of her mouth. Little witch! She had realised he was teasing her and was repaying him in kind.

Repressing an impulse to take her hand, William ran his fingers round several days of stubble. 'My lady, local customs notwithstanding, I feel unkempt.'

Nodding, she gestured for one of the girls. 'Juliana?'

'My lady?'

'We require a bowl of hot water, some soap and a razor.'

The maidservant gave William a dark glance. 'A razor, my lady? Are you certain?'

'Please.'

Curtsying, Juliana went to find water.

William rubbed his chin. 'Thank you, my lady. I feel like a brigand with a beard.' He lay back and fixed her with a look. 'Mind that when it is done, there are to be no remarks about eunuchs.'

A carefully plucked brow arched. 'You are not yet free—you are in no position to make such pronouncements.'

The Frank is exhausted, Anna thought, when he made no response to her comment. Instead, he closed his eyes and seemed to drop straight into sleep. *And no wonder. When did he last have a proper night's rest?*

'Here is the water, my lady,' Juliana said, setting a large ewer down on a wall table. She had several linen cloths over her arm. 'Will you wake him?'

A light snore reached her. *How strange. I know that his request for me to shave him was made largely to goad me into some reaction, but I feel a distinct pang that I am unable to do so. How ridiculous! Surely I am not looking for an excuse to touch him? How unladylike. And how inappropriate, this man is a slave, a Frankish slave.*

And yet, here I am, sitting at his side, unable to stop studying that strong, bristled jaw. Wondering what it might be like to touch him. I like his face, I like his form. And his mouth—how can so beautiful a mouth be so uncompromisingly male?

In truth, I wonder what it would be like to be married to such a man?

This is a wild idea. This is a burst of folly that does not belong in a sensible, practical mind. I know nothing about this man, nothing. There must be other solutions. When I see Father tomorrow—

'My lady?'

Anna started. 'My pardon, Juliana. What did you say?'

'Do you wish me to wake him?'

'Oh! N…no. It is likely he needs rest far more than he needs to shave.'

The look in Juliana's eyes was knowing. She had observed Anna's reaction to the Frank and had drawn her own conclusions. Anna's face burned.

This will not do. I am lady-in-waiting to the Princess Theodora, I should not be entertaining feelings of any kind for this man. He is a stranger, a barbarian slave. It would be much better if I resolved matters with my father without him.

I wonder, was he born a slave? That cannot be, he has the look of a warrior about him, a warrior who, despite appalling maltreatment, has honour enough to care for two small children. And the way he addresses one, there is little subservience in his tone. Why is he a slave?

This man is no slave.

'Let him sleep,' Anna said.

Thankfully, the door to the Princess's bedchamber opened and Juliana turned that knowing gaze on Katerina. Anna's mouth twisted. In Juliana's mind, the scandal of what Princess Theodora Doukaina had been doing in her chamber with Commander Ashfirth clearly outweighed Lady Anna's paltry fascination with the Frank she had found in the slave market.

Rising, Anna shook out her skirts. 'Princess Theodora has expressed a desire to visit the bathhouse,' she said. 'I shall be attending her.'

'Yes, my lady.'

'Juliana, should the Frank waken while we are elsewhere, you may offer to shave him.'

When Juliana's eyes went hard, Anna saw that she was in for an argument. Juliana was a servant, not a slave, and she thought the task beneath her.

'Must I, Lady Anna?'

Anna gave her a straight look. 'That was an order, Juliana, not a request.'

Juliana lowered her head. 'Yes, my lady, my apologies.'

And when Katerina and I have finished in the bathhouse, I shall have decided what to do with him.

* * *

William woke to the smell of loaves, fresh from the oven. Bright slashes of light poured through the windows and lay on the marble floor tiles, like stripes on a shield. No sooner was he sitting up than a serving girl approached.

'You would eat?' she asked, offering him a basket filled to the brim with bread, cheese and dried figs.

'My thanks.' Balancing the basket on his lap, William picked up the bread. Warm. Since this might be the last food he was given for some time, he was going to make the most of it.

Across the chamber, it was heartening to see Daphne and Paula being cared for by Sylvia and Juliana. Lady Anna was near a brazier at the far end, breaking her fast at one of the side tables with the Princess. She had put away the dowdy brown gown. Today, Lady Anna was wearing blue silk and was every inch the noblewoman—the *beautiful* noblewoman.

Lady Anna and her princess looked abstracted—William received the impression that they were in a hurry. Lady Anna's attention was certainly taken up with Princess Theodora, she didn't glance his way though she must be aware he had woken.

William squashed a twinge of disappointment,

it was best this way. He would be gone from the Palace this morning, at the first opportunity— there would be no regrets. During the night, he had come to a decision. The thought of staying in the Great Palace while he gleaned more about his mother's past was tempting, but too much was at stake, he had to get back to Apulia. He had his future to consider and he wanted justice—the man who had wronged him must not go unpunished.

And once that had been accomplished... Lady Felisa might have rejected him, but perhaps some other lady might consider his suit. It was likely such a lady would be less well-endowed than Lady Felisa Venafro, he had been aiming too high with her. Yes, a less well-endowed lady might consider him. Or...an older one. Some older ladies took young knights to husband and William knew he was not considered ill-favoured. If his lack of lands worked against him, perhaps his looks might work for him.

William's gaze had drifted back to Lady Anna, she was lifting a goblet to her lips, grace and elegance in her every movement. Her quiet beauty was most appealing. And far too distracting.

Reminding himself that an army marched on its stomach and that he must stay focused on his escape, he turned his attention back to his food.

The cheese was soft and white and as fresh as the bread. He chewed thoughtfully.

He would make his escape at the first chance. Lady Anna had said that she would free him, but he could not wait on the pleasure of a titled lady. He would go today, while their guard was lowered. No one expected him to make a move—they believed him to be recovering. He would have to take care where the Varangians were concerned, though. He would need arms, clothing…

A draught lifted William from his plans in time for him to see a flash of blue silk and the shimmer of a blue veil shot through with silver threads. Lady Anna was gliding past him, the Princess at her side. They left the apartment. He stared after them, stirred by an uncomfortable emotion he was unable to interpret. It was as though that brief moment of shared amusement the evening before had never happened. With a grimace, he rubbed his chin. He was in even more of a need of a shave this morning than he had been when she had teased him about resembling a eunuch.

'Excuse me?' The maidservant Juliana cleared her throat. 'Do you care for shaving water?'

William had opened his mouth to accept when it struck him that shaving might not be the best idea. If Lady Anna was to be believed, most men in the City wore beards, like Saxons. If he shaved, he would draw attention to himself and a runaway slave ought not to be drawing attention to himself.

'I would appreciate water to wash in,' he said, 'but I shall wait until I am stronger before I shave.'

The maid clapped her hands. 'Kari! *Kari!*'

The main doors of the apartment opened and a guard appeared. It was the Varangian he had noted earlier. Absently, William picked a dried fig and sank his teeth into it. The guard was a Varangian to be sure, but he looked very young.

How much experience can a boy like that have?

'Kari,' the maidservant said, 'when this man has finished breaking his fast, would you be so good as to direct him to the bathhouse on the ground floor?'

The maid was asking the guard to show him to a bathhouse? William could hardly believe his ears. His heart thudded. His moment had come—freedom was within his grasp.

William gave the maid one of his best smiles. 'Thank you, I confess I would appreciate a visit to the bathhouse after I have eaten.'

Daphne and Paula were safe—he could leave with an easy conscience. He would allow enough time for Lady Anna and the Princess to get well clear of the Boukoleon, and then…freedom!

* * *

When Katerina—in her guise as the Princess—had expressed a desire to escape the Palace for a while, Anna understood exactly how she felt. If Anna found it unnerving pretending to be serving the Princess when in truth she was serving an impostor, it must be even more unnerving for Katerina.

If we are caught, what will happen to us? Will it be enough to say we have been following Princess Theodora's orders?

The real Princess had insisted that Anna and Katerina carry letters that stated they were acting on her instructions, but Katerina was starting to show a distressing tendency to go her own way. It did not bode well.

They passed through the door of the Boukoleon Palace and into the first of the courtyards. A light rain was falling. By rights they ought not to leave the Palace unescorted, but Anna sensed that Katerina wanted to talk and they could scarcely talk openly with the Emperor's personal guard breathing down their necks.

Anna drew up her hood and led the way along paths that glistened with wet. As they left one courtyard and entered another on their way to the Chalke Gate, the hairs rose on Anna's neck. Where was everyone? The grounds were eerily empty of people.

It is far too quiet.

Through an arch, a lone peacock trailed across one of the lawns, its brilliant glory lost and bedraggled. When its shriek broke the silence, Anna almost leaped out of her skin. A slave was hurrying along the paths by one of the smaller palaces, but she could see no one else. Of course, with everyone absent, who would notice them wandering about without an escort? Her skin prickled. It felt unnatural—she had never seen the Palace so deserted.

Where is everyone? Can the rumours be true?

Anna had only been back in the capital for a couple of days, but disturbing news had reached her. The army had acclaimed General Alexios as Emperor, raising him on their shields in the traditional Roman manner.

It cannot be true, it cannot. We already have an emperor, Emperor Nikephoros! What will happen to him if General Alexios takes the throne?

Shivering, she drew her cloak more tightly about her as they walked along. The General was said to be camped outside the City walls, waiting for the right moment to make his move. Unsurprisingly, these developments were causing much unease, colourful stories were flying back and forth like the shuttle on a loom. It was impossible to say if any of them was true.

I must say nothing of this to Katerina, the poor girl has enough to contend with, pretending to be a princess in a world that is alien to her. Katerina's plight is far worse than mine.

Anna might not be on the best of terms with her father, but if it came to light that she was helping Katerina pose as the Princess, he was an aristocrat and that must count in her favour. Katerina, on the other hand, was a simple village girl, she had no one to speak up for her.

Except me. I will speak for her, if need be.

Saints, this afternoon I am meeting Father! This afternoon I must persuade him that I cannot marry Lord Romanos.

Katerina halted. She was lifting her brows as she stared at an ancient building where part of the roof had caved in. A row of antique statues lined the portico, ghosts from another time. Several of the statues had lost their arms, one its head.

'That was the Hall of the Nineteen Couches,' Anna told her.

Katerina shuddered. 'It looks derelict.'

'Yes, it's been empty for years,' Anna said, leading Katerina past several domed buildings towards the gate.

How brave Katerina is, to play the Princess in this way. Particularly since she is new to Court. If I had her courage, it would doubtless be easy to convince Father that I am not prepared to fall in with his wishes. She sighed. *If only he were less intransigent...*

In the past, Anna had tried calm discussion, she had tried entreaty.

My lord, I cannot marry Lord Romanos, I cannot.

Her father had been unmoved. The matter of her marriage had transformed him into a cold stranger, the man she had once adored might never have been.

'Enough of this!' her father had declared in a tone that had made her blood run cold. 'You will marry Romanos Angelos! The Angeli expect it. I expect it. Believe me, Anna, I will do what is necessary to ensure this marriage takes place. If I have to beat you into submission, I will. If I have to starve you, I will.'

That was the point she had left for Rascia to join the Princess. Two years had passed since then, it was possible her father had mellowed. She simply must convince him that Lord Romanos was not for her. If not, she would have no recourse but to take desperate measures.

Desperate measures. In her mind, Anna could still see William on the slave block. He was swaying slightly, that magnificent body of his was bruised, but not broken, and those horrible chains were rattling as he stood over the children.

So protective. So brave and determined. Such an indomitable spirit.

Anna had hoped that with the coming of the next day, the desperate idea that had been born in the slave market would have been supplanted by another more sensible one. Unfortunately, that had not happened.

Marriage with William would, naturally, be temporary. It would be contracted purely to convince Lord Romanos that she was not the bride for him. The problem was that Anna did not need to speak to her father to know that marriage to a Frankish slave would alienate him permanently. That was not what she wanted.

During her time in Rascia the change in her father had eaten away at her. *How wonderful it would be to be reconciled with him. It is just that I cannot marry Lord Romanos!*

'Creeping about in this way makes me feel like a criminal,' Katerina said, breaking into her thoughts. 'I suppose in the eyes of the Commander I am a criminal.'

'You told me you had admitted nothing!'

'Nor did I. But I do feel guilty for misleading him. Perhaps it was short-sighted of me, but I had not expected to feel quite so...bad.'

They reached the Chalke Gate, passed through it and entered the City. The broad, colonnaded avenue was worryingly clear of citizens. Anna's sense of foreboding grew, unease was an icy chill on her skin. Although no one was about, it was probably best they did not stray far from the Palace.

'Anna?'

'Hmm?'

'Yesterday I overheard something very strange...'

'Oh?'

'One of the grooms said that a soldier called Alexios Komnenos was making a bid for the throne.'

Anna gave her a startled look. 'I was hoping you wouldn't hear about that.'

'So it's true? Why on earth didn't you mention it?'

'I thought you had enough to worry about, and after we got back from the slave market I was somewhat distracted.' Anna forced a smile and pushed away the image of a pair of green eyes fringed by dark lashes. 'We both were. By the time the Commander had left your bedchamber, it had quite slipped my mind.'

'You don't think there will be fighting in the City, do you?'

'It is possible, but I do not think it likely.' Anna spoke firmly, though privately she had her doubts. The Imperial throne was at stake, and General Alexios had never been defeated.

They rounded a corner to enter the square and a rumble of voices rolled at them. A child's thin wail cut through the rumble, a dog yelped. *So this is where everyone is.* Justinian's bronze column was dulled by the rain, the base was all but hidden by the crowd milling around it.

Katerina gasped. 'No wonder the Palace seemed empty, everyone is here!'

Anna nodded. Hundreds of citizens, courtiers if the sumptuous gowns and cloaks were anything to go by, were pressing towards the great column, pushing past it to reach the door that led to the great church of Hagia Sophia. Caught up in the crowd, Anna and Katerina were carried along as though by an inexorable force, before they knew it, they had crossed the church forecourt and been swept inside.

Hagia Sophia was full of shadows and the low

murmur of the faithful at prayer. The air was wreathed with incense and the dome above flickered with the light of a thousand hanging lamps. Mosaic saints, haloes agleam with gold, watched from the walls.

Katerina glanced about wildly and clutched Anna's arm. 'Anna, the Empress is bound to be here. I cannot meet the Empress, she knew the Princess before she was sent to Rascia...I can't take the risk... Anna, get us out of here!'

In the apartment overlooking the Sea of Marmara, the young Varangian had called for a slave named Philip. Philip was wearing a short-sleeved tunic of bleached linen, as he escorted William to the bathhouse, William noticed many men in similar tunics, as well as a number of women wearing clothes made from the same undyed fabric. There must be hundreds of slaves here. But more to the point were the soldiers—guards were patrolling the corridors, not all of them Varangians. They were doubtless there to protect the Imperial family, but their presence must also keep the slaves in order.

William halted in the bathhouse doorway. It was empty and light was shafting down from a row of glazed windows set high in the walls. Instead of the bathtub he had been expecting, tiled steps led down to what was in effect a small pool, steam was rising from the surface of the water. A wooden bench stood at the poolside and linen drying cloths were draped over a rack.

'Your shoes, if you please.' The slave Philip gestured for William to remove his down-at-heel shoes.

As William kicked them off, he made another discovery. The floor tiles were warm. 'Hypocaust,' he murmured, flexing his toes. *Mon Dieu*, glazed windows, heated floor—what luxury!

The bathhouse walls were tiled as well as the floor and a geometric frieze ran round the walls. The air was perfumed with aromatic herbs. Philip picked up William's embarrassingly shabby shoes and put them on the floor next to the bench, handling them as carefully as though they were the Emperor's purple slippers.

'Your belt, sir?' Philip said, woodenly.

'No need to call me "sir", Philip,' William said, amused at the way the man had handled his shoes. 'My name is William.'

When Philip looked at William as though he were a madman, William realised no one had thought to tell him that he, too, was a slave. *Not for long though...*

'William, my name is William.'

'Yes, sir. I think I had better remove that bandage before you go into the water.'

William gave up and submitted, and Philip helped him undress. The man stared thoughtfully at his discoloured chest.

'I can give you a body massage after your bath, sir. There is an ointment that will ease those bruises.'

'Thank you, but that will not be necessary.' William had a squire in Apulia, but the thought of being given a massage by this slave made him uncomfortable. Had it been Lady Anna, however... He grinned. The thought of Lady Anna's hands smoothing away his bruises was much easier to entertain.

'The water has been freshly drawn, sir.' Philip waved at a tray of oils and soaps. 'Do you care for me to bathe you?'

'Lord, no, I can do that for myself.' The water was blue and inviting. Hurriedly, William stepped in—it was blissfully warm.

'Is the temperature to your taste?'

'Perfect, thank you.'

'Is there anything else I can do for you, sir?'

Water lapping at his waist, William discovered a ledge which formed an underwater seat. Lowering himself onto it, he reached for a block of soap. It smelled of rosemary and pine.

'No, thank you, Philip, I have everything. I shall call if I need you.'

'Very good, sir.'

'Philip?'

'Sir?'

'I should like to take my time in here.'

'Of course, sir.'

Bowing, Philip left the bathhouse, closing the door softly behind him.

William eyed the shadows on the tiled floor. Philip would probably give him half an hour before returning, but he couldn't rely on it. He must be quick, he would be gone from the bathhouse long before Philip came to find him.

Dipping his head beneath the water, he soaped himself from top to tail, then rinsed off. He was dry and had pulled on his braies and hose before he checked the shadow again. It had scarcely moved. His arm gave a twinge, having been half-wrenched from its socket by the slave master, it needed support. Finding the discarded bandage, he attempted to replicate the bindings as Lady Anna had done them. He made something of a clumsy job of it, but it would have to do.

It was a pity about the lack of a tunic. Shrugging—with the Palace crawling with guards, William minded the lack of a sword far more than he minded the lack of a tunic—he slipped his feet into his shoes and crept to the door. One of the larger drying cloths would do as a cloak.

Easing the door open, he peered through the chink and caught the rumble of nearby voices. He thought he recognised Philip talking, but could not make out what he was saying, or who he was talking to.

Not that way. Quietly closing the door, he narrowed his eyes and looked up at the windows, judging the height. His gaze dropped to the wooden bench.

In a matter of moments, he had upended the bench, scrambled up it and reached the window...

William's makeshift cloak must have passed muster, for once out of the bathhouse, he kept his head down and went through acres of Palace grounds without being questioned. Not that he saw many people, the courtyards, lawns and paths were largely empty. The sky was overcast, the air damp. A light rain was falling—it was more of a mist than rain—and there was a briny tang to the air. That last might have been his imagination, but

William knew the sea was close, he had glimpsed it through the apartment windows.

Heart thudding, braced for the shout that would warn him that his disappearance from the bathhouse had been discovered, William skirted a number of columned buildings. Rather to his irritation, he found himself wondering if he might catch sight of a blue veil shot through with silver threads. He received vague impressions of marbled porticoes, of fountains playing over nymphs and dolphins. Exotic birds wandered the lawns, their long tails leaving dark lines in the wet grass, but there was no sighting of a lady-in-waiting in a blue gown.

He was fortunate that Lady Anna had bought him, it was undoubtedly easier escaping from her than it would have been escaping from the merchant. The merchant had wanted a drudge. He would have kept him chained and maltreated him to keep him docile. And if the lady with the painted face had won the bidding? William shuddered to think what use she might have had for him.

Hearing the whinny of a horse, William broke step. A low whitewashed building lay on his left hand, cheek by jowl with the Palace wall. A long-jawed dog was tied to a ring in the wall and a couple of muscled grooms idled by a water trough. This must be the Imperial Stables.

What are my chances of stealing a horse?

A boy emerged from the stable with a forkful of dirty hay. He tossed it on to the muck heap and looked questioningly at William. 'Good morning, sir.'

'Good morning.' *No chance there.* Nodding casually at the stable boy, William passed on.

Was this all the Palace? It was like a city! Lord, somehow he had to get through the wall. Where in hell was the nearest gate? William couldn't ask, to do so would reveal a suspicious ignorance of the Palace, but if this went on, he was likely to find himself going round in circles. And the last thing William wanted was to find himself back where he had started, at the Boukoleon Palace.

Above him, the clouds were falling apart and the morning sun was breaking through. It was exactly what William needed. If the Great Palace was walled all around, surely it was reasonable to assume there would be more than one gate? He knew the Sea of Marmara lay to the south so… he would head north-east, there was bound to be a gate in the eastern wall.

Using the sun as his guide, William pressed on, hugging the side of a great hall, skirting one courtyard and another. He had no idea why the Palace was so quiet, but it was an unexpected blessing.

Some buildings looked to have been abandoned. He walked swiftly by and at last found a gate manned by four sentries. They were well equipped with helmets and mail tunics, with swords and spears...

William tried not to look too obviously at their arms. They were not Varangians, they had no battleaxes.

Again, his luck was in. Grave-faced, the guards had their heads together and were deep in discussion. William strolled languidly towards them. Concerned that the bruising on his naked chest and the bandage on his arm might cause comment, he drew the cloth firmly about him and prayed they were too preoccupied to notice that his cloak was a drying cloth from the Palace bathhouse. His pulse rate speeded up.

'Surely General Alexios won't fight it out in the streets?' one was saying. 'It's tantamount to treason.'

Another guard shook his head and made a sucking sound with his teeth. 'You don't think so? The General has been acclaimed Emperor by the army *and* he has the backing of half the Court. Emperor

Nikephoros is too weak to object.' Absently, he waved William through.

'Yes,' a third man chimed in as William forced himself to walk casually past, 'Emperor Nikephoros has alienated far too many. Wouldn't be surprised if...'

William stepped into a paved street and the voices faded. God be praised, he was free! Likely the guards would have been more disciplined and demanding if he had been trying to enter the Palace, but, thank God, he was out.

Free!

Heaving a sigh, William released his grip on his makeshift cloak. He knew the drill—he must walk naturally, he must walk as though he knew where he was going.

Head up, he turned briskly into a broad avenue. The rain had stopped. He had only gone a few paces when he noticed a fifth sentry outside the Palace. The man was facing the wall a few yards from the gate, a puddle at his feet. Adjusting the tunic beneath his mail coat, he gave William a sheepish grin. His gaze sharpened when he noticed William's discoloured chest. 'Sir?'

'Guard?' Dear God, it would take but one shout for this man to alert his comrades at the gate.

'Would you mind telling me your business, sir?' The sentry's hand hovered over his sword hilt.

William glanced quickly about him, the street, like the Palace, was largely empty. *Let the games begin.* Snatching off his makeshift cloak, William dived. He had the cloth round the man's head before the sword was unsheathed.

The guard struggled and pain shot up William's arm. Gritting his teeth, William held on grimly, cracking the helmeted head against the Palace wall. The man grunted and went limp.

William snatched the sword and was haring down a side street before a bemused passer-by raised the alarm.

'Guards!' Behind him came a shout. *'Guards!'*

Chapter Four

Heart pounding like a drum, William gripped the sword hilt and ran on, twisting and turning down a narrow series of passages that cut in between some wooden buildings. He turned left, he turned right, he turned left again—the City was like a maze. At last the shouts faded. When he stopped to draw breath, he found himself at the edge of a large ceremonial square. His chest heaved. Black spots danced at the edge of his vision.

On one side there was an imposing building faced with purple marble in the classic style the Romans had favoured. Myrtle bushes lined the avenue between the building and a pillared monument. There was movement behind the monument, a tantalising metallic gleam in the strengthening sunlight—the flash of light on a fan of spears, on a line of battleaxes.

Lord, Varangians, and he had all but run into

them. The Emperor's personal guard were out in force, in battle formation by the look of it. Still breathless, William backed behind a myrtle bush as snatches of the sentries' words came back to him. 'General Alexios…battle it out in the streets… the backing of half the Court.'

God have mercy, what was going on? Whatever it was, it was serious enough to have cleared the Palace grounds of courtiers, it had sent the Varangians to stand their ground in this square not a stone's throw from the Palace.

An ear-splitting scream pierced the air—a woman's. It had come from the tangle of streets behind him. Whipping round, William's gaze fell on a scrap of blue cloth caught in one of the myrtles. He tugged it free. Diaphanous blue silk, with silver threads cunningly caught in the weave.

Jesu! Lady Anna!

His stomach formed a tight knot as his consciousness narrowed down to the scrap of silk. The blue was an exact match—he remembered the glint of silver threads in her veil as she had left the apartment.

As another scream came from the mouth of the alley, William's instincts told him that Lady Anna was close.

A triumphant cry echoed off the walls of the

building. William felt sick. Several male voices... laughing, jeering, urging each other on. Lady Anna had just run into the worst kind of trouble, he was sure of it.

He was cold, cold as ice, yet perspiration was springing to his brow, he could almost feel his freedom sliding away from him. So much for returning to Apulia for justice, so much for winning lands for himself...

He could see her in his mind, grey eyes softening as she offered him the Venetian glass, mouth curving in a shy smile.

'Merde!' William braced himself and stepped back into the avenue.

He took a deep breath and before he had drawn the next, Lady Anna flew out of the head of the alley. Her breast was heaving, her fingers were clenched white on her blue skirts, holding them clear of the ground. Her veil had gone and her hair was streaming out behind her like a dark pennon. One foot was shoeless, William had time to register the disturbing vulnerability of bare toes before the men who were after her appeared.

Mercenaries. Three of them, howling like wolves. Predators. The uniform was unknown to him, but their eyes told William all he needed to know. These men were not fixed on any coming battle, they were focused on taking their prey. There was no doubt that rape was large in their minds.

Another scream came from the alley behind the building. Likely some other poor woman was being accosted by more of these devils. He prayed it was not the Princess.

William renewed his grip on the sword, the mercenaries halted and exchanged grins. They might as well have spoken aloud—they outnumbered him, they thought him easy meat.

'That would be a mistake,' William said softly.

There was movement behind him. Not Lady Anna. She had stopped mid-flight in front of the monument, her breath coming in shuddering gasps. Cold anger burned in William's guts.

He was woefully out of condition—his chest ached, his sword arm throbbed and it was one man against three. There was a chance he might prevail, but it was small.

The soldiers hesitated and William caught a whiff of soured wine.

They have been drinking. Good. That evens the odds a little...

As he summoned the strength to make the first move, William felt the walls of Constantinople close in on him. Picking out the lead mercenary, he raised his sword.

Oddly, the mercenary wasn't concentrating on William, he was looking past him. When his leer faded, William realised that something other than Lady Anna had distracted him.

Behind him, a harsh voice bellowed, 'Lady Anna! This way!'

Briefly, wary of losing sight of the mercenaries, William looked over his shoulder. A Varangian had appeared, it was the man who had emerged from Princess Theodora's bedchamber, the man he had seen in her company at the slave market. Commander Ashfirth.

The Commander unhooked his battleaxe and gestured Lady Anna towards him. The battleaxe glinted.

Lady Anna stumbled towards him. 'Commander! Thank God!'

William held steady in the centre of the avenue. *They will not have her, they will have to step over my body to reach her.*

The mercenaries' swords wavered. One of them took a step back.

Stay with the Commander, my lady. Be safe.

The lead mercenary spat. Another swore in a language that William did not understand. There was another backwards step, and another, and moments later all three had melted into the street round the corner of the building.

Warily, William turned. Lady Anna's hair was tumbled down about her shoulders, she had lost her hair pins as well as her veil, but thank God he could see no bruises.

'My lady—' Commander Ashfirth was frowning down the side street '—where is Katerina?'

Katerina? Who the devil is Katerina?

Lady Anna's mouth opened and shut, and the Commander gave her a little shake. 'My lady?'

'You...you know?' Lady Anna said, all colour leached from her face.

The Commander nodded and shook her again. 'The time for pretence is over. *Where is Katerina?*'

William frowned and stepped closer, he did not like the way the Commander was handling her. And why was he asking about Katerina? Surely he should be worried about the Princess? If William had guessed correctly, this man was the Princess's lover. Who was Katerina?

Lady Anna met William's gaze. 'She is safe. In Hagia Irene.'

'Thank God!' The Commander's relief was obvious. He looked at William. 'You there, slave!'

William did not lower his guard. 'Yes?'

'You will look after Lady Anna?'

'Yes.'

'Time is short,' the Commander said.

'I understand.' Lady Anna smiled at the Varangian. 'You had to know she was safe.'

Commander Ashfirth nodded. 'Do you trust this Frank?'

Lady Anna and William looked at one another.

'I will be safe with him,' Lady Anna said, her gaze flickering briefly to William's sword. 'Go back to your men, Commander.'

The Commander gazed coolly at William. 'You are to protect Lady Anna with your life. Take her back to the women's quarters in the Palace. Understand?'

Nodding, William held out his hand. 'I understand.'

Lady Anna moved towards him and Commander Ashfirth turned and sprinted round the monument towards his men.

The sunlight shone in Lady Anna's hair, it was glorious in its disarray. Her hand when it met William's was trembling and her breath was shaky, but she was safe.

Another whoop came from the side street, it was followed by the unmistakable sound of swords being banged on shields. Scare tactics. Lord, it looked as though Lady Anna was not quite as safe as William had hoped.

Her hand jerked free and she pointed. 'Look!'

Two of the mercenaries had returned, they were marching towards them, screeching like demons as they beat their sword hilts on their shields.

'Holy Mother!' Bundling Lady Anna behind him, William braced himself.

With only two mercenaries, the odds were turning in his favour.

The mercenaries nodded at each other, it must have been a signal, because one of them rushed at him headlong. He was over-confident and had little finesse. A butcher. As their swords clashed, the jolt sent black pain shooting up William's arm. He grunted and parried the next stroke easily. He might be out of condition, but they had barely engaged and already the mercenary was breathing hard. Too much wine, William suspected. Too much chasing after innocent women.

He parried half-a-dozen more strokes, feeling his way into the man's weaknesses, of which there were many. The other mercenary must be as drunk as the butcher, for he made no move to come to his comrade's aid, instead, each slash of the butcher's sword was accompanied with an unholy whoop and a thud on his shield. The strokes were wild, uneven. Slice, crash, hack, crash—like beats in in a devil's chorus.

It took only moments for William to begin to enjoy himself. It had been too long since he had held a sword and it was invigorating to realise that he had not lost his touch. This man was not his match. William was just through the warming-up stage—he no longer felt shooting pains with each clash of steel—when the mercenary overreached himself. William made a swift, decisive thrust and the man clattered to the ground. His shield rolled to the side, blood seeped across the paving.

Behind him, Lady Anna whimpered and the devil's chorus fell silent. The second mercenary stared at his comrade, eyes bulging.

William picked up the shield and beckoned. 'Come on, don't be shy, it's your turn. I could use more practise.'

The man had eyes as dead as his comrade's. His lip curled, he muttered something incomprehensible and retreated back the way he had come.

There was movement behind him. 'I...I thank you, William.' Lady Anna's cheeks were bloodless, she looked to be in shock as she watched him clean his sword on the dead man's chausses. It was a pity she had had to witness death at close hand, but William had had no choice.

'Come, my lady, we must hurry, there may be other mercenaries about. Which way?' That terrible screaming had started again, William gritted his teeth. *'Which way?'*

Her smoky grey eyes were wide with alarm. 'Do you think he went for reinforcements?'

'It is possible. *Which way?'*

She seemed held by panic and waved vaguely at the wall of the Great Palace. The domes of the Palace buildings were visible behind it. 'The Palace is too far, we might not make it.'

Shaking his head, William slung the mercenary's shield over his shoulder. With the sword firmly in one hand, he took hers in the other. Tugging her after him, he ducked behind the myrtle bushes and ran along the side of the building. The myrtle bushes were good cover. He stopped abruptly at the corner. A small structure resembling a storehouse stood a few feet away. There was no window, just a stumpy wooden door with fat hinges. He frowned doubtfully at it. It could almost be a prison cell.

Releasing Lady Anna, he handed her the shield and shouldered open the door. Inside, it was dark as night, he could see nothing. Behind them came the tramp of heavy boots.

'William!'

With a final glance at the sky, William bent his head and pulled her into the dark. Prison or not, this was the only hiding place. He had to be realistic. He could not fight an entire troop—if he were killed, who would protect Lady Anna?

It was ice cold inside, in an instant his skin was covered in goosebumps. The dim outline of a great cavern opened up before them, it was large enough to house a cathedral. William halted, staring in disbelief. He could smell water.

A small hand found his. 'See, William, the steps?'

As his eyes adjusted, he followed Lady Anna's pointing finger. A few yards ahead, a flight of steps fell into the gloom. Several feet lower down something sparked briefly, like a firefly. He caught sight of a vast stone column—no, a long line of them, marching into the murk, a legion of silent sentinels. There was another shadowy line of columns, and another, seemingly an entire army. The poor light made it impossible to see how many there were or how far they went. It was like staring into the hall of an underworld king.

'I see the steps.' Sensing that panic held her, he made his voice firm. 'Remember where they are, we are going down without a torch.'

Out in the streets, a bloodcurdling shout lifted

the hairs of the back of his neck. Just out of sight, the wolves were circling.

'Memorise the steps, my lady.' It was pitch black. Cold. It reminded him of the dungeons at Melfi. Taking the shield, he leaned past her and pushed the door shut. The darkness swallowed her. 'Stand still a moment,' he said, wedging the door with the shield.

'William?'

'I am ensuring no one will follow us. I don't believe we were seen, but…we cannot be too careful.' He found her hand again. 'The wall on your right will guide you,' he added, tugging her on.

The walls were slippery with damp, the air smelt…

'River,' he murmured. 'This place smells of river.'

Her small hand gripped his with surprising strength. Not wanting her to trip on her skirts, he took his time in the descent. It was like going down into Hades, it was bone-chillingly cold. He could do with a wool tunic, a padded gambeson…

'The water has been channelled here from the river,' she said, her voice sounding calmer. 'We are in the Basilica Cistern.'

'The Basilica Cistern?'

'Emperor Justinian built it so the Palace would have a permanent supply of fresh water.'

'Justinian? Surely that was centuries ago?'

'His cistern still feeds water into the Great Palace.'

Feeling with his feet, William groped on down. The sword scraped the wall, without a scabbard it presented something of a hazard, but he wasn't about to set it aside. If someone did manage to corner them down here, he would need it.

His instincts were shrieking at him, *be wary, be wary.* Was this a dead end? 'My lady, is there another way out?'

'If there is, I don't know it. This is the first time I have come down here. I recall being told there's a platform at the bottom.'

'Good. We can take refuge there, it will be out of sight of anyone who forces their way past that shield.'

'So we wait in the dark?'

He pulled her on, the warmth of her fingers was the only warmth in this dank Hades. 'Until we judge it safe to come out, I am afraid that we must.'

An image of the Varangians lined up in the square overhead flashed through William's mind.

'It looked as though there might be fighting,' she said, evidently following the train of his thoughts.

'Yes, we might have to wait until the dust has settled.'

'That...that could take some time.'

He felt a burst of regret. *Why did she have to leave the Palace today of all days? If it were not for her, I would be at the port by now, boarding a ship for Apulia.*

William could hear her breathing, he could hear his breathing, he could hear the soft whisper of silk as she came down the steps after him. He heard a splash and froze.

'That must be a fish.'

'There are fish down here?' Lord, what a place.

They fumbled on. So dark. So cold. He reached the last step and turned. Anna walked into him. His nose was briefly buried in hair that smelt tantalisingly of jasmine and spices. *Persephone in the kingdom of Hades.*

'My apologies.' He took his time drawing back, drawn to her warmth in this realm of cold and dark. The flowery fragrance sent tendrils deep into his mind. 'The steps have ended, this must be the platform,' he said, releasing her. 'We can go no farther, unless you have a mind to swim.'

'I wish we could see. How large do you think the platform is?'

'I am not sure. I am hoping it is at least a few

feet wide. I take it there's something like a lake down here.'

'I believe so.'

'How deep is it?'

'I do not know.'

If only they could see...

Manoeuvring her to the wall where she would be safest, William wrapped her fingers round the hilt of the sword. 'Hold this, if you please. Be careful, I don't want you to cut yourself.' He dropped to his knees.

'What are you doing?'

'Learning how much space we have before the water...ah! We shall be safe here, my lady, we have a couple of yards each way.'

The platform seemed to be made of wooden slats. The wall of the cistern and the steps rose up on one side, the other three sides led nowhere. About them came a constant drip, drip, drip of water.

Ensuring he kept himself between Lady Anna and the water, William found his way back to her and slid his hand down her arm till he found the sword. 'I'll take this.' Sinking to a sitting position against the wall, he pulled her down beside him. 'Since we are likely to be here for some while, we may as well take our ease. It's a pity I didn't have time to take the scabbard.'

'Where did you find the sword? What are you doing out of the Palace?'

William cleared his throat. He still had hold of her hand and he intended to keep it unless she made an objection, she would be safer if he knew her exact whereabouts. 'Its previous owner didn't keep good care of it, so I thought I would spare him the trouble.'

'You stole it?'

'Yes.'

'You…did you kill to get it?'

William listened carefully to her tone in order to gauge her feelings. Was she angry at him for attempting to escape her? She had seen him kill— did she fear him?

'No, but the guard will have a thick head for a time.'

'William?'

'My lady?'

'It is a terrible thing to see a man killed.' Her voice broke, he heard her swallow.

Putting his arm about her, William drew her to him. 'I did not do it lightly, my lady. Killing is never something to be undertaken lightly.'

'I know.' She leaned against him and he heard a small sniff. 'It is a terrible thing.'

'Don't waste your pity, that mercenary would not have given you, or me, a second thought.'

'I suppose not.' She sighed and, after a few moments, lifted her head. Delicate fingers touched his chest. 'Holy Mother, William, you are frozen! Here, have this.'

There was a rustling and some fabric was pushed at him. Her cloak.

'No, my lady, you need it.'

'But you have no tunic!'

'We shall be warmer together, so with your permission, we shall share it.'

'Very well.'

'Here...' Draping her cloak about them—it was a satisfyingly heavy cloak that felt as though it was lined with wool—William settled his arm about her. The light scent of jasmine filled the air.

'How did you escape the Palace, William?'

'The bathhouse windows were...insecure.'

'The bathhouse windows? Well, you chose a good day to make your move. Everyone is preoccupied with...' She trailed to a halt.

'General Alexios?'

'You've heard about him?'

He shrugged into the dark. 'A little. I do know the Varangian Guard would not be deployed in that square for nothing.'

'No.' She sighed. 'You were running away, so you don't trust me. I thought you understood, I have no intention of keeping you. As far as I am concerned, you are a free man.'

'You expect something from me, you admitted as much.'

'As to that, it is…a delicate matter. I am hoping to resolve it without you, in which case you will be freed unconditionally.'

William said nothing. Words came cheap, life had taught him as much. Several gold coins had exchanged hands for him at the slave market. Yes, words came cheap, but he had not. How likely was it that a slave would be bought and freed without having to do something in return?

It was black as pitch in the Basilica Cistern and William could not see, but he could feel Lady Anna's grey eyes on him. They would be earnest, open, honest.

'Lady Anna, I would like to believe you but…' even to his own ears he sounded cynical '…I have lost faith in my fellows.'

Warm fingers found his forearm, squeezing him in what he knew was intended as a gesture of comfort. 'William, you shall be freed. I would prefer that you stay, but after what you have done for me, if you choose to leave the City later today, I swear I will not send anyone after you.'

'The Commander ordered me to return you to the Palace.'

'The Commander does not own you!' Her voice softened. 'I will not hold it against you if you disobey him. And I shall simply find another solution to my dilemma. But setting my interests aside, it might be better if you do return to the Boukoleon.'

'Oh?'

Gently she shook his arm. 'So I might give you your document of manumission. You will need written proof you have been freed.'

William shifted and the hand fell away. 'My lady, since I do not accept that anyone had any right to enslave me in the first place, receiving your so-called manumission is, as I see it, an empty formality.'

'But, William...' She hesitated. 'Are you content that I address you as William?'

'As you choose, my lady.'

'William, you may believe such a document is worthless, but think...if you were questioned by someone who had chanced to see you at the market, it would be much better if you had the document with you.'

'I don't need a piece of parchment to know that I am a free man!'

She paused long enough for William to hear the slow drip of water close by. Cold from the wall behind them was seeping through her cloak and despite his irritation with her—he was a free man, he had always been a free man!—his instinct was to pull her closer. Briskly, he rubbed the chill from his arms.

'Very well—' her voice came softly through the dark '—I was only trying to help, as you helped me up there. I do thank you for that. I expect warding off those men was the last thing you wanted to do.'

William grunted. In all honesty, he couldn't deny it, his mind had been fixed on escape. 'I only wish you had stayed inside the Palace, you would have been safe there.' He hadn't liked the thought of her being hurt. 'I wasn't free for long, but I heard guards talking, you must have known that General Alexios was on the point of making his move.'

'I did hear whispers.'

'Then why leave the Palace today of all days? Why put yourself and the Princess at risk?'

'I...we had other things on our minds.'

'Such as...?'

'I...I cannot say.'

'Mon Dieu!' William had never shaken a woman

in his life, but he was beginning to understand Commander Ashfirth, he certainly felt like shaking one now. 'What could be more important than your safety?'

'William, your tone borders on insolence.' Her voice became distant. 'I am sorry I put your plans into disarray, but there is no need to speak to me in that manner.'

'I will speak to you in whatever manner I please! You endangered both yourself and the Princess, and I am stuck with the consequences.'

With a rustle of skirts, she shifted away, dragging some of the cloak with her. Cold air rushed between them. William grimaced. He had been enjoying the softness of her thigh against him, he had been enjoying the shared warmth.

'I am sorry to have inconvenienced you,' she said in that distant voice. 'But I do thank you, I know what could have happened. My father would have been beside himself if they had…taken me.'

Her words were startling, he peered into the dark, wishing he could see her expression. 'You are not saying your father would have chastised you?'

She gave a light laugh. 'I am certain that he would. Father expects me to go to my marriage in a pure, unsullied state.'

'But those men would have forced you! No father can chastise a daughter if a man forces himself upon her.'

There was a slight movement beside him, she
was shrugging her shoulders. 'It is important to
my father that I make a good marriage. If I am not
pure, my value is reduced.'

'I take it you mean your value as a bride?'

'Of course.'

The turn in the conversation was most unusual.
This was not the sort of discussion William had
ever thought to conduct with a high-born lady,
never mind one who was lady-in-waiting to a princess. In the past, while ladies had been happy to
tease and flirt with him, none had ever taken him
into their confidence. And this was a deeply personal conversation. Perhaps Lady Anna had need
of a confidant, perhaps she found it easier to talk to
a stranger. Well, since he was stuck down here with
her, he would listen. It was a small price to pay for
her kindness at the Palace. 'You were fortunate
then in more ways than one that the Commander
and I chanced to see you.'

'Indeed.'

'I am sure you are a daughter who makes your
father proud.'

'William, I wish that were true. But Father and

I…we have not always seen eye to eye.' She sighed. 'But you do not wish to talk about me.'

'Why not? With the City in turmoil, we are likely to be here for hours, we may as well entertain each other. Go on, tell me about your father.'

In truth, Apulia was beckoning and William would have liked nothing better than to get away. The cistern made his flesh creep, it was a dank and deathly place. However, he could not abandon Lady Anna to the mercy of marauding troops. It mattered little what her intentions towards him were, she might or might not intend to free him, but at heart he sensed she was a kind and gentle girl.

'You were saying that you and your father do not see eye to eye, I find that surprising. You are lady-in-waiting to the Princess—is that not a great honour?' William became conscious of a prickle of unease, something was nagging at the back of his mind. He had a strong sense that something important had eluded him.

'Yes, it is a great honour,' she murmured.

'An honour only given to a chosen few?'

'It is an honour I took for myself—my father does not consider that I earned it.'

'How so?' When Lady Anna gave no response, he added, drily, 'I am sorry, my lady, I am impertinent. A slave should not ask such questions of his mistress.'

'William, believe me, you are going to be freed!' She sighed. 'As it happens, I agree with you, we ought to talk. Since we find ourselves incarcerated down here for a time, what else might we do but talk?'

It was an innocent enough remark, but William found himself smiling into the dark. *What might we do? Oh, my lady, any number of things...*

The darkness might have robbed him of sight, but it was easy to conjure the image of her face and figure, it was a pleasure to recall her easy grace as she glided about the Princess's apartment. He hardly knew her, yet he could visualise her easily. They were sitting in inky blackness, but he could see her, clear as day...he could see those grey eyes widen as he loosed her gown and slid it from her...he could feel the softness of her skin against his. It would be warm as satin, soft as rose petals...those prim lips would relax, they would melt against his...her breasts would feel perfect against his chest...perfect...

A pulse throbbed in his loins. William swallowed. 'My lady, you may confide in me. Lest you are concerned, I give you my word that I shall not breathe a word of what we say. If...' he put a smile in his voice '...the word of your slave is acceptable to you? Talk to me, my lady.'

Mon Dieu, she had better talk to him, he needed distraction from thoughts that would surely shock her. And if nothing else, William might learn more about the Great Palace. He had often tried to imagine life at the Imperial Court.

'Very well. In short, Father and I fought over the question of my marriage. I could not like the man he had chosen for me and my father refused to change his mind. After several weeks of arguing, I left Constantinople and went to join Princess Theodora. At that time, she was living in Rascia, awaiting her own marriage. It was wrong of me to go against my father's wishes, but I simply could not stomach the man he had chosen.'

'Rascia is a long way to go to escape marriage.'

'Yes...' her voice came quietly through the gloom '...it took weeks to get there. When I set out I was very ignorant, I had no idea the Empire was so large.'

'And now both you and the Princess have returned to the Palace.' That irritating sense that he had missed something was still there, nagging quietly at the back of his mind. *What is it? Something, there is something I have missed...*

'We only returned the day before yesterday, I

have yet to greet my father. I have sent word—I expect to meet him later today.'

Her voice had changed, it was less confident, as though she was unsure of her ground. *There is more she might say, but she is concealing it...*

'You fear your father will insist on this marriage?'

'It seems likely.'

'What is the name of this unwanted fiancé?'

'Lord Romanos Angelos.'

William pressed her hand. 'You may discover you have outgrown the revulsion you felt for him.'

She gave one of her quiet laughs. 'I doubt it. I am in something of a mire over this because I am resolved to win my father's approval. I fear it will be a struggle.'

'You have been of service to the Imperial family—he must be proud of you!'

Anna heard the conviction in William's voice and smiled. She had insisted that Katerina should buy him and she did not regret it.

I could like this man, this mysterious Frank, but I must be wary of what I say to him.

Sitting in the dark, sharing her cloak with him, she felt extraordinarily at ease, so safe.

Therein lies the danger.

In truth, I know little about him. William is an

escaped slave from the Palace, one who has con-
trived to arm himself with a sword... I cannot be
certain I will be safe. His resemblance to Erling is,
now I am getting to know him, superficial. I must
not let the physical resemblance to Erling warp
my judgement. And above all, I must remember
my duty to the Princess.

I cannot be completely open with him.

What if he discovers that Katerina is not the
Princess? If I confess my involvement in a plan
to deceive the entire Court and word gets out...
Holy Virgin, if Father comes to hear of it, we shall
never be reconciled!

'William, I can say no more about my time in
Rascia with the Princess. Suffice it to say that my
father was displeased not only with my disobedi-
ence, but also with the manner of my going. I left
the capital publicly and without his express permission. By doing so, I shamed him before the entire Court. My father is the Governor of Heraklea
and—'

'Clearly, he is a proud man.'

'I can only pray he will forgive me.' Uncon-
sciously, Anna's fingers tightened on William's.
'Nor will it endear me to him if he learns that it
was I who urged the Princess to buy you. At first

glance you are very like a man called Erling. If my father meets you, he is bound to remember.'

'Erling? Who the devil is Erling?'

'Erling was a slave on my father's estate. In truth, he was my slave, but I never considered him as such—we were friends.'

'Lady Anna had to look to a slave for friendship?' His voice was teasing. 'That I find hard to believe.'

'Erling was a friend,' Anna insisted, regretting the defensive tone that had crept into her voice. 'He kept me company when I was a child.'

'What happened?'

'He…he died.'

'I am sorry.'

'I was very young and I made a foolish mistake.' She sighed. 'Had Erling lived, I suspect he would have resembled you.'

'That is why you pressed the Princess to buy me?'

'It is why you…caught my eye.' *I do not know William well enough to tell him what else ran through my mind…that I thought to use him to fend off marriage with Lord Romanos. And I certainly can't tell him after seeing that display of swordsmanship by the Augustaion. He is clearly no ordinary slave, he has had the training of a warrior.*

'My lady, you cannot leave it at that, you must explain.'

'There have always been slaves on the estate at Heraklea. Erling was…this may sound strange… but he was my companion. We were almost of an age. It was his task to keep an eye on me, to accompany me when I rode round the estate, to—' Anna broke off with something that sounded suspiciously like a sob.

'How did Erling die?'

'My father had house guests, and Lady Ma… one of the ladies had a bracelet I admired. I borrowed it without asking her permission. When the lady discovered it was missing, she accused Erling of stealing it. I didn't realise until it was too late. He was beaten. He died that night.' Anna's throat closed up.

'Was your father involved in the beating?'

'I…I have said enough.'

'You grieved for Erling.'

'Yes.'

'How old were you when this happened, my lady?'

'Ten years of age. I always felt there was something I could have done to prevent his death.'

'But you were only a child!'

'As I said, I regretted not being able to save him.

I suppose that's one reason why, when I saw you on the slave block, I had to buy you.'

'One reason? Will you not tell me your other reason?' His question was little more than a whisper.

'I...I am not prepared to say.'

There was a short silence.

'My lady, you were motivated by more than wanting to redress past wrongs.'

She pulled her hand away, guiltily aware she was telling him only half of the truth. 'I know it is foolish, I know you are not Erling, but part of me did want to set the balance straight.' *While another part saw you on that slave block and saw my salvation...*

Chapter Five

'It appears you have a soft heart, Lady Anna,' William said, wishing she would tell him everything.

'What nonsense!'

'You are kind.' It was the sort of gently flattering remark a knight might make to a lady with whom he was conversing, but in Lady Anna's case it had the ring of truth about it. Lady Anna was unlike any noble lady he had ever met. He sensed a rare sensitivity in her, she gave the impression of genuinely caring for the well-being of others, whatever their rank. She had been fond of the slave called Erling, she had grieved for him.

However, she was not purely motivated by kindness, there was a hint of self-interest in the mix. The cynic in him mocked his desire to see the best in her. This was partly about atonement, Lady

Anna had bought him because guilt from the past had darkened her soul for years.

There was the question of the task she had for him. It must be discreditable, otherwise she would surely explain what she had in mind. William's lips twisted. Self-interest motivated most people, he would be the first to admit it motivated him. Yet his naïve self, the part of him that wanted to see the best in her, would not be silenced...

Lady Anna gave every sign of being a caring woman. She had ensured he was well treated in the Palace, she was sharing her cloak—would Lady Felisa be as mindful of her servants as Lady Anna seemed to be?

Lady Felisa Venafro was the Apulian lady who had misled William into thinking that she might accept him as her husband. At the time William had been delighted. Marriage to Lady Felisa would have given him the surety of a roof over his head, he would have had lands, a future, heirs.

He should not have been surprised when Lady Felisa had betrothed herself to another knight instead. William's birth counted against him. He was not only landless, but his parentage was uncertain. Of course, he understood why Lady Felisa had pretended to consider him. She needed someone to keep unruly neighbours in check, in short, Lady

Felisa needed a husband who was strong and determined, qualities William liked to think he possessed. As a result he had interpreted Lady Felisa's interest in him as genuine. It had been no such thing. Lady Felisa had used the threat of a possible marriage with Sir William Bradfer to lure another knight into offering for her. A landed knight, one of good birth.

William had not cared particularly for Lady Felisa, his proposal had been born of ambition and her rejection had stung at the time, but no longer. Nevertheless, he could not help wondering how Lady Felisa treated her servants. Would she go out of her way to help them?

A dank darkness hung about the platform, thick, black and impenetrable. Until this moment, William had not given much thought to Lady Felisa's personal qualities. She was an heiress, any marriage between them would have been political. Admittedly, she was comely, if he had married her he would have had a wife with beauty as well as lands—what more could he expect in a wife? Meeting Lady Anna was throwing new light on long-held ambitions.

Were lands and beauty all he required in a wife?

It would be interesting to learn what had been uppermost in Lady Anna's mind when she had bought him—the desire to help others, or the desire to atone for past failings? *What can she want of me?*

'Tell me, my lady, how long were you at the market before you bought us?'

'We had just arrived.'

'So we were the first slaves you saw?'

'Yes.'

Unsettled, he stared into blackness. 'I think you would have persuaded the Princess to buy whoever stepped onto that block—it was our good fortune that you saw us first.'

'William, that is more than enough about me. If you please, it is past time for you to tell me something of yourself. I should like to know how you came to be in the slave market.'

William hesitated. What might an itinerant knight tell a well-bred court lady? She was talking to him because he had saved her from those soldiers, because they had been forced to take refuge in this cavern beneath the streets. She was whiling away the time.

'I know you were not born a slave,' she prompted. 'First, tell me about your early life, of your mother and father.'

'My lady, I never knew my father. My mother

was, like you, a noblewoman. She lived for a time in the Great Palace.'

She gasped and small fingers found his arm. 'Your mother was Greek?'

'Yes.'

The fingers tightened. 'So that is why you speak our language with such ease, I did wonder. Your mother...' Lady Anna's voice trailed off thoughtfully before strengthening again. '*Tell me!* Tell me everything!'

'My lady.' William grimaced, he felt extraordinarily self-conscious. No darkness was deep enough to hide the fact that he was not used to talking about himself to anyone, and he was not sure he wanted to start. 'I am no bard to while away the time with a pretty story. My birth is doubtful, mired in shadows. In short, it is not a fit tale for a lady's ears.'

'Nonsense!'

There was a rustling of silk and she moved closer, bringing more of that tempting warmth with her. Her body nestled against him, soft and feminine. Confiding. Trusting. Desirable. Lady Anna was just as beautiful as Lady Felisa, maybe more so. It did not help that she was almost in his lap.

She was treating him as though he were a longstanding friend. She was confusing him with this

Erling of hers. And there…more temptation…that tantalising fragrance. Jasmine. Spices. That hint of spring.

Before William could order the words to explain that his story really was unfit for gently bred ears, she leaned her head against him. A lock of her hair swung across his chest and belly, it felt like a caress.

Groin tightening, he sucked in a breath. It had been so small a movement, he was certain she had no idea how her hair was teasing him, yet his blood heated.

'It is most odd, William, how I feel at ease with you…'

'I am not Erling, my lady.' *And you should not feel at ease with me.*

'I know that.' Her head moved against his arm and again that springlike scent reached him, he ached to have his arm about her again. 'However, I shall not question my instincts, they proved right in any case…you saved me. Tell me how you came to be a slave.'

It was undoubtedly an order for all that it was uttered so softly.

Lord, she ought not to lean so trustingly against him, she ought not to let her hair drape over his belly. If she realised the effect her nearness was having on a certain part of him, if she knew her hair had broken free of its pins and was stroking his belly—but how could she? It was like midnight in here.

William prided himself on his self-control, but sitting in the Basilica Cistern with this woman was becoming something of a trial. He found a lock of hair and brought it surreptitiously to his nose. She could not know, she could not see him any more than he could see her...

Slowly, he inhaled. Spring flowers, a rich honey scent, Lady Anna... Lord, he was rampant, hard as rock. Abruptly, he dropped her hair, biting back a groan as it feathered sensuously down his chest. An image jumped into his head...of her kissing his stomach in exactly that spot. Her mouth was moving slowly down his skin, down, down...and he was a brute. This kind, innocent lady would not appreciate the road his mind was taking. He must talk to her, talking might keep his lust in check.

'Very well, my lady. Like you, my mother served in the Great Palace.'

Her head moved, the cloak shifted. Hair tickled his stomach. 'What is her name?'

'I never knew her name, not her real name. I barely knew her.'

Slim fingers curled into his and his throat went

dry. He felt another impulse to gather her into his arms and pushed it back. Each time the impulse returned, it was stronger and more insistent.

'You never knew your mother? How sad.'

William wanted to bury his head in her neck, he wanted to taste her. Instead, he found some words and forced them out, words that might, given her conventional nature, make her pull back. 'I knew her no more than I knew my father. My lady, I was born out of wedlock. Believe me, my story is not one for a lady's ears.'

He kept his head firmly upright, bracing himself for the moment when she would surely pull away from him. When those small fingers remained where they were, his heart lifted in the most ridiculous manner.

'I want to hear your story. Please go on.' A smile entered her voice. 'You cannot refuse me, William, if you do, I shall command you.'

'If you insist.' For once he would set aside his reticence. What harm? It was hardly as though they moved in the same circles. Within days he would be leaving Constantinople. Soon his time in the Empire would be but a memory.

Her head came back, a pleasing heaviness against his upper arm. Silken hair swirled over his chest and he was enveloped in a cloud of scent. He groaned.

'William, I am sorry, did I hurt you?'

'It would help if you would simply *sit still*.' His voice was sharper than he intended, he felt her freeze.

'I am sorry.' Her voice was contrite.

I am a brute. William gritted his teeth. 'I shall tell you what I know of my parents.'

'Please.'

'Like you, my mother served in the Great Palace. As I understand it, her father was an admiral in your navy, she was of good family.' Realising that his head was leaning towards hers, he abruptly jerked it upright. 'I cannot swear that any of this is gospel, my recollections are from what I was told in earliest childhood.'

'Where were you born?'

'In the Duchy of Apulia and Calabria—for most of my life I have lived in Apulia.'

'Why did your mother leave Court?'

'It's unlikely I shall ever know for certain. I believe there was a border dispute between the Empire and Norman lords in the Duchy. A deputation of knights came to the Imperial Palace to negotiate terms. I assume that my father was among them.' He paused for her response, but the only sound was water dripping nearby. 'My lady, this is surmise, but I imagine that my father persuaded my mother to form an illicit relationship with him.'

'Perhaps they fell in love.'

He had no response to that. The nobility did not marry for love. In Apulia they married for lands, for dynastic reasons. The marriage William had sought with Lady Felisa would have been just such a marriage. It was exactly the sort of marriage that Anna's father had been trying to arrange for her.

'I shall never know, my lady. What I do know is that when my father left the Imperial Court, my mother chose to go with him.'

'They never married?' Her voice held a note of disapproval.

'No.'

'Why not?'

His lips twitched—William was coming to suspect that Lady Anna was a firm believer in the proprieties.

'Who knows? My father may have had to make a political marriage. And if he was in love when he left Court, he may have fallen out of love when he reached Apulia. Lady Anna, there could be many reasons why my parents never married, but I am not privy to them.'

'Your mother should have told you more—at the least you ought to know your father's name.'

William gave a short laugh. 'You think he should have been made to face his responsibilities?'

'*Yes!* He had a son… Your mother should not have been left to bring you up on her own.'

Forgetting she could not see him, he made a swift negative gesture. 'I am glad I was not foisted on him. Imagine how an unwanted brat would have been received.'

'I also think that your mother could have given you the name of her family here in Constantinople. That is perhaps the strangest part.'

'It is understandable if you hear the whole tale. Whatever happened between my mother and father, it caused my mother to leave Apulia and go to Calabria. Calabria is wilder and more isolated than Apulia. I have often wondered if it was in her mind to return to Constantinople, but when she discovered she was having a baby, she no longer felt that was possible.'

'So she stayed in Calabria.'

'She entered a convent there and, not long after, took the veil. Women are rechristened when they become nuns. A bride of Christ does not bear her family name, which is why I never learned about

my mother's family. In the convent my mother was
known simply as Sister Martha.'

Water dripped, something splashed—another
fish?—while she digested what he had told her.

'You were born in this convent?'

'Yes, until I was six, I was cared for by nuns.'

'Were they good to you?'

'They were kind, but I did not belong there. My
mother—Sister Martha—treated me in exactly the
same way as all the other nuns.' He put a smile in
his voice. 'In a sense, I was blessed with several
mothers.'

Lady Anna gave an unladylike snort. 'Several
mothers? It sounds as though you had none! Did
your mother not tell you anything about herself?'

'Sister Martha never spoke of her sinful past.'

'She taught you Greek, though.'

'I have often thought about that in the years since
then. Teaching me to speak Greek must have been
one way to remember her previous life.'

'It is possible she wanted to give you a connection with your heritage, something that you might
explore, should the chance arise.'

Something he could explore? Lady Anna seemed
to be suggesting that his mother expected him to
learn about the Greek side of his family. The idea
was tempting, but the more he thought about it,

the more difficulties he found. As far as William could judge, his mother's relatives had never shown the slightest concern for her welfare—contact had been severed the moment she had left Constantinople. Her family would have had no idea what had happened to her. Certainly they would be unaware of his existence. Lady Anna didn't know what she was talking about.

She sighed. 'I expect you had many questions for her.'

'In the convent I was too young to appreciate the…unusual nature of my upbringing. Afterwards, as a young man, I did have questions, but by then it was too late. My mother was dead, there was no one else I might ask.'

'You said the nuns cared for you until you were six—what happened after that?'

'A knight—Sir Bruno Senecal—came and took me from the convent. He had brought his sister to join my mother's order, and whilst he was there, my mother persuaded him to take me into his household. Sir Bruno is steward of the castle at Melfi.'

'That must have been something of an adjustment for a six-year-old boy brought up by nuns.'

'It was the best thing that could have happened to me. Sir Bruno is an exceptional man—he trained me as his squire and, later, he saw that I was knighted.'

'You are a cavalry officer!' Small fingers pressed into his arm. 'Why did you not tell me? I had no idea.' The fingers relaxed. 'If you are a Frankish knight, I ought not to be calling you "William". Surely you are known as "Sir William"? Is that not so?'

'My lady, I am content that you call me William.' And that, William realised with a frown, was no less than the truth. He had fought long and hard to earn the right to be called 'Sir William', yet he liked the way she called him 'William'.

'So this Sir Bruno removed you from the convent and trained you as a cavalry officer?'

'I owe everything to him.'

'He was the father you never had.' Her voice was thoughtful.

William leaned his head against the wall and stared into the blackness. 'You are perceptive, my lady. I have never thought of him in those terms, but Sir Bruno has been like a father to me.'

'But he could not answer your questions about your family?'

'No. And when finally I returned to the convent in Calabria to ask them, my mother had died.' He took in a deep breath. 'So you see, my lady, the details of my parentage are likely to remain shrouded in mystery.'

'Yes,' she murmured. 'While you are in Constantinople, I wonder if it might be possible to discover your mother's relations? They may wish to meet you.'

'I have decided against it.' Being a slave for even a short time had taught William how he was likely to be seen by his Greek relatives. In Byzantium, Franks were considered barbarians. And even if his mother's family were unusually tolerant, what reason would they have for welcoming a complete stranger into their midst?

'William, what age are you?'

'Twenty-two.'

'William.' The grip on his arm tightened, her voice rose. 'William, I have an idea…if we can work out when your mother left the Palace…we might be able to discover—'

'No.'

'Don't you wish to find your family?'

'No!' He bit out the response and at once her hair slid across his stomach as she pulled back. He felt hollow inside. 'I am sorry, my lady, but I have no desire to meet them. Your people view mine as foreigners—barbarians. It's more than likely that my mother's family rejected her for taking up with a Frank, she probably left to escape their disapproval.'

'This is pure surmise. Will—'

He curled his fingers into a fist. 'I have neither the time nor the desire to meet them. Lady Anna, it is as you pointed out—Sir Bruno is the closest thing to a family that I shall ever have. I have no need for any other.'

'You sound very certain.'

'I am.' He had to get away. Someone in the Duchy wanted him dead, and the longer he remained here, the less chance he had of learning who they were and why they saw him as their enemy. The longer he remained here, the less chance he had of claiming justice.

A soft sigh whispered out over the black water. 'I cannot help thinking that you are missing an opportunity. William, since you find yourself in Constantinople, I am sure it would be possible. We are great keepers of records.'

'I don't even know my mother's name. Leave it.'

'Very well.'

An uneasy quiet settled over the platform. The dripping seemed louder, the splashing more frequent. Behind him, the wall grew harder, icier— the cold bit deep in the Palace Cistern. Leaning forwards, he rolled his shoulders. The damp was getting to him. He adjusted the cloak more tightly about them.

'Your arm is paining you.'

Lady Anna's voice was small. It occurred to William that his rebuttal had hurt her feelings, which had not been his intention. He wasn't going to change his mind, though. Whatever she had planned for him, he had to return to the Duchy. 'No, the pain is almost gone.'

'William, what's that noise?'

Somewhere above them he heard a dull thudding. 'Sounds like battle drums. Your friend the Commander must be rousing his men.'

He felt her shudder. 'The Varangian Guard...yes, of course. I wonder what is happening up there?'

A draught feathered down the side of his neck. Tipping his head to one side, William craned his neck to peer up the stairway. No light was leaking from the top—the shield was holding. They would certainly hear it if it fell, but perhaps they were not as safe here as he hoped...

'My lady, are you certain there is no other entrance?'

'Not as far as I am aware.'

'The water must come in somewhere,' he said. 'Is it piped in?'

He felt her shrug. 'I do not know...probably.'

William's stomach chose that moment to growl.

'You are hungry,' she said. 'I think that you did not eat well for some time before we found you.'

'I admit I could do with more food. When the drums stop, I shall see if the coast is clear.' He put his hand on her arm. 'I fear we must be patient awhile longer, there is no point looking while they are sounding. The Varangian Guard have obviously dug in beside that monument. It didn't look as though the Commander was expecting a speedy resolution.'

He paused, hoping to learn something about the turmoil in the City, but all she said was, 'The Milion—that monument is known as the Milion. It measures the miles to cities and ports in every corner of the Empire.' Her fingers twined with his. 'Since we have time, you can finish your tale. Tell me how you came to be enslaved.'

William shoved his hand through his hair. 'I would rather not.'

'Sir William, you are yet my slave.' Her voice was light, teasing. 'In theory you have to obey me until the document of manumission is in your hands.'

'My lady, it is not wise to taunt me. I am illegitimate, that I cannot deny, but I was born a free man. No one has the right to steal my freedom.'

'William, my apologies, I should not have said that.' She spoke quietly. 'It is just that I feel so at ease with you, I think it must be your resemblance to Erling—we spent much of the time teasing one another. I assure you I meant no harm.'

Inordinately pleased that she felt at ease with him, William recalled a previous teasing comment of hers. 'In the Palace you called me a eunuch.'

'That was only because of your Frankish love of shaving.'

A light touch on his cheek had him almost leaping out of his skin. Careful fingertips were exploring his face, running over his chin and jaw. His blood heated.

'Careful, my lady, I am far from a eunuch.'

A soft laugh ruffled his hair. Her fingers wandered over his cheekbones. 'William, you speak our tongue so well, I confess it is increasingly hard to think of you as a Frank.'

Her voice was husky, as though she wanted… as though…

'You never did shave.'

'I visited the bathhouse, but, no, my lady, I did not take time to shave.'

'Too busy planning your escape, I expect.'

One did need light, William was learning, to judge whether a lady was interested in kissing him.

His body seemed to know it. The blood was rushing to his chausses, his mind was fixed on one thing, he wanted to pull her—gently, gently—into his embrace.

In the eternal darkness of the cistern, he only had his instincts to go by. As a knight, William had learned to trust his instincts, they did not often let him down...

A peculiar hunger had him reaching for her. She met him halfway and the shock of delight stole his breath for a moment. Those delicate fingers were burrowing into the hair over his ears, light fingers that were little more than a whisper of summer wind. Warily, mindful that in her mind he was a barbarian, William found her arm and stroked his way to her waist. In the dark, their lips found each other and clung.

Warm. All the warmth of the world was there in her mouth. Soft. That feminine fragrance filled the air. She had perfumed her hair, the scent of spring clung to it. Holding himself firmly in check, for he found himself wrestling with a powerful surge of desire, he kissed her cheek. He must not lose control, he was a trained knight, not an ill-disciplined page boy. He found her earlobe...the side of her neck. Pressing kisses on her skin, he inhaled, drawing in her scent. He licked her and held down a moan.

She seemed fascinated with his hair, stroking, smoothing, she was tracing circles round his ear, rubbing an earlobe between thumb and forefinger. His ear warmed.

He would miss this woman when he left. The thought knocked him back. What was he thinking? By the law of this land, he was her slave. There was no genuine feeling here, no sentiment. To her he was only an entertainment to while away the time.

He pulled back, setting distance between them. When her hands continued with their tantalising caresses, he made a half-hearted attempt to push them away. Her touch was making him ache in places that had no business to be aching given that she was lady-in-waiting to a princess and he was a barbarian knight with no status whatever at the Imperial Court.

Lady Anna did not seem to have noticed his retreat. Light strokes feathered across his chest, delicately exploring. His breath stopped. It was becoming more of a struggle to call to mind the fact that he would soon be leaving Byzantium. Lady Anna's hands were causing havoc with him, body and mind.

Had she led him astray with that prim and innocent air? Had he misjudged her? William had taken her for an innocent, but she had spent years in the entourage of a princess. A composed and beautiful court lady, Lady Anna could just as easily be experienced as innocent. Was she innocent, or experienced?

William had little knowledge of the goings-on of courtiers. Gossip about the Imperial Court was hard to come by in the Duchy, and he had been half out of his head while she had been tending him in the Princess's apartment. He had learned more today, as he had hurried through the courtyards and gardens of the Great Palace.

All those fountains and statues and exotic birds… all those marble halls and tiled bathhouses…they must need armies of soldiers and servants and slaves just to keep the place running.

Life in the Great Palace must be full of intrigue and complexity. Was Anna—disconcertingly he was starting to think of her as Anna in his mind— was Anna in the habit of toying with slaves? When she was young, she had clearly adored Erling. Had she taken this a step further when she had become a woman?

The painted face of the lady at the slave market pushed into his mind. The woman in the cherry-coloured gown had wanted him for her bed. He would have realised it at the time if he had not been half out of his mind.

There was a bitter taste in his mouth.

Her finger was exploring his upper lip. Had Lady Anna been corrupted? It could not be easy for a woman living amidst such decadence to keep her innocence. Was she innocent?

'Did you persuade the Princess to buy me for your entertainment, my lady? Is that why you bought me?'

The finger stilled and she made a small choking sound. 'I told you, you reminded me of Erling.'

'Your slave.'

'Yes.'

'Did you kiss Erling?'

A peal of laughter echoed round the cistern. 'Kiss Erling? I was only a child, so naturally I did not kiss Erling. I am, however, interested in trying another kiss with you. Kiss me again, William.'

Her bluntness caught him off guard. Was it a command? A request? He had no idea. Before he had time to respond, she had caught him by the neck and pressed her lips to his.

She was slender, he could feel her ribcage through the silk of her gown and span her waist with his hands. Holding the image of those smoky grey eyes in his mind, William deepened the kiss. Her jaw relaxed almost immediately and their tongues met. She gave a fluttery sigh, her tongue withdrew before returning to flicker along his.

Innocent? Experienced?

Command? Request?

Hell's teeth, if only he could *see*.

Chapter Six

And then it no longer mattered whether Lady Anna was innocent or experienced, it no longer mattered whether she thought she could command him or not. A moan of encouragement sent hot blood rushing to his loins. Her breasts shifted against his chest and the blue silk gown whispered in the darkness. It was as though she was trying to climb onto his lap.

Who was he to deny her?

He gripped her waist and lifted. A bright laugh rolled out over the dark lake, warm arms curled round his neck, angling his head so they might kiss and kiss and kiss.

She had his full attention. Every part of him was filled with desire—one part in particular ached to the point of pain. Yes, she had his full attention, more of it than she could possibly want. His attention was pressing against her belly, hard and proud and eager.

William dragged in a breath. If he did not ease away soon, he might lose control. The rush of lust was overwhelming, he had never felt the like of it before. Lady Anna might consider this a game of dalliance to while away her time down here, but for him it was fast becoming dangerous. He wanted her, more than he had ever wanted Claire. Claire was a maidservant who, long ago in the stables at Melfi, had given William much pleasure. But this need to possess, this burning ache, he had never felt this with Claire…

The Frankish slave's tongue was entangled with Anna's. *Delicious, why has no one told me that a man can taste delicious?* Anna felt a dizzying rush of feeling, her thoughts were scattered, fragmented.

I must not think of him as a slave, he is a knight, Sir William.

His mouth—how can it be so firm and yet so gentle?

William murmured something—a Frankish love word? Anna had no idea of its meaning. Twining her fingers in his thick hair, she kept him close. Her heart was beating fast, her breath coming in shaky gasps. Noblewomen were protected in the Empire, even in Rascia her freedom had been limited and this was her first real kiss.

She was completely unprepared for the rush of feeling. And the pleasure. *It is as though William is speaking with kisses. Kissing is a form of speaking, it does not matter that I do not understand his Frankish words, I know what he is saying in his kisses.*

William is telling me to relax. He is telling me that he likes me, that he will fight for me if those mercenaries return.

He nibbled her upper lip.

William is telling me more…he is telling me that there is no need for me to worry, that the Emperor will not chastise me for the deception Katerina and I have practised on the Court. William will stand by me, he will support me when I explain that we have been doing Princess Theodora's bidding.

William's mouth was also, it seemed, telling her that she need never fear that her father would force her to accept Lord Romanos Angelos as her husband. And his mouth, Anna realised as she dragged in air, was not the only part of him that was speaking to her. For there, pressed against her side, jutting proud, she could definitely feel…her limbs began to weaken…

Strong hands gripped her shoulders as he pushed her from him. A musky male scent—aroused man—filled her nostrils, his breath was warm on her cheek. Under cover of her cloak, she leaned into him, aching to be close.

He finds me desirable. With a jolt, Anna recognised that she found William equally desirable. She felt deliciously weak. *I never felt this when Romanos tried to approach me. I should not be feeling it now, but William is a knight, a man of honour, I am safe with him.*

'This will not do, my lady.' William sounded as though he were smiling. Anna might not be able to see his expression, but she caught the subtle lift in his voice.

Firmly, heedless of her protesting murmur, William, *Sir William*, set his hands on her waist and lifted her easily to the side. 'You are a cosy armful, my lady, but this must stop.'

How dare he call me a cosy armful!

'As soon as I get you back to the Palace,' he went on, 'I shall be leaving.'

William's words, his actual words, were so at variance with what she had read in his kisses that it was a moment before she could speak.

He is leaving. As soon as he has escorted me to the Palace. Vaguely, Anna recalled him saying as much. *I did not believe he meant it, not when he has kin in the City. I cannot believe a man like William, one who has never known family, does not want to meet his relatives.*

'You cannot leave until I have freed you.' Knight or not, he was her slave!

'I have duties in Apulia, my lady, duties that have been neglected. Which is why we must not allow ourselves to get carried away. If that happened, you might find yourself facing unwanted consequences on your own.'

Well, that certainly put her in her place. William's kisses were nothing but lies, he had no intention of helping her with anything. Jerking away from him, she felt a sharp tug on her scalp—her hair was caught.

'I should like my hair back.'

'Certainly, my lady.' William inched away so their thighs were no longer touching. Gathering up her hair, Anna smoothed it into some sort of order and knotted it at the nape of her neck. By retreating, he had surrendered the whole of the cloak to her, and whilst she did not want him to be cold, she was reluctant to move back.

She straightened her skirts. 'This gown will be ruined after this, ruined.'

'I expect so, my lady.'

He was laughing at her! 'Clod,' she muttered. *Thank heaven he cannot know my cheeks are on fire!*

'Yes, my lady.'

The darkness in the cistern was suddenly a blessing—William could not see how thrown Anna was to find that he would not be persuaded to search for his relations. *Nor can he see how much he inflamed me. Heavens, why is this so upsetting?*

Chewing her lip, shocked at how easily William seemed to have awakened the wanton in her, Anna stared blindly into the blackness and wished she had not been kept so cloistered. *Thank the Lord, he is unaware of the effect he has on me. This wanting, this achy wanting must be lust. It is a sin. What a sin, though! One touch and my limbs melt, one kiss and I am weak with desire. This is not me. Lady Anna does not feel desire in this way. I am not myself.*

Why does William have this effect on me? It must be because he is a barbarian. No wonder Father warned me to have nothing to do with them!

A metallic clink came from somewhere above them.

'What's that?' At her side, there was movement, Anna could not know for certain, but she would swear the sword was fast in William's hand.

'The door.' William's voice was clipped. 'Someone is trying the door.'

She reached instinctively for William before she realised what she was doing and checked herself. She twisted her fingers together. *Have the mercenaries found us?*

'Wait here,' William said, moving away.

Heart in her mouth, Anna got to her feet. To keep her bearings, she placed a hand on the stone wall and listened to William making his way up the stairs. After a few moments she heard another clink and a scraping sound. A shaft of light sliced down from the top and the forest of columns sprang into being. They looked as though they had been there since the beginning of time, great pillars rearing up out of water that gleamed like a mirror of jet. William was but a shadow moving about at the head of the stairs.

'William?'

'One moment.'

The light increased. From where Anna was standing, she could see most of the Basilica Cistern. Dozens, if not hundreds, of columns rose out of the water, stretching up towards a cathedral-like roof where the shadows clung like cobwebs. The water rippled. A dappled shifting of light moved past under the surface—a shoal of fish.

Leading off from the platform, a wooden structure like a jetty ran off into the lines of columns.
Anna had not noticed it earlier when they had been
stumbling about in the dark.

Something thudded and the light was gone. Then
came that scraping sound—William replacing the
shield.

'William?'

'Do not be alarmed, I am coming down.'

Hand on the damp wall, Anna waited. It seemed
an eternity went by before she felt the light touch
of his hand on hers.

'William.' She moved closer. 'What's happening outside?'

'I couldn't see much, just the backs of some people running away from that square.'

'The Augustaion?'

'The one by the Milion Arch...they must have
tried the door as they went past. I am afraid we
shall be stuck here awhile longer,' William said,
his breath warm on her face.

'How long do you suppose we have been down
here?'

'I have no idea.'

Anna sighed. 'Oh, Lord. Do you think it is past
noon?'

'I should think so—why?'

'I am meant to be meeting Father this afternoon.'

'Your father will have to wait. It can't be helped, I'm afraid, it is not safe to venture out yet. Your father must realise that none of this is your fault.'

'You...did you hear screaming?'

William hesitated and that told its own story— he had heard screaming. Shuddering, Anna tugged at his hand. 'We shall take our seats as before and you will share my cloak.'

It was snug under Lady Anna's wool-lined cloak, particularly with one arm about her and her head on his shoulder. William leaned back and stared blindly into the dark. He had heard screaming somewhere in the City, he had also smelled smoke. There was no way he was going to permit Lady Anna outside until he was certain she would be safe—the General's mercenaries had yet to be called to heel.

Before William had rammed the shield back into place behind the door, he had taken stock of the cistern. The forest of columns—the size of the place!—had taken him aback. They had carved capitals—one was covered in acanthus leaves, another with bold geometric patterns. They looked very old, perhaps they dated from the time of the Romans. Even the bases were carved. A grotesque upside-down face with hard stone eyes had glared up from the glassy surface of the water, it had hair which seemed to writhe like a nest of snakes. The Medusa. William had seen similar carvings in Apulia.

Resting his head against Anna's, he fell into a doze. He dreamed he was kissing the Medusa, only his Medusa's lips were warm and soft, she had ungovernable brown hair and smelt deliciously of spring flowers. When he woke, Anna was cuddled even more closely and her arm had found its way round his waist. From the rhythm of her breathing she must be asleep. The battle drums were silent.

At least there was no danger of them dying of thirst in the Basilica Cistern. To drink, all they had to do was lean over the edge of the platform and dip into the water. If they were here much longer, though, it was hunger that was likely to be the headache. William's stomach had been clamouring for food for an age already. He closed his eyes, and in a moment the image of a feast appeared in his mind's eye...he was taking a slice of roast boar from a platter, there was a haunch of beef, a dish of salmon...

Several hours passed, William had no way of judging the time. What was happening in the City above? Was it safe to emerge?

Gently, he touched the head pressing into his shoulder. 'My lady, are you awake?'

'Mmm...'

'I am going to see if the coast is clear.'

She straightened. 'Very well, but I want you to have my cloak.'

'My lady, it is not nec—'

'Yes, it is, you are half-naked—you must take my cloak.'

The cloak was pressed into his hands and, once again, William climbed the stairs to see if it was safe to leave.

'We can go out, then?' Lady Anna asked, her face a blur.

She had joined him at the top of the steps and was standing in the half-light on the landing. Her eyes gleamed as they watched him, her trusting smile warmed him better than any cloak. William swallowed, the sound seemed loud in the quiet of the cistern. He had spent hours in the dark with this woman and now that there was some light he couldn't tear his eyes from her. The top of her head reached his shoulders. He noted the fall of her hair as it framed her face and something that felt alarmingly like longing shivered through him.

She drew in a breath and her breasts lifted. 'Will—'

He reached out to touch her mouth with his fingertips and that gentle smile didn't waver. His stomach rocked.

'A moment, just one,' he muttered and bent to take her lips with his.

Her mouth was as soft as it had been before, it was as welcoming. Spring—she even tasted of spring.

Her hands settled on his shoulders. 'William.'

William's blood pounded in his ears and when, with a murmur of disapproval, she pushed the cloak aside and found his skin, his muscles bunched and jumped under her fingertips. Her touch, though light, left fire in its wake. She was gentle and refined—why did he feel this fire for her? She was sweet and innocent, he should not be touching her.

He groaned, the sensual throbbing in his veins would surely alarm her. But he could not draw back, not yet. Taking her firmly by the chin, he guided her mouth back to his. She gave a little moan.

One small kiss was met, eagerly it seemed. She was pure delight.

Then another kiss. And another.

William knew he was leaving Constantinople,

but he could not stop. Pushing guilt from his mind, he took the kiss deeper. And, improbable though it was, she allowed each kiss to become more intimate, more devastating than the last. His tongue teased hers, her tongue teased his. He bit her bottom lip, she bit his. She gave a gurgle of laughter he felt in his toes.

With a jolt, William became aware of voices outside. Abruptly, he released her.

Lady Anna gave a little cough and stepped back. William could not help it—he had to touch her just once more. He contented himself with simply running a finger down a beautifully flushed cheek.

Pushing the shield aside, he gripped her hand and turned for the door.

'Why the kiss, William?' she asked quietly.

Breaking step, he turned. Smiled. This woman was easy to smile at. 'Last chance.'

Her eyes glittered, her expression was puzzled. In the light streaming in through the door, her lips were rosy from kissing. Bringing his head closer, he drew in the scent of spring. 'You, my lady, are ripe for kissing, and that was likely my last chance. Once we reach the Palace, you will be surrounded—the Princess, your father, ladies, servants...' he raised an eyebrow '...and in case you need reminding, I am returning to Apulia.'

'It was a farewell kiss?'

Smiling was suddenly not as easy as it had been a moment ago. 'Of course, my lady, what else might it be?'

Until Anna poked her head through the entrance of the Basilica Cistern, she had had no idea how long they had spent underground. She emerged, blinking, into daylight.

Morning light. It is early morning, we have spent a day and a night in the cistern! Lord, look at all those people...

The square was alive with people pushing this way and that. Recoiling in surprise, Anna instinctively moved closer to William—the contrast with the quiet in the cistern could not be more marked. His body was warm and solid and his hand slid round her waist, steadying her. She struggled with a most improper impulse to lean against him.

'It is safe, my lady.'

His hand lingered, his thumb gave her waist a small, secret caress. She had no inclination to push it away. There must be something wrong with her—she had never felt the slightest desire to permit Romanos Angelos the liberties she permitted this Frank. *I enjoy kissing William and, what is worse, I should like to kiss him again. I am sad-*

dened that he is so eager to leave the City. A barbarian! My father would be so disappointed in me.

'If you look carefully,' he continued, 'these are townsfolk, not soldiers.'

A measured glance confirmed this. A man with the build of a blacksmith was carrying a child on his shoulders, a woman was leading a mule piled high with trunks and boxes, another had a baby slung in her shawl. Ordinary citizens. There was a burly man hauling a hand-cart packed with clay amphorae, there were a couple of black-robed priests...

'Everyone is smiling,' Anna said, much struck by the contrast to the anxious expressions she had seen near Hagia Sophia. Had that really only been yesterday? Had they really spent a night in the cistern?

A laughing woman ran up and thrust a spray of laurel leaves at her. 'Such news! Such *good* news!'

As the woman made to run on, Anna caught her sleeve. 'What has happened?'

'We have a new Emperor!'

'General Alexios?'

'Yes! Emperor Nikephoros has abdicated!' The woman bobbed a curtsy and ran off, leaving a trail of leaves and flowers in her wake: daisies, violets, laurel, bay.

Emperor Nikephoros has abdicated? Worries crowded in on her. *What might this mean for Katerina and me? Princess Theodora was related to Emperor Nikephoros...isn't she also a distant cousin of General Alexios's wife? Sweet Mother, I need to think about this...*

This could be disastrous! Emperor Nikephoros was old and feeble, but at least with him as Emperor we had a chance of covering up Princess Theodora's absence from the Palace. We cannot hope to fool a man like General Alexios, he is far too astute.

Wide-eyed, Anna exchanged glances with William. 'Can this be true?'

William shrugged.

'William, you don't understand, Emperor Nikephoros can't have abdicated—it's almost unheard of!'

'Be thankful, my lady. It was likely the only way to avoid bloodshed in the streets.'

William was watching her, the spring sunlight full on his face.

Lord, he is tall. And how fair his hair is. William is a giant of a man, just like a Viking. And how green his eyes are! So green. Anna had been struck by their colour in the slave market. She had thought William's eyes were a match for Erling's, but out here in daylight she realised her initial perception had been flawed. *William's eyes are clearer and brighter than Erling's ever were. Sunshine after rain. And how carefully he studies one...*

His hand fell from her waist. 'So General Alexios is now Emperor? I take it he is the man the army acclaimed?'

'Yes.'

'A new Emperor,' he murmured, looking towards the Milion Arch.

The Varangian Guard were holding their position in the Augustaion. Anna could see the morning sun glittering on the crescent-blades of their battle-axes. The Guard looked as immaculate as they had done when she and William had entered the cistern, they were ready for whatever Fate flung at them.

William tapped the sword against his calf and looked down at her. 'Those men are not holding their ground for nothing, there may yet be trouble and I want you out of harm's way. Come on, my lady, it is past time I returned you to the Palace.'

'If only I had not lost a shoe,' Anna said, limping along at the edge of the square.

'Are you certain your foot isn't hurting?'

William's eyes gleamed. 'I can carry you if you like.'

'Thank you, but that will not be necessary, my foot does not hurt in the slightest.' *Imagine the scene should Father hear I was carried into the Palace in the arms of a half-naked barbarian!*

Fortunately, William was swathed in her cloak and thus far his half-naked state had passed unnoticed, as had the sword. Uneasily aware that it was dangerous for William to be bearing arms within the Palace, Anna turned towards the Palace gate. *Somehow I must get that sword off him, every moment he carries it, he risks arrest.*

'Not that gate, if you please, my lady,' he murmured.

'Why ever not?'

Through the cloak, the sword hilt gently nudged her thigh. 'I may be…remembered, particularly by a guard with a dent in his helmet.'

'Very well, there is another gate farther along.'

William trusts me enough to escort me back to the Palace. The question is—does he trust me enough to allow me to disarm him?

They skirted the Palace wall, coming to a street where the air was heavy with rich scents—musk, sandalwood, spices…

William's eyebrows rose and he looked enquiringly at her. 'The local brothel?'

'Sir William! No such establishment would be countenanced so near the Great Palace.' Anna pursed her lips, really, at times the man was impossible! 'This is the street of the perfumiers.'

Sweeping past him, she spoke to the guards and they went through an arch and into a courtyard.

William kept close, mouth edging into a smile. He inhaled deeply. 'I see the fragrance of the... perfumiers carries right into the Palace.'

Anna sent him a severe frown. 'They *are* perfumiers, I swear it.'

'Of course they are.'

His tone of disbelief drew a withering look from her, but she held her tongue, William seemed to enjoy baiting her. It was a supposition that was borne out when they crossed one of the busier courtyards.

Anna had just nodded at an elderly courtier whom she recognised as a friend of her father's, when the edge of William's cloak fluttered in the corner of her eye.

'William!' she hissed, as that broad chest, that broad *naked* chest, was revealed. 'Keep the cloak fast, you cannot wander the Palace half-dressed! I have my reputation to consider.' *And someone may notice that sword…though I dare not mention that here, I cannot risk a public argument.*

Green eyes were lingering on her mouth in a way that reminded Anna of his farewell kiss and made her forget the dangers for foolhardy slaves who carried swords in the Palace. Then he shrugged and tugged the edges of the cloak together. 'As you wish, my lady.'

'You are a wretch, William.' *He expects me to give him his freedom straight away, but I do not know that I can. God knows I want to free him, but first I must find a better way to escape marriage with Lord Romanos.*

He gave her an unrepentant grin and her toes curled. 'So I have been told, my lady.'

Anna maintained a stoic silence until they reached the entrance to the Boukoleon and had climbed up to the Princess's apartments. The wind from the sea was swaying in the curtains, bringing the screaming of the gulls into the reception chamber. Polished floors dazzled where the sun fell on them.

Anna eased off her remaining shoe. Juliana was sitting at the other end of the chamber, sewing in the light from one of the windows. Other than Juliana, the apartments seemed empty, Anna sensed immediately that Katerina was not there.

Oh, no! Did she not get back safely?

Juliana set her sewing aside and scurried over. 'My lady, are you all right?'

'I am well, I thank you.'

'Praise God, you are in one piece! We feared for you when you did not return yesterday. But just look at you! What happened to your veil? And your gown is torn, and—' Juliana broke off, disapproval springing into her eyes. 'Saints, why have you given that slave your cloak?'

'Never mind that.' Anna waved Juliana's disapproval to one side. 'Where is the Princess? Did she not return yesterday?' She was conscious of William stalking the length of the apartment, throwing open doors, peering into bedchambers.

Juliana began wringing her hands. 'Why, yes, my lady, she did. Commander Ashfirth found her in Hagia Irene. He sent her back with one of the Palace guards.'

'Thank God.' Anna was transfixed by Juliana's wringing hands. *Why is she doing that?* 'Where is the Princess this morning?'

'Last night Commander Ashfirth came to the apartment himself and, when he left, he took the Princess with him.'

Anna's eyes widened. 'Have they not returned?'

'No, my lady.'

'And this was last night, you say?'

'Yes, my lady.'

'Where did they go?'

'They didn't say.' When Anna made a sound of exasperation, Juliana added, 'I am sorry, my lady, they left in such a rush that—'

Anna brushed Juliana's excuses away. 'Never mind. Commander Ashfirth will doubtless keep her safe.'

At least I hope he will. Katerina, what have you done? Holy Mother, help me. General Alexios is bound to want to meet Princess Theodora and I am not confident we shall be able to deceive him. Yet deceive him we must, if we want to protect the real Princess. I can only pray that matters of state will keep our new Emperor so busy that he has no time to worry about meeting a distant cousin of his wife's...

'Lady Anna?' William strode back to her, eyes serious. 'Where are Daphne and Paula?' He frowned at Juliana. 'Did the Princess take them with her last night?'

Juliana looked taken aback to be addressed so directly by a slave. 'N-no.'

'Then where in hell are they?'

'I...I am sorry, I do not know. I went out for a

moment and when I returned there was no sign of them. Sylvia had gone, too.'

William's brow wrinkled. 'Sylvia?'

'Sylvia is the wet-nurse,' Juliana told him.

Anna blinked. 'Juliana, you must have some idea where they went?'

'I...I am sorry, my lady. Sylvia was here at cock-crow, but I have not seen her since. She...she left no message.'

William swore. 'God help us!' Rounding on Anna, he took her by the elbow and marched her to the brazier at the far end of the apartment. His mouth was tight, his eyes bleak. 'You assured me the children would be safe.'

'They are, I am sure of it! Ka—Theodora swore to look after them, she would never allow anyone to hurt a child.'

'Then where the devil are they?' Jaw set, William waved at the empty pallet where Paula had slept. The copper bath was leaning against the wall nearby, the willow basket of baby cloths was tipped on its side, linens trailing out over the marble tiles. *They left in such a hurry that some-one dropped it.*

There was a lump in her throat. Anna tried to swallow. 'William, I am sure they are being looked after.'

His fingers were crushing her elbow, his eyes were like chips of green ice. 'They had better be.'

The children mean so much to him. Too much for there to be no connection between them...are Daphne and Paula his daughters? The suspicion had no sooner formed, than the words tumbled out. 'You are very fond of Daphne and Paula.'

'What of it?'

'William, are they yours? Are Daphne and Paula your daughters?'

Dark lashes came down, shielding his eyes, and beneath the growth of several days' beard, his cheeks flared crimson.

Chapter Seven

'Are they mine? What a question!' William leaned in, mouth tight. 'No, my lady, they are not. Jesu, what kind of a man do you take me for? When I saw you by that monument I was on my way home, I had no intention of returning. Is it likely I would leave my daughters behind me?'

Anna's heart thumped. *He is carrying much anger. I will not let him see that he is alarming me. I will reason this out calmly. William is a warrior, he will have been trained to be dispassionate, yet that is not what I see. How can he have so much feeling for two small girls, if they are not his?*

A cold lump settled in her stomach. *Is William lying?*

'For God's sake—' his voice was hard '—can't a man admit affection for a child without confessing paternity?'

Juliana's eyes were narrow as she watched them,

curiosity was fighting with disapproval at Anna's shocking behaviour. Her lady was allowing a slave to argue with her!

I had better be careful of what I say, rumours spread round the Palace like wildfire...

'Yes, yes, naturally you feel affection for them,' Anna said, in as soothing a voice as she could muster. 'After all, they shared your captivit...' A muscle tightened in William's jaw and Anna trailed uncomfortably to a halt.

Stupid. Mention of his captivity had merely added fuel to the fire of his anger.

Releasing her, William raked his fingers through his hair. 'Since I have not actually left Constantinople, I thought to see them once again. I hoped to see them *safe.*'

Anna tipped her head back to meet those hard green eyes. Lord, but he was tall, the man towered over her. *Are all Franks as tall?* When Anna had first seen William in the slave market, she had not realised quite how large he was. And later, when she had tended him, she had been more concerned about the possibility of broken bones than to take his measure.

Despite the privations he had suffered, he was an exceptionally vigorous man. *What must he be like in full health?* As Anna stared at him, she realised that this was the first chance to study him properly. They had spent hours talking in the cistern, in truth, because of their time alone together, Anna had spent longer talking to William than she had to any man. Most of that time they had been in the dark. His physical nature had been hidden from her.

Except when we kissed...

Put those kisses out of your mind.

Compelling though those kisses had been, Anna had kissed him because…because she had been frightened by those mercenaries…because William had saved her…because—

Now it is you who are the liar. You kissed him because you are attracted to him, dangerously attracted.

This man is a Frank, a barbarian! You scarcely know him. You are still in the dark concerning his nature, those little girls might well be his daughters—he might even be married! You would not like to think so, but what sort of a man is he? Put those kisses out of your mind. Set your mind to devising some other way of avoiding marriage with Lord Romanos.

A muscle was jumping in that strong jaw, the green eyes watched her, hard as glass. Determined. Anna could see how William would have fought to become a knight. A man like William would brook no opposition....

With a sigh, he looked away, rubbing his forehead.

His head pains him. It is because he is hungry.

'We should eat,' she said softly.

The fair head nodded. 'That would be good, perhaps then I will be able to think straight.' The anger was fading from his eyes. 'Although I have to confess I would rather see the girls safe.'

Anna looked at Juliana. 'Juliana?'

'My lady?'

'Please send to the kitchens, Sir William and I are ravenous.'

Juliana's eyes bulged. '*Sir* William?'

'Yes,' Anna spoke firmly. 'This is Sir William Bradfer, he is a knight visiting from Apulia.'

'I thought...but...but...my lady...he's a Frankish *knight*?'

'He is.'

Juliana shook her head, her jaw gaped. 'But, my lady, you cannot give a Frankish knight the run of the Princess's apartments! It...it is not done, it is not seemly!'

Anna sighed. 'Juliana, neither of us has eaten in an age, we shall worry about the conventions later. In the meantime, we would like fish, and bread, and cheese…bring fruit, pastries, whatever you can lay your hands on.'

'And beef,' William murmured. Anna's listing of food had filled his mouth with saliva. 'I would kill for beef.'

Juliana gave a grudging curtsy. 'Very well.'

When Juliana had gone, Anna looked William's way. 'Daphne and Paula are being well cared for, of that I have no doubt,' she said, even as it dawned on her that she believed him when he said that the girls were not his. William was no liar. It was likely he felt protective towards them because he had known fear and uncertainty himself as a child. However fond of Sir Bruno he had become, it could not have been easy when his mother sent him away. 'But as for you…' Reaching up, she unclasped his cloak.

William caught her hand. 'Careful, my lady, what about that reputation of yours? What about those conventions the maid is so concerned about?'

Colouring, she brushed his hand aside. 'Don't be ridiculous. I want to see if your bruising is fading, and then we shall find you fresh clothing, *proper* clothing. We can't have a knight looking as though he has joined a troupe of tumblers.' She gestured imperiously at a guard hovering by the great double doors. It was the young Varangian that William had met the day before.

'You there, Kari?'

'My lady?'

'Sir William needs new clothing—hose, a shirt, a tunic, that sort of thing. And a cloak. I should like everything to be of good quality.' She frowned at his feet. 'And new boots. You might find spare ones in the armoury.'

Kari looked as startled as the maid had done. 'Commander Ashfirth will not like—'

'I shall take full responsibility.'

'Yes, my lady, I'll see what I can do.' Kari hesitated. 'I may need to pay for some of those things...'

She nodded. 'One moment.'

Anna hurried into the bedchamber, hair in a glossy tangle that hung down her back and swayed with her every step. William realised that in her concern to find clothes for him, she had forgotten that she had lost her veil and her hair was unpinned and...

She is beautiful! William's chest constricted in an uncomfortable muddle of confusion and desire. Anna emerged from the bedchamber and quietly pressed something into Kari's hand. William's gaze sharpened, it looked like a gold bangle.

'My thanks, Kari,' she said.

Kari bowed. 'I may not need it, the sergeant may supply me without question.'

'Just do your best, Kari.'

'My lady?' The guard threw a wary glance at William's sword. 'Ought Sir William to be bearing arms in the Palace?'

Wide grey eyes met William's, she gave him an apologetic shrug. 'Kari is in the right, William. In view of the as yet...unresolved nature of your status here, it would be best if you surrendered that sword.'

William's fingers clenched convulsively on the sword hilt. Give up the sword? He would feel naked without it. William's own sword had been taken from him after the ambush in Apulia and the lack of a weapon in the days of his slavery had added to his feeling of helplessness. Surely she would understand? A moment ago William had thought her concern for him touching...but had it really been concern? Or had she been biding her time, waiting for the right moment to disarm him?

'Give up the sword, my lady?'

Holding out her hand, Anna gave him one of her quiet smiles, William had no way of knowing whether he might trust it. He wanted, he *ached* to trust it, but...

'That would be best,' she said. 'While you are a guest in the Palace, I would not want you to risk arrest. You might not know this, Sir William, but the right to bear arms here is not universal...for example, if a slave were found carrying such a weapon, he might be executed.'

William called to mind the guards posted at the doors of the Boukoleon, the guards in the barracks on the lower level, the guards on the stairways and outside the apartment. The Palace was crawling with them and Lady Anna of Heraklea probably only had to lift a little finger for an entire regiment to come running.

Was she threatening him?

'Of course, that does not apply in your case,' she added quickly. 'Nevertheless...'

Nevertheless you would be wise to surrender that sword, because if you do not you are out-manned. Is that what she is saying?

William wanted to trust her, it was galling to discover the extent to which he wanted to trust her.

She had given the guard something—one of her bracelets?—to buy him clothes and had asked Kari to ensure they were of good quality. Surely she would not do that if she thought of him as her slave? Slaves here wore stuff that was little better than homespun.

Guts in as great a tangle as his thoughts, William slowly held out the sword.

'My thanks, William.' She passed it to Kari.

As the guard's footsteps faded, William caught her gaze. 'Earlier, I saw you give him something— what was it?'

'Nothing of any note.'

'It looked like a gold bangle.'

She shrugged. 'It was just a trifle.'

A gold bangle was a trifle? Lord, he would be in her debt for that gold bracelet—however was he to repay her? His hands clenched. 'My lady, I am overwhelmed by your generosity. Already I owe you much and you must know that I do not have the means to repay you.'

'Please do not mention it, it really is of no account. Now, about that bruising…'

She steered him to a chair and William held himself still while she unwound the bandage and examined him. He watched her face and prayed that he had not misjudged her as she went to fetch a basket of pots and clean bandages. Lady Anna treated him with every consideration. She had gone out of her way not to demean him, pointedly calling him 'Sir William' in front of her maid and the guard. She cared for his physical well-being. He had not misjudged her. She must know he didn't like being beholden to her, though, because she wouldn't look at him.

She clapped her hands and called for water and sponges. A painted screen that was alive with birds and flowers appeared out of nowhere and before he knew it, William found himself hustled behind it. While he washed, he was aware of her slipping into one of the bedchambers.

When he came out from behind the screen, she was waiting for him. She had tidied her hair a little and put on another pair of shoes, but the gown was still the blue one with the tear in the skirt. Gesturing him back to the chair, she selected a clay pot from the basket and handed it to him.

'I shall give you this salve, you should use it when you next bathe, William.' She deliberately averted her eyes from his.

'Yes, my lady.' William tried to catch her gaze, but those long lashes swept down. Her fingers were as shapely as her body, her touch as she gently probed his bruises set off tiny shivers in his belly. Pleasant shivers. Shivers that Sir William Bradfer should not be feeling for Lady Anna of Heraklea.

She had a lady's hands, unmarked by hard labour. The skin was smooth, the nails unbroken. And there...William breathed in carefully...yes, he caught a hint of the fragrance he had noticed in the cistern…

'Good, there is no swelling,' she murmured, again managing to avoid his gaze.

'What scent is that?' he asked, saying the first thing that came into his head, hoping that a direct question would lure those smoky eyes into meeting his.

She kept her gaze firmly averted. 'Scent?'

It was damned odd how much William ached for her to look into his eyes. The more she refused to do it, the more he wanted it. A chilling thought occurred to him. Was she ashamed of what had passed between them? Was she afraid of him? When he left, he did not want her to think badly of him. Suddenly it was most important that he found a way of repaying the money he owed her.

He kept his voice light, perhaps teasing might help. 'I see you have been visiting those…establishments near the Palace gates, my lady. I can smell flowers.'

Cheeks flaring crimson, she took the pot from him.

There was a slight crease in her forehead. 'They are perfumiers, William, I told you.'

'As you say, my lady.' He inhaled loudly. 'You smell delicious, I noticed it before. What scent is it?'

She wrenched the cork from the pot. 'It…it is jasmine, a blend of jasmine and spices and—'

'Musk.'

Her mouth tightened. 'Turn around, please. Show me your back.'

Meekly, William did as she asked and, moments later, cool ointment was smoothed into his skin.

'How does it feel?'

It felt wonderful, her delicate touch made his blood run hotter than Claire's ever had. 'Much better, I thank you. How does it look?'

'Colourful,' came the curt reply. 'However, I expect you will live.'

William shut his eyes, the better to enjoy the stroking as she rubbed the ointment into his back. 'That stuff doesn't smell half as sweet as you.'

She made a small huffing sound. 'Its purpose is to heal.'

Her fingers lingered. Her strokes, tentative at first, became bolder. Up over one shoulder, across to the other, and down, following the length of his spine. Were there bruises that low? No matter, Lady Anna could rub that stuff all over him if she had a mind to.

Provocative images leapt into William's head— images of Lady Anna leaning over him, of a long tress of hair spilling free of its knot, of her leaning so close she could cover him with kisses...

William shifted, he must stop thinking of her in this way. It was making him burn for her and she was not for him. 'Do you think you will meet your father today?' he asked, trying to distract himself.

What must Lord Romanos Angelos be like for her to have taken such a violent dislike to him? He could not be that bad. Her father must see some good in the man, he would not have picked him out unless he came from a good family and could offer her wealth and security.

The stroking paused. 'My father? I am uncertain, I shall have to send him a message. I expect so.' Her hand resumed its slow, sensuous path across his back. Was she enjoying the contact as much as he was? If only he could see into her eyes. But no, however much he twisted round to look into her face, she would not meet his gaze.

The scent of jasmine mingled with the medicinal tang of the ointment and for some extraordinary reason the combination was stronger than any love potion. Hot blood was racing to his chausses. Resting his arms on his knees, William gripped his hands together. Lord, he was pulsing and throbbing like a green lad dreaming about his sweetheart.

Her breath warmed the back of his neck.

The stroking stopped and when he turned, she was replacing the cork in the clay pot.

'Get dressed.' She waved at a pile of clothes that had appeared on a side table, Kari must have brought them while he had been washing. 'You may use the screen.'

Rising, William went to the table. A pair of soft leather boots sat on top of a leaf-green tunic and a cream shirt. His brows rose, the tunic was silk, the shirt linen. Lord, even the hose were silk. He grimaced, Kari had not returned her bangle.

'My lady, clothes like these do not come cheap.'

She shook her head. 'If you speak about debts, William, I will not hear you.' A curtain was billowing at one of the tall windows. Moving towards it, she caught hold of the curtain and tied it back.

While William was dressing behind the painted screen, he overheard her talking to the young Varangian. 'Kari?'

'My lady?'

'Be so good as to send someone to enquire whether my father, Lord Isaac, has been seen in the Palace this morning. If so, would you convey my warmest greetings to him and suggest that, if it is convenient, we might meet some time this afternoon.'

'Yes, my lady.'

When William stepped out from behind the screen, Anna was leaning against a window frame. Joining her, he found himself staring out over the Sea of Marmara. A small, walled harbour lay directly below the window.

His military instincts awoke. There was a harbour in the Great Palace? He could not see any warships. A gold gonfalon hung limply at the stern of a small galley, a pair of dromons were moored fore and aft. Two towers flanked the harbour entrance, standards bearing the double-headed Imperial eagle were flying from the flagpoles. There were sentries in the turrets as well as the walkways and quays, a row of statues—lions and oxen—watched with them from the main landing stage. If there was a harbour in the Palace, he might not need to trawl the City looking for a trader bound for Apulia. Maybe, just maybe, what he needed was right under his nose…

'My lady, is this the Imperial harbour?'

'Yes.'

Gulls were everywhere, circling over the harbour, perched on the backs of the stone lions. The quays were paved with what looked like marble and a flight of steps ran up from the harbour, presumably to an entrance in the Boukoleon. The entrance was out of William's line of sight, but something told him that it would be marble, too. 'I take it the main port lies elsewhere?'

'Mmm.' Anna had taken up a comb, she was drawing it through that rippling fall of hair. 'The City has several harbours and most of them lie in the Golden Horn. There are landing stages on both sides of the shore.'

Anna's hair looked so soft, for a moment the longing to touch it was stronger than William's need to learn as much as possible about the layout of Constantinople. When the opportunity came for him to make his way home, he must be ready for it. He only had to confirm that Daphne and Paula were in good hands. Irrespective of what Anna might want of him, he was eager to be on his way.

'Does the Golden Horn lie towards the north?'

'Yes, the Horn lies across the City to the northeast.'

As Anna went on with her combing, William permitted himself the pleasure of watching her. When loose, her hair reached well below her waist. It was, he was learning, something of a temptation. The sight of her parting a glossy strand and working her way down from crown to tip brought an uncomfortable tightening to his chest. He had felt a similar sensation once or twice before when in Lady Anna's company and he could not account for it. Earlier, he had put it down to hunger, and he was certainly hungry now…but he did not think hunger was at the root of it. It was in some way connected with her—he found her utterly beguiling.

William's experience of high-born women was limited. His early years in the convent had been somewhat unconventional, and in any case, he could scarcely remember them. He could not recall his mother in any detail, he could only conjure a shadowy face that remained a studied blank, devoid of emotion. The rest of her was shrouded behind a dull habit, a nun's veil.

Later, when William had been accepted into Sir Bruno's household and had grown into a young man, there had been a girl or two. However, William had never been profligate, he had no wish to bring unwanted children into the world. When he had befriended Claire, the young maidservant at Melfi, she had seemed delighted to accept him as her lover, her *careful* lover.

However, meeting a maidservant in a stable was one thing, this fascination with Lady Anna of Heraklea was quite another. Claire was not, bless her, a lady. Claire was a sweet girl, an earthy girl who had been born knowing how to please a man, one who took pleasure in doing so. In all the time

William had spent in the stables with Claire, they had hardly exchanged more than a dozen words. Spending hours, *hours*, talking to Anna had been something of a revelation. It struck him that speaking with a woman could be far more intimate than knowing her in the carnal sense.

How could that be? And yet, it was so. William cleared his throat. He had spent hours with Anna in the dark, and the handful of kisses they had exchanged had moved him far more than Claire's knowing ones. It was a mystery.

As for this, standing by the windows in the Boukoleon Palace, watching Anna comb that glossy, perfumed hair…no lady had ever accorded him half as much honour. He felt as though he might watch her for ever.

It struck him he was watching something extraordinarily intimate. He was scarcely managing to breathe, it was as though he were afraid of breaking a spell. Anna's maid, if she returned, would doubtless be scandalised.

Anna herself had forgotten his presence. And when she recollected it, he would be cast into the outer darkness…

Mon Dieu, his common sense was deserting him, this woman meant nothing to him, nothing!

All at once, she recollected herself. 'My apologies—whatever am I thinking!' Flushing like a rose, she shot William a glance and hastily bundled her hair over her shoulders. 'A veil, I must find a veil.'

'What harm? There's no need to be shy on my account.'

'No, no, it will not do.'

William wanted to take her hand, but they were no longer alone in the Basilica Cistern so, of course, he did no such thing. No one was looking their way, nevertheless, Anna would be conscious there were others nearby.

His mouth twisted. So much for congratulating himself on the honour being done to him, so much for believing she trusted him. Clearly she thought so little of him that she had forgotten his existence the moment she had put the cork back in that pot of salve. Anna of Heraklea was a noblewoman, a lady of exceptional birth. His questionable origins must shock her, it had been a mistake to confess them. To her he must still be a slave and an object of charity, that was why she was able to overlook his presence. When it suited them, aristocrats ignored servants and slaves. William knew this—in the past he had done it himself.

A twinge of something very like pain went through him as she snatched a veil from a chair and pinned it hastily in place, it was another delicate blue one, of a darker hue than the one she had lost by the monument at the edge of the Augustaion.

'I understand,' he said, smiling politely. 'You have your reputation to consider.' Anna must make a good marriage to please her father.

She was saved from making a response by the return of Juliana and a stream of servants bearing trays and dishes. William knew them for servants rather than slaves because their clothes—dyed in rich, earthy colours—were of a better quality than the slaves'. While the dishes were arranged on a table by a window, he fingered the cloth of the green tunic she had got Kari to buy for him. Silk, heavy samite. He took it as a sign that she really did intend to free him. What must it have cost? How was he to repay her when his money was back in the Duchy?

Then Juliana leaned past him to place a loaf of bread on the table and the urge to eat pushed all else from his mind. Fresh bread. Butter...

He swallowed. There were eggs, a platter of meats, another of cheeses, fruits...

'A feast, my lady.'

'Please, Sir William, it is past time we broke our fast. Do be seated.'

The blue veil fluttered as she waved him to a

chair. As his stomach noisily reacted to the sight of the food, her lips twitched. He pushed the platter towards her and she shook her head.

'Help yourself, William. There will be no formality here.'

He set to eagerly and waited until they had taken the edge off their hunger before speaking again. 'I am glad to have met you, my lady.' He grinned. 'And not just for the food.' He looked pointedly about him, raising a brow at the rich curtains gently shifting in the onshore breeze, at the polished marble floor and the gilded tables. 'When I return to the Duchy and describe my stay in the Boukoleon Palace, Sir Bruno will think I am fevered. He is a down-to-earth man and my tales of eating in the seaside apartment of a princess, in the company of a beautiful lady, will seem strange indeed.' Reaching across the table, he took her hand. 'When I leave here, I shall be in your debt, my lady, in more ways than I can count.'

Her smile set off a warm glow inside him. 'Sir William, you are most welcome, I am only s—'

The apartment doors opened. It was the young Varangian, Kari.

'Lady Anna.' Kari bowed. 'Lord Constantine Angelos is outside, he wishes to speak to you. He has your father's permission to enter the apartments.'

'Show him in.'

Lord *Constantine* Angelos? Who the devil was this? Anna had mentioned an unwanted fiancé named Romanos Angelos—could this be his brother?

The newcomer was wearing a red tunic, a heavy court tunic, such as a nobleman might wear in the Imperial Palace. It was slit at the sides and embroidered with gold threads that glistened as he moved. His hair was dark and wavy and cut close below the ears and his lips were curved in a warm smile.

Anna's face lit up. 'Constantine!'

Chapter Eight

Lord Constantine Angelos came towards them. When his dark eyes took in Anna and William's clasped hands, his brows lifted. 'I was with your father when your guard gave him your message. Welcome home, Anna. It is good to see you.'

Rising, Anna looked quickly towards the door. 'Father is here?'

Politely, William immediately rose, too.

'No, my dear. Lord Isaac is very busy on your behalf.'

'On my behalf?'

'He returns your greetings and asked me to tell you that he will meet you later, as you suggested.'

Anna stared. 'But what is he doing?'

'Finding a number of suitors for your hand in marriage, as I understand it.'

'I...I beg your pardon? What about Romanos?'

Lord Constantine grinned. 'My brother married

Lady Pulcheria of Limnos shortly after you left for Rascia.'

'Romanos is married?'

She had gone very still. Ever the courtier, her expression was under tight control, but after what she had told him, William knew she must be pleased. He was glad for her sake. The idea of Anna being forced into a marriage with someone she did not care for had been distasteful.

Lord Constantine drew his head back. 'I thought your father would have written to tell you.'

'No, no, he didn't. Saints, Constantine, I had no idea. So all this time...' her voice trailed off before strengthening again '...is Romanos happy in his marriage?'

'Indeed, already he has a son and another child is expected at harvest time.'

'I am glad. Romanos and I were not suited, but I am glad he has made a good marriage.'

'He is happy. And now Lord Isaac is looking for a husband for you, he has been talking to a number of suitors on your behalf.'

Anna touched Lord Constantine's arm. 'How do you know this?'

'My dear, there is little that goes on in the Palace that I do not know about.'

'He must still be angry with me, he has not forgiven me for leaving without his permission.'

'Anna, I think he has forgiven you.'

'That cannot be true. If he had forgiven me, he would have told me about Romanos being married.'

'My dear, I cannot claim to read Lord Isaac's mind, but I do believe you are forgiven. For one thing, his approach to finding you a husband has quite changed.'

Smoky grey eyes fixed on Lord Constantine's face, tiny lines had appeared in her brow. 'How is it you know so much about my father's affairs?'

'Lord Isaac is making quite a show of choosing a number of suitors who will try for your hand. What has changed since you were last betrothed is that this time *you* will be the one who makes the final choice.'

'Me?' Her eyes lit up and she gripped Lord Constantine's arm. 'Father will let *me* pick my husband? I never thought he would permit me to choose!'

'I believe your father wants a reconciliation as much as you do,' Lord Constantine said, with a slow smile. 'It is his way of making amends.'

Smile widening, he lifted her hand to his lips.

She held back. 'Constantine, you never answered my question.'

'Which question was that?'

Slowly, she withdrew her hand from his. 'How do you know so much about my father's affairs?'

As William watched them, his stomach sank. He knew the answer before it was uttered.

'I know, my sweet,' Lord Constantine said, 'because I happen to be the first man your father approached.'

A chill crept over William's skin.

'You? My father has offered me to you?' White teeth were biting that pretty mouth, her eyes were alight, dancing. She was trying not to laugh.

Her smile was infectious, the relief instantaneous. The idea of marrying Lord Constantine amused her. A grin escaped William even as he recognised that Lord Constantine did not share Lady Anna's amusement.

'Anna, I tell you I am chosen as one of your prospective suitors…and you laugh?'

'Of course I am laughing. You…my suitor?' She made a dismissive gesture. 'Constantine, I could never marry you. I am very fond of you, but you are like a brother to me.'

'I thought…' Lord Constantine's lips curved, but his eyes were watchful. There was no question but that this man did not share Anna's amusement. 'A brother—you think of me as a brother.'

Lord Constantine was making light of this, he was smiling to hide that he was hurt by her reaction. *Whilst I...* William brought his brows together. This should mean nothing to him, he was not interested in the outcome. Lady Anna of Heraklea and Lord Constantine Angelos were strangers whose paths he had crossed. By the time she married, William would be back in Apulia. He was interested because chance had flung them together for a time, he was glad she was to be given a choice.

Lord Constantine recaptured her hand and kissed it. 'Lady Anna,' he murmured soulfully, 'I am desolate. I beg you to reconsider.'

She tossed her head and a long brown curl escaped to tumble over her shoulder, she was so intent on Lord Constantine that she didn't notice. 'You cannot expect me to take you seriously?'

Lord Constantine put his hand to his heart. 'My lady, I would be honoured if you would consider me.'

'Constantine, who are the other suitors?'

'That is for your father to say.' Lord Constantine turned to William. 'Anna, who is this? You know full well you ought not to be entertaining men in the Princess's apartment—you are no longer in Rascia.'

'Don't worry, Constantine, this is my friend, William.' The men nodded at each other and Anna continued. 'William, my apologies for not introducing you at once. I think I mentioned that I was betrothed before I left for Rascia. As you will have gathered, Romanos has married someone else. This is his brother, Lord Constantine Angelos.'

Anna smiled at Constantine. Constantine was one of her oldest friends and although she had not put it in so many words, she knew, she just knew that William had understood from their brief exchange that while she had not been fond of her previous fiancé, she had been very fond of Constantine. It was as though he could see into her mind.

'You look well, Anna,' Constantine said, as they settled around the table. 'Your travels among the barbarians do not seem to have dulled your beauty. In truth, rather the reverse. I am glad I overheard the guard speaking to your father, I had not looked for the pleasure of meeting you so soon.'

When Constantine smiled, his dark eyes sparkled with amusement and affection. With a twist of unease, Anna was aware that William was less than relaxed. Constantine's unguarded reference to barbarians must have offended him, he would not be disturbed by Constantine's flirting. In any case, Constantine always flirted, it meant nothing.

Apparently oblivious of any undertones, Constantine directed a polite smile at William. 'William, eh? You must be a Frank—that's a name favoured by the Normans. If it were not for your name, Anna's friend, I would have taken you for a Viking.'

'I come from the Duchy of Apulia and Calabria,' William said stiffly.

'Come, Constantine, don't start with your questions.' Anna glanced at William. Her mind was struggling to take in all that Constantine had told her.

Father is going to allow me my choice of husband! Thank God William never knew the plans I had for him, what a fool he would have thought me. It is better this way. Much better.

It was most perplexing, though, how her heart felt like lead. 'Constantine has the most insatiable curiosity,' she managed brightly. 'Constantine, you are not to pester William with your questions. William is a knight, that is all you need to know.'

'A knight? So you are Sir William of…?'

'Bradfer, Sir William Bradfer.' With something as near as smile as anything Anna had seen since

Constantine had joined them, William flexed his sword arm. 'Bradfer means—'

'Strong arm, I know.' Constantine grinned. 'It doesn't tell me much else about you though, does it?'

William cocked a brow at him, refusing to be drawn, and the silence stretched out.

After a moment, Constantine sighed. 'Never mind. Anna, Sir William may be a close friend, but you really should not have invited him up here.'

'Do not concern yourself, my lord,' William said. 'I shall be leaving soon.'

'Not yet, I hope,' Anna got in, quickly. 'Sir William, you cannot have forgotten that I have to find that…document for you. You will not want to leave without it.'

'My lady, you are most kind, but I do not consider it essential. It is but a formality.'

Anna stared at him for a moment and gave a brusque nod. There was a faint prickling at the back of her eyes, she blinked it away. Saints, she could wish that William was less eager to get home. She genuinely liked him but he…he simply couldn't wait to leave.

Still, this morning had seen one problem solved—she need no longer use William to avoid marrying Romanos. One of her suitors must be acceptable, and if not...well, she could do worse than consider Constantine. She and Constantine had always had a liking for each other.

Her other problem remained. Katerina. Where had she got to? Leaning forwards, she caught Constantine's eye and, conscious of the servants, lowered her voice. Such was the habit of openness between her and Constantine that she had to remind herself that he was unaware that Katerina had taken the Princess's place. 'Do you know anything of the whereabouts of Princess Theodora? She was in the City with me when some German mercenaries threatened us. I ran one way, she ran the other and—'

Constantine frowned. 'You were separated? When was this?'

'Yesterday. I was afraid...afraid...and...oh, Constantine, it's a long story but some of the General's mercenaries were after us and we had to split up. I haven't seen her since. Juliana swears she returned, but she seems to have vanished again. Have you heard where she might be? I am worried for her safety.'

'She is well, I believe,' Constantine murmured. 'Commander Ashfirth took her to safety.'

'Thank heaven.' Relief rushed through her, but worry remained. *Katerina is safe! But what shall we do? It was one thing to pull the wool over the eyes of an old and feeble Emperor, but now... If our deception is uncovered, my reputation will be damaged beyond repair—I will be lucky not to be banished! No one will take me as a wife, and as for my father...if this scandal breaks, he will never forgive me.*

'One of my men told me that Commander Ashfirth saw fit to hide her somewhere in the Palace after the General's men scaled the City walls.' Constantine shrugged. 'It is something of a mystery. Some preposterous rumours are floating about, no one is making much sense.'

'What is being said?'

'That Commander Ashfirth locked her in the Treasury and the moment Emperor Nikephoros abdicated, he carried her out again and claimed her as his own.'

'No!' Anna put her hand on her churning stomach. 'Surely that is not possible?'

'My dear, you forget, Varangians swear loyalty to the Emperor in person. They swore to serve Emperor Nikephoros and until the new Emperor sits on the throne and they have sworn their oath to serve him, they are masterless men.'

'But...the Princess...he cannot have claimed the Princess!'

'He must be evoking the Varangians' right to plunder,' William said, leaning an elbow on the table. 'Even in Apulia, we have heard of it. When an Emperor dies, is it not the Varangian tradition that they may help themselves to treasures from the Palace?'

'They call it palace pillaging,' Constantine said. 'However, they may only keep what they can carry.'

'But…but we are speaking about a woman here, not a casket of gold!' Anna said. 'And in any case, Emperor Nikephoros is not dead, he abdicated.'

Constantine grinned and reached for an apple. 'From what I heard, Commander Ashfirth didn't stop to make the distinction.'

Anna waved toward the doors. 'Why does Kari remain on duty?'

'My guess is that he is acting on the Commander's orders, it is not in the Commander's interest to alienate General Alexios by allowing a complete breakdown of order.'

'And the rumour is that Commander Ashfirth has taken the Princess?' Anna rubbed her brow. *If this is true, we are ruined! What shall I do? My only hope is that General Alexios will be so busy with the coming enthronement that he will not have time to summon his wife's distant relatives to an audience.*

'The Commander was seen coming out of the Treasury with her in his arms.' Constantine spread his hands. 'I admit it sounds implausible.'

The attraction between Commander Ashfirth and Katerina was clear from the moment they had met, but Katerina must know that she cannot simply run off with the man!

Green eyes were fixed on her, Anna forced a smile. 'I cannot believe this outlandish tale. It is almost as unlikely as Emperor Nikephoros abdicating.'

'The abdication is most certainly true. The Patriarch—the bishop—feared there might be a bloodbath and to prevent it he advised Emperor Nikephoros to abdicate. The miracle is that Nikephoros listened, he must have realised control was slipping from his grasp. Frankly, I had not thought he had so much wit.'

'Constantine!'

Constantine bit into his apple.

Anna hoped she looked calm. There were so many emotions roiling about inside her and she was very much afraid that the one that was gaining dominance was terror. Now she had time to think about it, she realised that the abdication changed everything.

'So General Alexios really is the new Emperor,' she murmured.

'Yes.'

'My lady…' William was studying her '…what's wrong?'

'Wrong? Nothing is wrong. It is just this coup… I did not think General Alexios would succeed.'

'You would have done if you hadn't been stuck out in the provinces,' Constantine said conversationally. 'The General is nothing if not ambitious. Did you know he has never lost a battle?'

Nodding, Anna gazed at the sea and tried to remember what she knew about General Alexios and his young wife, Irene.

The new Emperor is not cast in the same mould as Emperor Nikephoros and his wife is a distant cousin of Princess Theodora. God help me, General Alexios will want to meet Katerina, he will have questions for her. And if General Alexios is as clever as his reputation suggests, he is bound to find out that she is an impostor!

The food in her stomach congealed into an indigestible mass.

When I agreed to take part in this pretence, the

Emperor was an elderly man who kept largely to his apartments. But now...

'The enthronement is to take place on Easter Day,' Constantine added. 'We are a couple of days away from having a new Emperor.'

'So soon?' *Heavens.*

Constantine set his apple core aside. 'Anna, have you had enough to eat? You look a trifle pale.'

'I have eaten plenty, thank you.' *And I could not manage another bite.* She stared out of the window, her mind so full she neither noticed the shimmer and shift of sunlight on the sea, nor the seagulls rocking on its restless surface. 'I take comfort in the thought that the Princess was seen in the company of the Commander, that is something to be thankful for. He will protect her.'

William crumbled bread between his fingers. He had been listening to this exchange with some interest and his skin was prickling. Something was wrong here, very wrong. Lord Constantine was right, the colour had leached from Anna's cheeks— she was hiding something. She was in some kind of trouble and it was more than the difficulties she had mentioned with her father. Something other than the choosing of a husband was worrying her.

'Anna...' Lord Constantine leaned confidentially towards her '...I cannot swear as to where the Princess was last night, but I can definitely tell you that she and the Commander were seen leaving the Palace this morning.'

Lady Anna's eyes were intent. 'Where did they go?'

Constantine grinned.

'Tell me!'

'The Princess is...' Lord Constantine's voice was scarcely above a whisper '...presently at Commander Ashfirth's house. He has set a contingent of his men to guard her. You need have no fears on her account—your princess is quite safe, though what effect these rumours will have on her marriage prospects I cannot say. Duke Nikolaos will be most displeased.'

William leaned forwards. 'Duke Nikolaos?'

'Duke Nikolaos of Larissa is betrothed to Princess Theodora,' Anna murmured. 'He is not at Court at present.'

Constantine took Lady Anna's hand and raised it to his lips, lingering long enough for William's jaw to clench.

'I have pleased you in bringing this news?' Lord Constantine murmured, his voice as smooth as honey.

'You have indeed, thank you, Constantine.'

William did not know how it was, because Lord

Constantine seemed to be a likeable enough fellow, but he was suddenly filled with a burning need to hit him in the face. William was staring woodenly at what was left on the meat platter when it came to him that Lord Constantine might know what had happened to the little girls, to Daphne and Paula.

'Excuse me for interrupting your courting, Lord Constantine,' he said drily, 'but do you know what became of the children whom the Princess adopted? Are they with her?'

Lord Constantine shifted in such a way that William could no longer see Anna. Without thinking, William moved to put her back in his line of sight—he liked looking at her. The realisation hit him like a dash of cold water.

Mon Dieu, the sooner he left, the better, he had no business gazing at a lady of the Imperial Court. He must remember his ambitions. If he did not return to the Duchy soon, he would lose all chance of learning who ordered him killed. And he was determined that his enemy would not escape justice.

But there Lord Constantine sat, the Devil blast him, stroking her hand. She had laughed and said she thought of him as a brother, so why was she not objecting?

'Children?' Lord Constantine paused thoughtfully. 'One is not weaned while the other is only this tall?' He held out his hand to the level of the table.

'Their names are Daphne and Paula, Constantine,' Anna said, smiling warmly into Lord Constantine's eyes. William felt as though a dagger had been planted in his gut.

'I believe they have also been taken to Commander Ashfirth's house, they went with a couple of maid-servants to keep the Princess company.'

'There, William!' Expressive grey eyes filled with relief. 'The girls are unharmed. The Princess is kindness itself, she will take good care of them. She has a...special understanding of their plight.'

William nodded. It was time to leave, the girls were safe. The sense that something was elud-ing him was still there, hiding in a dark corner of his mind. He had harboured the feeling for some time...surely if it were important it would have come forwards, into the light?

No matter, the girls were safe. He could leave Constantinople with a clear conscience.

Empty inside despite the food, William pushed to his feet. 'It is time I was on my way. The Palace will doubtless be in an uproar when the new Emperor arrives.'

'William, you cannot leave!' Smoky eyes frowned up at him. 'I...I have not dismissed you.'

'You refer to that service you wished me to perform for you?'

For a moment, she would not meet his eyes. 'No, I find that is no longer necessary. But you cannot leave without the document, I want you to have it.'

'My lady, I told you, the document is irrelevant to me.' William must go and the sooner the better. It seemed that every moment in her company made it harder for him to leave.

'You will not stay for the enthronement?'

'I am sorry, my lady, urgent affairs await me at home.' William extricated her hand from Lord Constantine's and bowed over it. A subtle drift of jasmine caught in his nostrils and the dagger in his belly turned. 'I am in your debt, my lady. When I can find a way, I shall repay you.'

'Sir William, I meant it when I told you not to consider it. I am sorry that you are to leave us, but I wish you a good journey. Here...' reaching for the pot of salve, she pressed it into his hand '...you may find this of use.'

William turned away, his throat tight. 'My thanks, Lady Anna.'

The cloak she had provided for him was draped over the painted screen, he scooped it up in passing and headed for the doors.

The great double doors opened and again the

dagger twisted. The urge to look back was unbearable, resisting it caused more pain than the battering he had received in the days of his slavery. Fortunately, blocking pain was something William had mastered in his knightly training. He strode through the apartment doors and they snapped shut behind him.

Anna stared after William, her mind was in turmoil. 'He has no money. I don't know how he thinks he will pay for his passage home.'

'He's a Frankish knight, he probably thinks he can bludgeon his way on board. Maybe he hopes to find a captain who is a sailor short.'

'You have not seen his bruises.' Rising, Anna walked distractedly to the brazier. The sight of the marks on William's naked back as he fought that mercenary near the Augustaion leapt into her head. She swallowed. 'He will try, of course, it is not in his character to surrender. But he… Sir William has suffered much of late. His sword arm is damaged and it is possible he has a broken rib or two. He should be resting, not thinking about hauling sailcloth about on a ship!'

'You exaggerate, I am sure, the man looks as strong as a lion.'

'He has been trained to make light of his hurts.'

Constantine tipped his head on one side and held his hand out. 'Anna, come here.' He was wearing the most crooked of smiles.

'What?'

'You don't want this knight to leave, do you?'

'I don't want him to injure himself!' Retracing her steps, she took Constantine's hand. It was a little disturbing to realise there was truth in Constantine's statement, but this was not the time to think about it. 'Constantine, it is quite ridiculous, William can be as stubborn as a mule. He says he has family in Constantinople, yet he shows no desire to find them. I am sure if he were to contact them, they would provide him with everything he needs for his passage home.'

Constantine's gaze sharpened. 'Sir William has family in the City?'

'So he said, but he will not stay to meet them. I have not known him long and there is much he has not told me, but it seems likely that someone in Apulia has wronged him most dreadfully. His mind is taken up with the thought of returning to reclaim his rightful place in the world.'

'Someone in Apulia wronged him? How?'

'Constantine, he has not told me everything. I would like to help him though—can you think of anything we might do?'

'*We?*'

'Could...could you not find him...employment of some sort?'

Constantine gave a bark of laughter. 'The man is a Frankish knight! He trades his strength and his skill at arms. If his strength has been compromised, I cannot see that he has much to offer.'

'Think, Constantine, I beg you, there must be *something* he could do. I wish I had money to give him, but the few coins I took with me to Rascia have long gone.' She grimaced. 'My jewellery is of little value, I gave Kari my last gold bracelet so that he might find William some clothes. Quickly, Constantine, think!'

'You really do care for him,' Constantine said slowly.

Her face burned. 'Yes. Yes, I do.'

I like him far more than I ought to like a Frankish knight, I like him enough to wish that he was not a barbarian who lived far beyond our western borders. And the thought that I shall never see him again is almost unbearable.

'Very well. Though I shall be hard pressed to find work that a Frankish knight will feel able to accept.'

Thinking aloud, she stared at Constantine. 'You have always shown an interest in the peoples living at the edge of the Empire. In the past, you have often lamented the lack of a strong Emperor who might share your interest and make better use of your knowledge. Soon, we will have a strong Emperor...'

Constantine's eyes became hooded. 'Your point being...?'

'General Alexios will, I am sure, appreciate your talents far more than Emperor Nikephoros ever did. And think how impressed he would be if you spoke Norman French.'

'Anna, I must tell you, my Norman French is already fairly tolerable.'

'Tolerable? You can settle for fairly tolerable?' She tipped her head to one side. 'Wouldn't you rather be fluent?'

'I suppose, for you, I could let the Frank teach me the refinements.' Constantine looked thoughtfully into the distance. 'Anna, I think you may have hit on something... Sir William could earn his passage home by tutoring me in his language—'

'And in the meantime his body will have time to heal properly.'

Constantine reached forwards and kissed her on the cheek. 'I know you are not suggesting this for my sake, but this could be useful. I shall be glad of the chance to improve my Norman French.'

Spirits lifting, Anna tugged at Constantine's hand. 'Hurry! He will be halfway to the gate by now.'

Constantine swung his cloak about his shoulders. 'Do you know which gate he will use?'

Her cheeks warmed. 'The one by the street of the perfumiers.'

Chapter Nine

William had left the Boukoleon Palace by the
main north door and was halfway across one of
the courtyards by the time he was hailed.

'*Sir William!* Sir William, a moment, if you
please!'

William swung round to see Anna on Lord
Constantine's arm, they were passing a group of
courtiers by a fountain. Anna was holding her blue
skirts clear of the ground in a grand manner that
was only slightly marred by the jagged tear in the
fabric. Vaguely, William wondered why she had
not taken the time to change. Looking at her, it
was as though a weight he had not known he was
carrying lifted from him.

'Lady Anna!'

Conversation round the fountain ceased. Heads
turned.

'A moment, sir, if you please,' Anna spoke into silence, her veil drifting about her like blue mist.

'Lady Anna, Lord Constantine.' Conscious of the eyes watching their every move, William gave them his most formal bow—this *was* the Imperial Court.

'Sir William, we should be grateful if you would care to accompany us,' Anna said, indicating a curving path that led away from the fountain. 'Let us walk awhile.'

They followed the path across a broad swathe of grass and came to a halt in an area where the grounds were less well tended and apparently deserted.

William looked curiously at her. 'My lady?'

Her hand fell from Lord Constantine's arm. 'We have been discussing how you planned to book your passage for Apulia, and wondered if you might need some...assistance.'

'Why should I need assistance?'

Grey eyes looked anxiously up at him. 'What were you going to do, William, fight your way onto a ship and force the captain to give you passage?'

'Something like that.' He lifted his shoulders. 'In truth, my only thought was to get clear of the Palace. After that...well, I shall take things as they come. I can always hire myself out as a deck hand.'

A small hand touched his sleeve. 'William, you must not think of such a thing, you are in no fit state. We would be honoured to help you.'

He watched them exchange glances. This was about money—Anna knew he had no money. It made him uneasy to know they had been talking about him. 'I don't need any more charity,' he said stiffly. 'My lady, I am already in your debt.'

Anna opened her mouth, but Constantine set her gently to one side. 'Anna, it might be best if you explored the gardens for a while, I can take it from here. It shouldn't take long.'

Anna met Constantine's gaze and, with a slight frown, removed her hand from William's arm. Nodding at them, she continued down the path towards a grove of trees. The ribbons of her cloak streamed out behind her, her veil fluttered. She had an elegant and sinuous way of walking, her whole body swaying...

Abruptly, William noticed that Constantine's dark eyes were on him, running over his green silk tunic, the new cloak.

'You have no purse, Sir William,' he said, bluntly.

'You are observant, Lord Constantine, but you do not need to concern yourself on my behalf.'

'On the contrary, I do. Anna worries about you, and what concerns Anna concerns me.'

Lord Constantine's proprietorial manner towards Anna was irritating. She might think of Lord Constantine Angelos as a brother, but she clearly had a high regard for him and the man knew it. He must be confident she would eventually choose him as her husband.

'Lady Anna has already been more than generous,' William said, gesturing at his clothes. 'I have no intention of asking for more. Particularly since I am certain she sacrificed a gold bracelet to acquire these for me.'

'She was right then, you do need money.'

William's hand went to where his sword-hilt should be. 'Lord Constantine, I would prefer that we do not continue this conversation. Lady Anna had no right to discuss my affairs with you.'

'Relax, man, she was discretion itself. However, one doesn't need the wisdom of Solomon to see that you are in need of a friend.' With a glance down the path that Anna had taken, Lord Constantine held out his hand. 'And that is what I offer you: friendship. For Anna's sake.'

Warily, William clasped the outstretched hand. 'I won't take your money, my lord.'

'No charity, of course not. Wouldn't dream of offending you by offering it.' Lord Constantine grimaced. 'A man has his pride. Women never seem to understand that, that is why I suggested Anna walk in the gardens for a time.'

William narrowed his eyes. 'You sound as though you have something in mind.'

'A small proposition,' Lord Constantine said.

They strolled past an abandoned building as, with a whir of wings, a pigeon flew out from under the portico. Broken statues flanked a boarded-up doorway, ivy was winding up the marble columns. Despite the dereliction, the building had an air of grandeur. It must be an ancient palace that had fallen into disuse.

'My lord?'

'In Apulia you are a knight, a horse-soldier, I seem to recall?'

William grunted assent.

'And you hire yourself out, do you not?'

'Ye…es, but—'

'How do you feel about putting yourself up for hire here?'

William drew his head back. 'As a cavalry officer? Are you suggesting I enlist in the Imperial army?'

'That wasn't exactly what I had in mind…' Lord Constantine lifted an eyebrow '…although I am sure you would be well paid to show off your prowess in the Hippodrome.'

William's lip curled. 'Circus tricks.'

Lord Constantine grinned. 'Thought that would be your response. No, Sir William, I have something else in mind. I have always had a—how should I put this?—a hunger to learn about the peoples who live outside the Empire. I would be in your debt if you could teach me as much as possible about your country, particularly your language.'

'I am not certain I have a country,' William said, carefully. 'My mother was Greek and I have no idea who my father was. I was told he was a Frank, but I have never set foot in Normandy or France.'

Dark eyes held his, steady and determined. 'You speak three languages, I assume.'

William rested a foot on the cracked bottom step of the ruined portico and nodded. His upbringing at the convent and later with Sir Bruno had ensured that he spoke Greek, Latin and Norman French.

'Sir William, I already know the rudiments of Norman French and I am eager to learn more. Will you stay long enough to teach me? Name a fair fee and I will pay it. Well? What do you say?'

William hesitated. He could certainly use some money and the red purse hanging from Lord Constantine's belt was reassuringly plump. This was a battle, and he must do what he could to return home and discover the identity of his enemies. And if he were realistic, he was somewhat out of condition—accepting this man's money for a few days' tuition might not be such a bad idea...

If he held back his plans for, say, a couple of weeks, he could easily help Lord Constantine. He might also help Lady Anna, the debt he owed her for freeing him was incalculable. It was obvious that something was preying on her mind—when they had been breaking their fast in the Boukoleon, she had gone chalk-white. Her concern seemed to revolve around Princess Theodora. The military coup, which by all accounts had resulted in a popular and efficient general seizing the Imperial crown, seemed to be causing her no little distress. Why? William didn't begin to understand what was going on, but he was certain Lady Anna needed a friend almost as much as he had when he had stumbled on to that auction block. He would be happy to assist her in any way he could.

'Very well, Lord Constantine, I shall give you two weeks of my time if you cover my passage home.'

'Agreed.'

'My lord, there is one caveat...'

'Oh?'

'Of late there have been a number of disagreements between your people and mine on the borders of the Duchy. I would have you note that I am not prepared to do or say anything that might compromise the holding of any Frank. As long as you understand that, we have an agreement.'

Lord Constantine gave him a broad grin. 'I understand. Tutor me in Norman French for a couple of weeks and you shall have your fee.'

'I would also like money for a bracelet for Lady Anna.'

'I beg your pardon?'

William's cheeks grew warm. 'You may give it to her, but I want her to have another bracelet.'

'Agreed. In the meantime…' Lord Constantine tugged at the strings of his red purse and handed him several heavy gold bezants '…take these as a token of my good will. Anna expects me to find you lodgings, too, but Lord knows how I shall do that—the Palace will be in turmoil until power has been transferred to General Alexios. The General's men will be expecting billets, and his wife, the new Empress, has her own entourage. Normally the Empress would be expected to take up residence in the Boukoleon, but that is, I hear, undecided.' He shook his head. 'Whatever happens, there aren't likely to be spare beds. Lady Anna might be able to help you—'

'No!' When Constantine's eyebrows lifted, William expanded. 'I have troubled Lady Anna too much already, I will not ask for more.'

'Sir William, Anna enjoys helping people.'

'That may be, but I am already beholden to her.'

Lord Constantine made a sound of exasperation and was on the point of replying when his gaze shifted to something behind William. His expression froze.

Two men, one in his middle years, the other a stripling, were at the head of a ragged procession as it wound its way down the path that led from the Boukoleon. Fur-lined cloaks and jewelled cloak-pins marked the leading two out as aristocrats, the others were dressed as servants or slaves.

'Lord Isaac!' Constantine bowed to the older man. 'What an unexpected pleasure to see you again so soon.'

Lord Isaac? Was this Anna's father? The man's hair was streaked with grey, his beard was neatly trimmed. As for the boy, William was disconcerted to note his eyes had been carefully outlined with some black cosmetic.

'Yes, yes, good to see you, Lord Constantine,' Lord Isaac said. Perceptive grey eyes ran quickly over William and, equally quickly, dismissed him.

'I am looking for my daughter, she was seen coming this way. I thought she was with you.'

'She was, my lord.' Lord Constantine exchanged unsmiling nods with the stripling, who was dark-complexioned with glossy black hair and a beard. 'Good day, Lord Michael.'

As William's attention returned to the older man, he became aware of an unsettling sense of familiarity. Lord Isaac's eyes were similar to Anna's, they were harder and more calculating, but the colour was the same.

'Your daughter went through the trees there, my lord,' Lord Constantine said, directing them towards the path. 'She will not have gone far.'

'Thank you. Come, Lord Michael.'

Lord Isaac favoured William with another curt nod before he and his companion stepped back onto the path. The gaggle of servants followed.

'Lord Constantine?'

Lord Constantine glanced irritably at him. 'For God's sake, man, I thought we had established that you and I are to be friends, Constantine will do.'

'Very well, and you must call me William.' William watched the two men and the train of servants walk into the trees. 'I take it that is Lady Anna's father?'

'Yes, that is Lord Isaac, the Governor of Heraklea.'

'And the younger man?' He must be the reason Constantine looked as though he had been forced to drink a vat of sour wine. Poor fellow, Constantine looked to be in a worse state than William had been when Lady Felisa had spurned him for the knight with the large estates. But if that painted boy was another of Anna's suitors, he was surely no threat. Perhaps Constantine was not as confident of winning Anna's hand as William had assumed. 'Is he one of Lady Anna's other suitors?'

'Yes, that is Lord Michael of Brusa. And as you may have gathered, he is, hell fry him, high in Lord Isaac's favour.'

The path into the trees was empty again. William felt a pang of sympathy for Constantine, courting when one's heart was engaged was clearly a painful business. And if William felt this bad simply because he understood what the man was going through, he must ensure that, when he next went courting, his heart would not be involved.

'In the Palace you said that Lady Anna was to be given a choice?'

Constantine sighed. 'So Lord Isaac has sworn, but Anna is desperate to please him, to make up for their years of estrangement.'

'You think that will sway her?'

'Don't you?'

William stared towards the wooded area, hoping to catch a flash of blue silk. Nothing. Just cypresses, more cypresses and a glimpse of grey— the great walls that protected the Imperial Palace from sea-borne attack.

'Has Lady Anna met Lord Michael before?' he asked. He was certain that the painted boy would never appeal to a woman like Anna.

'I have no idea.'

'I assume he has land?'

Constantine gave him a disgruntled look. 'He has land, a lineage that goes back to Rome, bulging coffers and a face to rival that of Adonis.'

'It is a painted face and one she does not know. Surely she will choose someone for whom she feels some warmth?'

The idea of Anna marrying Constantine was faintly unpalatable, however, the thought of her marrying Lord Michael was far worse—it completely repelled him. Lord Michael might be pleasant enough, William had no way of knowing, so how was it he found the thought of Anna marrying the fellow so unacceptable? Clearly, he was sympathising with Constantine far too much.

'Perhaps marriage is best when it is a matter of duty,' he said. 'Perhaps it should be undertaken for dynastic reasons, for building up one's lands, one's fortune. It should not be confused with love.'

Constantine sent him a strange look. 'Some warmth between a husband and wife is desirable though, you just said as much.'

'Yes.' William felt at odds with himself. Love was what had happened in the stables between Claire and himself. Love was simply a pretty word for the carnal pleasures to be found in the arms of a willing woman—it was no more than that.

'Anna will choose to please her father.' With a sigh, Constantine squared his shoulders. 'She wants to make amends for earlier mistakes.'

'Such as leaving for Rascia to serve the Princess.'

Constantine gave him a searching look. 'I see she has talked to you at some length.'

William grunted. The memory of Anna fast in his arms in the cistern was suddenly as vivid as a freshly painted icon—it could have happened mere moments ago. She had been so warm, so soft, so…giving… Would she be as yielding in Lord Michael's arms? In Constantine's? He frowned— the thought of Anna in anyone else's arms was repugnant.

Turning abruptly, he scuffed one of his new boots against the bottom step of the ruined hall. 'About my accommodation,' he began, making a show of examining the walls, 'I take it no one has plans for this ruin?'

Whatever the building had once been, its days of grandeur were long gone, decay was setting in. Tumbles of brick and stone lay at the foot of the walls, yellow weeds flowered in cracks between stones. The rendering was fractured and eroded with tentacles of ivy crawling across it.

'It's not likely—it's been empty for years.'

'Fine, it will suit me very well.'

'William, it's derelict!'

'I am a knight, a horse-soldier.' Walking round the side of the building, William found that some of the rubble had been piled in front of a worm-eaten door. As a crude attempt to block entry, it was pitiful. Clambering onto the rubble, he leaned experimentally against the door. The wood creaked and moved about an inch. He straightened. 'As General Alexios would doubtless inform you, soldiers are trained to make camp anywhere.'

Constantine was watching him, hands on his hips. A dark brow lifted. 'You plan on bedding down in here?'

'I assure you I have bedded down in worse places.' William gave Constantine a straight look. 'It will save you the trouble of having to bribe a Palace official to find me a bed.'

'It's not such a bad idea,' Constantine said, thoughtfully. 'I wonder if the couches are still inside?'

'Couches?'

'This was once a reception hall, it is known as the Hall of the Nineteen Couches.'

William lifted a brow. 'Seriously?'

'Seriously. Envoys and ambassadors from every corner of the Empire and beyond were received here. The Emperor presided over feasts where he and his guests ate from couches in the Roman fashion, hence the name.'

William grinned. 'Judging by the state of the outside, I'll wager the couches are long decayed. Do you care to find out?'

Constantine scrambled up beside him and together they put their shoulders to the door.

'My lord!' Anna sank into a deep curtsy next to a tall cypress, scarcely daring to look into her father's face. The moment she had both longed for and dreaded was upon her. Was her father ready to forgive her? She prayed for reconciliation, but he would be irritated that she had failed to meet him yesterday—that would surely weigh against her. However, after what she had learned from Constantine—that her father was ready to grant her the husband of her choice—she had reason to hope.

Warily, she looked up. A young man was standing with some servants by another cypress. Anna had eyes only for her father and when he held out his hands to her, she slowly placed hers in his.

'You look well, daughter.' Her father raised her, keeping her at arm's length so as to look her up and down. 'If a little…unkempt.'

Anna grimaced, naturally, her father would notice the tear in her gown. *I should have changed my gown, only there was no time because I was afraid that if Constantine and I did not hurry after William, we would lose him...*

However, it was heartening that her father had not mentioned their missed meeting. It was possible he was unwilling to chastise her with the young man listening. She rushed into speech. 'I wasn't expecting to meet you until this afternoon, but it is good to see you, my lord.'

And so it is. The thought startled her. She studied him. *My father, Lord Isaac, Governor of Heraklea.* Two years had passed, years that had left their mark on her father's features. The streaks of white were more plentiful in her father's hair, his beak of a nose was more pronounced and the lines on his cheeks more deeply graven.

'Is there peace between us, my lord?' Anna held her breath, waiting for his reaction. Adept at schooling his expression, her father was a hard man to read. It occurred to her that in her childhood she had had no trouble reading him, the difficulty had begun after Erling's death. He had accused her of excessive grieving for someone who was 'only a slave', he had told her such emotions for a slave were unfitting.

After that, everything twisted between us.

Her father made a growling sound low in his throat. 'Peace? We shall see.' He squeezed her fingers and a smile flickered briefly across his lips. It was gone so quickly she was uncertain whether she had imagined it. 'You are a woman now, let us see if you have learned to act like one.'

'I shall do my best, my lord. I did not like…displeasing you. It is just that…Lord Romanos… I could not like Lord Romanos for a husband.'

Tucking her arm in his, her father nodded. 'He frightened you.' His expression was so benign, Anna could only stare. *Has he changed so much? Is that possible?*

'Yes, Father, he did.'

When the young man standing by the cypress made a movement, Anna realised he had been listening to them with an intensity that was far from casual.

Who is he?

He looked somewhat younger than William. Like William, he was impossibly handsome, but there the resemblance ended—where William was fair, he was dark.

This boy is beautiful, a dark angel. A cold shiver ran down Anna's back. *Is this one of the suitors Constantine mentioned? Does Father think to please me by giving me a beautiful boy?*

The young man stepped forward. 'Lord Isaac?'

Her father waved him aside. 'I should like a moment with my daughter, if you please, Lord Michael.'

'My lord.' The boy returned to stand with the servants by the cypress.

Saints, that boy has painted his eyes! And he is still staring, he must be one of the suitors....

Anna's heart lurched. *I do not want to kiss this boy, I will never want to kiss him. If only it were William standing there...*

'You should not have run away,' her father was saying. Placing his hand on hers, he led her a little way down the path, back towards the Hall of the Nineteen Couches.

'I was not ready for marriage, my lord, and when

I heard that the Princess needed more ladies…I…
I am sorry, my lord.'

'I trust you performed your duties well?'

'Yes, my lord.'

'And I am sure that the Princess taught you the importance of obeying your betters?'

Anna stared fixedly at a laurel bush growing next to the path, she loathed it when her father spoke in this vein. He had never done so when she was a child, it was only later, after everything had soured between them…

'Yes, Father.' Lord Michael was following them at a discreet distance. Shivering, Anna drew her cloak tightly about her, she hoped she was wrong about him and that he was not one of her suitors. Her instincts told her that this boy did not like women. It was common knowledge that some men preferred male lovers, Anna was sure that Lord Michael was one such man. Anna had never given the matter much thought, it was simply how things were, but she had no wish to be married to someone who took men as lovers. 'Why is he staring?'

'Later. First I will hear of your time with the Princess. Do you know why she was so reluctant to come home?'

Anna felt every muscle go rigid. *The Princess is reluctant to come home because she is hiding an illegitimate child, a child whose very existence would likely shock the entire Palace. The Princess is grieving for Prince Peter, and, like me, she is afraid of being forced into a marriage she has no taste for...*

Anna looked her father straight in the face, for the sake of both the Princess and Katerina, she must lie, and lie convincingly. 'I do not know, my lord,' she said. 'Princess Theodora does not always confide in me.'

Her father came to a halt. The Hall of the Nineteen Couches came into view at the top of the rise. It looked deserted, there was no sign of William or Constantine. *Where have they gone?*

'Anna, don't tell me you fell out with the Princess? In the light of the General's coming enthronement, that would be most unfortunate.'

'My lord?'

Her father made an impatient sound. 'Think, Anna. Princess Theodora is a member of the Doukas family. General Alexios is married to Irene Doukaina.'

'My lord, I do know that.'

'Good, then you will appreciate that if the Doukas dynasty were powerful before the coup, the General's accession can only confirm their influence. It would not be wise to offend them.'

'Father, I have not fallen out with anyone!'

'That is a blessing.' He sighed. 'I was afraid your impetuous nature had led you into trouble again, and that you might need help to be reconciled with the Princess.'

Impetuous? Her father though she was impetuous? It was a sobering thought. Anna had never thought of herself as being particularly impetuous. However, she knew what this was really about— her father was concerned about his standing at Court. Status had always been important to him, he did not wish her to do anything that might jeopardise his position as Governor of Heraklea. Anna understood that, but she wished that, for once, her father would not place so much importance on what others thought of him.

She shook her head. 'The Princess and I remain on good terms.'

'I am glad to hear it. So, the Princess has returned to Constantinople with but one lady in attendance. You.'

'Yes, my lord.'

'And rather than falling out with you, she does in fact hold you in high regard?'

'I believe so.'

'Yet you expect me to believe she does not confide in you?'

Anna put up her chin. Inside she was squirming, she hated having to lie, particularly when she wanted to mend things between them. 'Consider this, my lord. If Princess Theodora were to confide in me, I would not betray that confidence.' *And that is as much truth as I am prepared to give you.*

A gull swooped past. The lines deepened round her father's mouth—he was debating whether to chastise her for being obstructive, or to praise her for doing the Princess's bidding.

'Anna, it is true that I was both angered and shamed when you left. I was angered because you had disobeyed me and shamed because you forced me to break the betrothal agreement I had made with Lord Romanos.'

Anna focused on a pebble on the path, nudging it with the toe of her shoe. 'My lord, I regret angering you, but I saw no other way forward.'

'Let us not rake over old coals. It pleases me to say that I have heard good reports of your service to the Princess. What troubles me today is news that Princess Theodora has vanished from her apartments. The most extraordinary stories are flying about, linking the Princess with Commander Ashfirth of the Varangian Guard. Anna, where is the Princess? Surely she cannot have taken up with that barbarian?'

Anna's breath caught at her father's tone, the very way he pronounced the word 'barbarian' was an insult to all foreigners. He made it sound as though anyone born outside the Empire was incapable of behaving honourably. She knew otherwise.

'Father, how can you speak in that manner? Particularly when the Princess was to have married Prince Peter?' As a foreign prince, Peter of Rascia had been a barbarian. His betrothal to Princess Theodora had been a political necessity—surely even her father would think twice before criticising it?

Her father's brows came down, his mouth worked. 'The Princess had a lucky escape when the Prince of Rascia was killed,' he muttered.

'Father!' Temper was beginning to get the better of her—she must not give into it. Gritting her teeth, she struggled for control.

Her father made a dismissive gesture. 'Enough of this. You are trying to distract me and I will not be distracted. Answer my question, if you please. Has Princess Theodora taken up with Commander Ashfirth?'

What can I say? I cannot confess that the woman everyone believes to be Princess Theodora is an impostor. Nor can I confess that the real Princess does not intend to return home for some weeks because she has had an illegitimate baby!

On the other hand, if I confirm that the Princess is lodging with Commander Ashfirth, an outraged Court will descend upon them… I doubt Katerina could cope with the questions.

Her father's eyes were boring into her when it occurred to her that part of the truth might satisfy him while she worked out what to do. *Remain calm, do not let him goad you into losing your temper, you will achieve nothing.*

'I have not seen the Princess this morning, my lord. Yesterday whilst out in the City we had the misfortune to cross paths with some of the rougher elements of the General's army—'

'The barbarian element, no doubt.'

Anger was a tight fist in Anna's stomach. Taking a steadying breath, she nodded. *Remain calm.* 'They were German mercenaries, I believe. The Princess and I were separated. Fortunately, the Princess found her way back to the Boukoleon, but I was forced into hiding. I only returned to the apartment this morning, by which time the Princess had…she had gone out again.'

Her father's lips tightened, his eyes dropped to that betraying tear in her skirt. 'You took no real hurt?'

She managed a smile. Did her father care—did he *really* care? Or was this once again about appearances, about her value as a bride? 'No, my lord, I was not hurt. A Frankish knight came to my aid.'

'Holy Virgin, this gets worse and worse! Where was your escort that you had to call on a Frankish knight to help you?' Her father glared at her. 'There is no need to answer that, I can see from your face you had no escort.'

'No, Father, the Princess did not wa—'

'Anna, for God's sake! What happened?'

'The knight fought off the mercenaries, my lord, and we went into hiding.'

'Where did you go?'

'We took refuge in the Basilica Cistern.'

Her father's jaw dropped. 'Anna, you cannot be telling me that the reason you missed our meeting yesterday was because you spent the entire night in the cistern, alone with a barbarian?'

Chapter Ten

'Sir William overcame one of the mercenaries, but there were others on the prowl. Father, we had to hide somewhere—the cistern was the nearest place.' Saints, Anna might have distracted her father from questioning her about the Princess, but she had no liking for this twist in the conversation. Her father had always viewed foreigners with suspicion, to his mind they were wild and uncivilised.

'By the Rood, girl—'

'My lord, would you rather I had been molested? Raped? Murdered?' Anna gritted her teeth, wishing, not for the first time, that her father were not so prejudiced. 'Sir William is brave and honourable—he got me safely away from the General's mercenaries.'

Her father's mouth worked, his cheeks suffused. 'And who protected you from him while you were alone in the cistern with him?' He brought his head close. 'Did this barbarian touch you? Did he…tamper with you in any way?'

Anna's cheeks scorched and she felt a rush of anger on William's behalf. William might be a Frank, but he would not dream of hurting any woman. Heaven help her, she must lie again. 'No, Father, he did not, he was a perfect gentleman.' *Perfect in more ways than one.* She shrugged, pushing away the memory of William's kisses.

The anger in her father's face was diffusing. Relief flooded through her. Virgin be praised, she did not want to have to argue with him, not at this, their first meeting in years. She shot a glance towards the abandoned hall. *Where are they? I thought they were going to wait for me…*

'Thank God for that, you were most fortunate.' Her father lowered his voice. 'Anna, I must advise you. Never make mention of your encounter with the mercenaries, nor of spending the night with a Frank. Your reputation…' he jerked his head towards the handsome youth hovering in the background '…you put your marriage prospects at risk. It is simply not worth it. Anna, are you listening to me?'

'Yes, my lord.'

'Then you might look at me instead of staring

towards that ruin, Constantine wandered off some time ago.'

'You saw him?'

'It was he who told me where to find you.'

Anna looked curiously at her father, wondering whether he would comment on the uncanny likeness between William and Erling. When no comment was forthcoming, she said, 'My lord, did you see Constantine's companion?'

Her father looked sharply at her. 'Handsome brute, looks like a Viking?'

'Yes, my lord...' Anna spoke through a tightly clenched jaw '...that is Sir William, the Frankish knight who fought off the mercenaries.'

'I didn't wait to be introduced.'

'Did he remind you of anyone?'

'The Frank? Why on earth should a barbarian remind me of anyone?'

Calm, Anna, remain calm.

'When I first saw him, he put me in mind of Erling.'

Her father's eyes bulged. *'Erling?* Have you lost your wits? That man looks nothing like Erling!'

It was Anna's turn to stare. 'You don't think so?'

'Absolutely not. Anna, stop wasting time, I wish to know...' her father's gaze flickered to the spot where Constantine and William had stood

'…whether Lord Constantine discussed anything of…importance when he came to greet you in the apartment this morning.'

'Yes, Father, he did. Constantine mentioned that you have discussed the possibility of a marriage between us. He also said that he is not the only man with whom you have opened negotiations.'

'That is so, I am indeed considering others.' Lord Isaac drew her slightly to one side, before continuing quietly. 'Did Lord Constantine tell you that I have decided it is you who will have the final choice?'

'Yes, Father, I am very grateful.' Anna smiled, it was such a relief to hear confirmation of what Constantine had told her. Thank goodness she had kept a rein on her temper. Except…in a corner of her mind, a pair of gut-wrenchingly beautiful green eyes were gazing steadily at her. *Handsome, certainly, but not a brute.*

'Anna, I am giving you a choice because I feel you should have a final chance to prove that you have matured into a thoughtful and considerate woman….'

In a trice goosebumps had formed on Anna's arms, it was as though the wind from the sea had, in a moment, turned wintry. *But it is spring, it is not midwinter.* 'F-Father?'

'...I will be happy to guide you, Anna, and to that end you should know that I approached Lord Constantine first because we owe his family an apology after you so rudely turned your back on his brother. I must say I was somewhat surprised by his favourable response—it is more than you deserve.'

Anna rubbed her arms to get rid of the goose-bumps as the dreadful realisation sank in. *Father has not changed, at heart he remains the same.* She felt cold, she felt sick. 'Constantine and I have always had a fondness for each other, my lord.'

'Yes, yes,' her father said, testily. 'I recall that very well, but that is of little moment.'

'Father?'

'Try to remember the honour due to your position. You are the daughter of the Governor of Heraklea. As such I expect your marriage to further the family's interests.'

'Lord Constantine's lineage is impeccable!'

'That goes without saying, although I have to say that Lord Constantine lacks the...steadiness of his older brother. You will not know this as you have been out of the City, but lately Lord Constantine's behaviour has not been quite as...exemplary as I would have hoped. In short, I do not really believe he would make the ideal son-in-law.'

'What can you mean?'

Lord Isaac grimaced. 'Lord Constantine is far too interested in people whose affairs should not concern a decent man. In short, he spends too much time consorting with foreigners.' He jerked his head towards the Hall of the Nineteen Couches. 'Men like that Frankish knight.'

Anna's jaw dropped. 'William saved me!'

Her father's face darkened. '*William?* You are so familiar with this…this barbarian that you call him *William?*'

Anna gripped her hands together. This was terrible! This meeting was going badly wrong, and not simply because it was dawning on her that the 'choice' her father was offering her was turning out to be no choice at all. 'Sir William risked his life to help me, my lord.'

'It is no use you looking at me like that, my girl. I want you to listen to me, and listen most carefully. Your reputation will suffer if it becomes known that you are consorting with foreigners. I am telling you this for your own good.' He wagged his finger in time with his words. 'For your own good. Understand?'

Anna knew she was frowning, but she could not help it. 'Yes, Father, I understand.' *But I do not agree! If Constantine has persuaded William to stay I shall want to see him...and why shouldn't I?*

Her father's face softened. 'I want you to make a good marriage.'

'A dynastic marriage.' Anna's lip curled.

'That's it in a nutshell. You are not a peasant. You are a lady with responsibilities to your family as well as to yourself. I well remember that you had a fondness for Constantine, and that is why, in part, I approached him first.'

Anna swallowed. 'You have just admitted that your main reason for approaching Constantine was to redress the wrong you say I did Romanos. You do not want me to choose Constantine, if I do, you will forbid the marriage.' *My father's approach to Constantine had nothing to do with my fondness for him, Father was simply setting the balance straight with the Angeli. And to think I had hoped that Father might have mellowed—to think I hoped he was going to let me choose a husband! When Father talks about allowing me to choose, he is only paying lip service to the idea.*

In the corner of her eye, the young man shifted from one foot to the other. *If I do not choose the man he wants—and assuredly, this is he—my so-called choice will be rejected.* A lump of ice formed where her heart should be.

'As I see it, Father, nothing has changed.'

Her father looked at her in a puzzled way. 'Everything has changed.' He took her arm and squeezed it gently. 'You are my beloved daughter and you have at last come home where you belong. Later you shall tell me what you thought about life outside the Empire. You must have suffered great privations.'

'Not at all, my lord.'

'I see you have learned to be diplomatic.'

'No, my lord, I meant what I said—I enjoyed my time in Rascia.'

He raised a brow. 'You seem to have grown into a resilient young woman—one might almost say an alarmingly resilient young woman.'

'Father?'

'Later you shall tell me the whole. I have questions about the Princess, too, but this is not the time for them. First, Anna, you must think about your marriage. I am hoping that—with your agreement, naturally—we may soon have cause to celebrate.'

Anna sighed. Sometimes it was as though she and her father spoke different languages. It would seem that relations between them were going to be even more challenging than ever.

Oblivious of her disquiet, Lord Isaac gestured

at the young man with the kohl-darkened eyes. 'Anna, here is someone I should like you to meet.'

He is very young, far younger than I had at first thought. And I cannot like him, he will not meet my eyes...

Smiling to hide her misgivings, Anna allowed Lord Michael to lead her towards a grassy space between the trees and the sea wall. When she saw her father heading down the path away from them, her misgivings increased. *Father has such a concern for the proprieties—why isn't he escorting us? He must really want this marriage...*

'Your father tells me you have recently returned from Rascia,' Lord Michael said, as they strolled up and down. The sunlight flashed on his cloak brooch, on his finger rings. 'I hope the voyage was smooth, the wind can make the sea treacherous at this time of year.'

'Mercifully, we were blessed with fair winds.'

'You must be pleased to be back in Constantinople.'

'Yes, it is good to be home.' Anna stifled a yawn, she had barely slept in the past couple of days and had no desire to waste time exchanging niceties with Lord Michael. It had not taken her more than a moment to make up her mind about him.

What was her father thinking? The entire Court

must know that Lord Michael had a liking for men—she could not marry him. She didn't care if his family and his record as a soldier were impeccable. Lord Michael was also far too young, she needed someone like...someone like...

'You couldn't have returned at a better time, in my view,' Lord Michael said, studying a large sapphire on one of his rings.

'Oh?'

'You will be here for the enthronement—'

'Excuse the impertinence, my lord, but what age are you?'

'Age? I am twenty, my lady.'

Twenty! He is younger than I. 'How long have you served in the army?'

Lord Michael straightened his shoulders. Shoulders which were, now Anna stopped to observe, broad, although not quite as broad as Sir William Bradfer's. Not that she could compare William with Lord Michael. With her father's prejudice against foreigners, he would never accept a Frankish knight as a prospective son-in-law. Even she could see how unsuitable William was. *He has no lands.*

Constantine was her best choice, if she could only change her father's mind about him. She liked Constantine very much, but remembering the hurt in his dark eyes as he had declared he was serious in his intent to marry her was giving her pause. *I am fond of Constantine, but...what if he is in love with me? If he is, I do not feel I should marry him, it would not be fair to Constantine.*

Instinct was telling Anna, very loudly, that she could never love Constantine in the way he needed to be loved. *I love Constantine as a brother, not a lover. If it is wrong to marry a man who has a liking for other men, it must surely be wrong to marry a man knowing one cannot return his love.*

'Four years, my lady,' Lord Michael said. He was staring at a ruby now, angling it so it glowed in the light. 'I have served in the army for four years.'

She fought down another yawn. 'Brothers and sisters?'

'One of each, my lady. And you?'

'I have a younger brother, he is fifteen.' *In truth, he looks about your age.*

'Is he in the army? Which regiment?'

If I were to marry Lord Michael, this is how it would always be between us. Polite questions and answers. No real meeting of minds. Nothing remotely like the instantaneous connection I felt when I saw William on that slave block.

How could Father not see the resemblance between William and Erling?

When Anna's foot caught on a stick that had fallen from a plane tree, she realised that she had, all unawares, led them back to the wooded area near the Hall of the Nineteen Couches. She bent to retrieve the stick and stared wistfully at some green buds, which were on the point of unfurling. Gently, she touched one of them.

'My lady?'

'My apologies, Lord Michael—you were saying?'

He gave her a courteous smile. 'I was asking about your brother, my lady, but it is of no moment. I can see you are...distracted. It cannot be easy returning to the Palace after so long away.'

'I confess I am finding everything here rather... overwhelming,' she said, seizing on the excuse he offered. She studied Lord Michael's youthful features, wondering whether she could trust him to speak frankly. *He is very young. This boy will not understand my fury with my father, nor will he know what to say if I try to enlist his help. Discretion is surely called for.* 'I did have a restless night last night, Lord Michael. If you will forgive me, I should like to return to the women's quarters.'

I need to think!

Lord Michael gave her an immaculate bow. 'I shall look forward to our next meeting, my lady.'

'And I too, my lord.'

'May I escort you back to the Boukoleon?'

'Thank you, but that will not be necessary.'

Lord Michael turned and signalled for his entourage. His slaves had, Anna only now realised, been a few steps behind them the entire time. She watched them trail back up the path after their lord with a hard knot of determination taking shape inside her. *I cannot possibly marry Lord Michael. How am I to convince my father to give me a real choice?*

A movement by the entrance to the Hall of the Nineteen Couches caught her eye—William was sitting on the top step, arms resting on his knees. He gave her a quizzical smile.

'William! How long have you been sitting there?' *He was watching me!*

'Long enough. Is that pretty boy one of your suitors?' He came down the steps to stand at her side.

Anna tipped her head back to meet his gaze. *Tall. William is several inches taller than Lord Michael. And much broader—I do like that in a man.* 'What of it? I am expected to make a good marriage.'

'Your courting techniques look a little rusty.' He gestured at the stick and grinned. 'What did you think you were going to do with that, brain the man?'

Anna tossed the stick aside. 'Don't be ridiculous!' Why did William take such delight in needling her?

'I offer tuition in courtship rituals, should you require it.' He shifted, bringing his lips to within inches of hers. His voice became husky and intimate. 'Much of my time has already been spoken for, but I am sure I can make space for so charming a student...'

By this time, William was so close she could feel his body heat. She was looking at his mouth, her body warming in anticipation, when she recollected where they were. She jerked back, cheeks ablaze.

'Don't do that, William! We are in full sight of...' Anna waved vaguely at the hall and surrounding grounds.

'Of?'

'Of everyone!'

He stepped back with a grin. 'They've all gone, there's no one here but us, my lady.'

She shook her head at him. 'William, did you and Constantine come to an agreement?' She had to ask. It wasn't that she could ever number William among her suitors, but for all that he teased her, she was starting to feel a real fondness for him. *I do not want him to leave, not for a long time...*

Behind that thought was a darker thought, one that did not fit with the first. *This man for whom you are learning to feel affection is still your slave, you have power over him. You may yet have a use for him.*

The problem was, if Anna used that power, she would lose his good will. Her father might not care about losing the good will of a slave, but Anna did, particularly when that slave was Sir William Bradfer.

'Hmm?' He was smiling, staring at her mouth as though he wanted to devour it. Her stomach swooped.

'Did you come to an agreement with Constantine?'

'As I am sure you already know, Constantine asked me to tutor him in Norman French.'

'And you have agreed?'

When the fair head dipped in acknowledgement, a rush of happiness had her smiling back at him. *He is staying!*

'How long will you remain with us?'

'I have promised him a couple of weeks. After that I really do have to leave.' He offered her his arm. Warily, half-afraid of what he might do next, Anna placed her hand on it. *Two weeks. I wish it were longer.* As he led her up the steps of the Hall of the Nineteen Couches, she gave him a sideways glance. William's sheer physicality was impossible to ignore, if she had not spent so much time alone with him, she might be afraid of him. But this was William, the Frankish knight who, even though he had been half-naked, had fought off a fully armed mercenary for her. The worst she had to fear from him was his teasing.

William stayed with me in the Basilica Cistern when his only thought must surely have been escape. He looked after me. Briefly, Anna found herself wondering if all Frankish knights were as well favoured. To some he would look every inch the foreigner. *To my father, for example, that shock of fair hair signals the possibility of barbaric Norse blood, and those green eyes...*

'Is my face dirty, my lady?'

She flushed. 'No, it is just that my father—you must have seen him, he said he saw you...?'

'I saw him,' William said, helping her over the heap of rubble in the doorway.

She frowned. 'I know you are a Frank and not a Norseman, but you do look like a Norseman.'

'Vikings and Franks come from the same stock.'

'Oh? Well, that explains it. I do not know how it is, but my father could not see the resemblance between you and Erling. To me it is obvious.' *How could Father not see the resemblance? How could he not see the kindness in the man; the sense of honour; the devotion to duty?*

As Anna stepped over a block of masonry, it lifted her eye to eye with him. *He has breathtaking eyes. They are so vivid, they are alive with flecks of light and they crinkle at the corners when he smiles. I want him! I want William for my husband.* The shock of the thought almost sent her tumbling from the block.

'Careful, my lady,' he said, patiently assisting her over the rubble and through the doorway. 'Some of this is unstable.' Seizing her by the waist, he lifted her easily past the last of the stones.

Anna's next thought almost had her on her knees. *Officially, he is still my slave. Could I compel him? Two weeks, he said he would stay for two weeks... I cannot want William! My father would kill me!*

'There!' William made an expansive gesture. 'Welcome to my new quarters, my lady.'

The Hall of the Nineteen Couches stretched away in front of them. The long walls on either side were pierced by several apses, some of which were complete with the ancient couches that dignitaries of a former age had reclined on while they dined. The couches were covered in leaves and dust. The grandest and least decayed of them, the one the Emperor must have used, stood in the largest apse, facing the door.

I cannot want William! Carefully, Anna removed her hand from his arm. *I scarcely know him, I certainly do not love him. Of all the men I know, this one is capable of putting others before himself. Witness the way he cared for those children, witness the way he cared for me.*

'Your quarters?'

Daylight was streaming in through two tiers of windows, there were a number of holes in the roof and there, high in the apex, a disintegrating bird's nest. The floor was uneven, grime and more leaves obscured the mosaic floor. Overall, though, the hall looked remarkably sound.

'Constantine informed me that beds were likely to be scarce over the next few days so I thought this place might suit. In fact…' his eyes darkened '…the more I think about it, the better it seems.'

Anna looked blankly at him, the oddest of litanies was running though her mind.

I do not love him, how can I? William is attractive, dangerously attractive, but there are many barriers between us. Father would never countenance such a match, William has no land, he is

*determined to return to Apulia. Why? Why is he so
determined to return when he has no land there?*

*He might win lands here! Yes, William could
win lands here and... Be realistic, William has not
mentioned marriage, all he has done is kiss you.*

Father would never countenance such a match...

When William caught her hand and tugged her
to him, she scowled suspiciously up at him. 'Why
did you bring me in here?'

'To show you my quarters, to see if you thought
them suitable.'

Anna held her breath, a wicked light in his eyes
was having an extraordinary effect on her pulse.
'Suitable for what?'

His head lowered, his mouth stopped scant
inches from hers. 'Lessons in courtship,' he murmured. His low, sensual voice sent shivers down
her spine.

*I refuse to kiss him. I do not want him to kiss
me, I want...*

'This hall must have been built with you in
mind,' he muttered, whirling her about until they
were standing in the nearest of the alcoves.

Her mouth had gone dry, she swallowed. 'It
was?' *Lord, I cannot deceive myself, I ache for
his kiss.*

Lowering his head that final inch, William touched his lips to hers.

She had been going to object. She had been going to be strong and push him from her, but that first touch sent her fine resolutions flying from her mind. There was a dizzying rush of feeling in her belly. *For such a large man, he can be very gentle, almost...too gentle.* With a murmur she reached for his shoulder and pressed closer. She wanted to be enfolded in his arms, she wanted to be held, tightly held. 'William.'

So tall, he is so tall. She had to go up on her toes to reach him properly. She wound an arm about his neck. When she pushed her fingers into his hair, her palm tingled. Breathless, she drew back. 'What was that?' His eyes had been closed, he opened them and gave her a slow, toe-curling smile.

'That, Lady Anna, was lesson number one. It is a pity most of the couches have been broken or lost...' he looked thoughtfully at the grand central couch '...we might need a good one for the later lessons.'

'Couches?' *Later lessons? What on earth is he talking about? All I want is for him to hold me.* 'Why do we need couches?'

'For your tuition in courtship rituals. You really should not have threatened to club that poor boy.'

He shook his head. 'It is no way to win a husband. Next time, you might try kissing him. Your kisses are extremely...stimulating.'

'Lord Michael didn't want to kiss me and I certainly didn't want to kiss him!'

'You didn't give him a chance. You didn't want to kiss me a moment ago, did you, my lady?'

'That was because...because...' Anna closed her mouth with a snap. She hadn't wanted to kiss William, but the reason she hadn't wanted to kiss him was because she had wanted to kiss him! 'That was...different.'

William towed her into the second alcove. Here, the couch was leaning on a slant, it was missing a leg. Setting a booted foot on the lopsided seat, he pulled her close, manoeuvring her until her hip was warmed by his thigh. 'Why was it different?'

'I...I...' Anna struggled to find a suitable response before it occurred to her that she need not answer him. 'William, you have no right to behave like this. You are teasing me and I do not like it.'

'Very well, there will be no more teasing. Now, let us progress—with due seriousness—to your next lesson.'

'No, this must stop. This instant!'

Chapter Eleven

Breaking out of William's arms, Anna stepped away from him. She had to, because otherwise he would realise how she burned for another kiss. *His touch is too disturbing, it is far too seductive.* Anna had often wondered how it was that so many women permitted themselves to be seduced—this man was giving her much insight. It might not reflect well on her strength of character, but she feared that if William put his mind to it, he would find it all too easy to seduce her. She would, quite simply, not want him to stop.

'Stop?' He lifted a hand to his heart. 'My lady, I am devastated. Your touch is the only warmth and light in a life that is sadly dark.'

Hiding a smile, she sighed and made as if to leave. *Too seductive, he is far too seductive.* 'I don't know how ladies are expected to behave in your Duchy, William, but you should know that I am flouting Palace conventions simply by being alone with you. If you insist on behaving like this, I shall have to leave. I had hoped that we might be friends, but you are making me behave in the most unseemly manner. What if someone had walked in on us a moment ago?'

'That door grates abominably, we would have heard it open.'

'Unless you are prepared to be sensible, I shall have to return to the apartment.' *At least I shall be able to think in the apartment, when I am with you, all coherent thought flies from my head.*

His expression sobered. 'Stay, my lady. If the price of your company is that I am not to tease you, then I shall not tease you.' Smiling ruefully, he extended a hand and came towards her. 'Please stay. I have no wish to drive you away, I enjoy your company.'

And I enjoy yours, far too much.

His eyes smiled into hers, and the sincerity Anna read in them had something twist inside her— she was dreading the day when she would have to bid him farewell. 'You said you will stay for two weeks, I think? To help Lord Constantine improve his Norman French.'

'Yes.' With a grin, he dropped to his knees and

put his hand on his heart. 'Don't go, my lady, I will behave, I swear it.'

Disarmed, Anna allowed herself to be ushered towards the largest alcove. A quiet gleam of gold caught her eye, some of the ancient gilding on the Imperial couch was intact. William wiped away a scattering of leaves.

'Please sit, my lady.'

She raised an eyebrow. 'On the Imperial couch, Sir William?'

His lips twitched, his eyes dropped briefly to her mouth and Anna discovered that he did not have to be touching her to evoke those small tingles in her belly.

'I have promised to behave, we shall not move on to the more…advanced lessons without your consent. Besides, this is the soundest couch, unless you sit on the floor, which is filthy, there is nowhere else.'

Anna settled herself amid a rustle of skirts and William took his place at her side. She noted that he made a point of ensuring there were several inches between them.

'My lady, since my plans have changed and I am to be staying in the Palace, there is something I need to ask you.'

'Oh?'

He grimaced. 'I am not planning to make much noise about my presence here, but neither am I prepared to skulk in the shadows. It is possible that someone may recognise me from the slave market. Apart from the Princess, two other people were bidding, a man who looked as though he was a merchant and a woman who might be attached to the Court in some way.'

'Yes, I saw them.'

'It could become awkward if they noticed me wandering the Palace grounds.'

'I see what you mean—you don't want to get arrested for being a runaway slave. I must ask the Princess to sign your document of manumission.'

'I would be grateful. As I said, I shall need that document if I am to remain here. If I am challenged, you may not be nearby to bear witness to the fact that you have freed me.'

Anna nodded, even as guilt twisted inside her. She was unable to bring herself to confess that she might not, after all, be quite ready to grant him his freedom. *I need to think about this. In one sense, William is more suitable as a husband than I realised when I saw him in the slave market. He is not merely a slave, he is a knight. I need to think...*

'I understand,' she said, temporising. 'I shall try and find your document. Ka—the Princess left it at the apartment. When I go back, I shall find it and, as soon as I can, I shall get her to sign the manumission.'

'My thanks, you are most kind.'

Anna swallowed. She was not kind, she was misleading him and she did not like it. Guilt, it seemed, was a heavy burden. Giving him a weak smile, she realised he was staring at her speculatively. 'Whatever is the matter?'

'You have done that more than once, you know.'

'What? What have I done?'

His expression was thoughtful. 'When mentioning the Princess, you stumble over her name.'

'Nonsense!'

The fair head shook. 'No, I do not think it is nonsense. I almost missed it the first time because I had other things on my mind. But there is more than merely stumbling over her name—I get the definite impression that you are in some kind of trouble. My lady, what is it?'

'Nothing!' Anna's voice was high, quickly she moderated it. 'You are mistaken, it was a slip of the tongue.'

'A slip you made more than once.' Astute green eyes held hers. 'You are hiding something, and you are afraid.'

Her chin went up. 'I am not.'

'Something is troubling you, I am sure of it. My lady, I should like you to know that if I might assist you in any way, you only have to ask. You have been so generous to me, I should like to return the compliment.'

'Thank you, Sir William, but you are mistaken, I do not need your help.'

'You are not in any difficulty?'

'I am not.' Anna hoped she was not blushing, it was almost impossible to force the lie past her lips. She had never liked lying, and for some reason it was particularly hard lying to this man. Especially when he was offering her assistance. *Holy Virgin, help me.*

He gave her a crooked smile. 'My lady, your secrets would be safe with me.'

'I am sure they would, if I had any worth telling.'

He lifted his broad shoulders. 'Very well, you are not to be persuaded, but please remember that if you change your mind, I would be honoured to help you.'

'There is nothing to tell.' There was a lump in Anna's throat. The idea of having someone to whom she could unburden herself to was very tempting. *It is not my secret, though, it is Princess Theodora's secret and I will keep it as long as I can. Katerina and I must be the only ones who*

*know that the Princess has gone into hiding.
Commander Ashfirth must have realised it by now,
but no one else must know. No one.*

*William has realised I am lying, I can read it in
his face, a tiny line has appeared between his eyebrows.* Her pulse quickened. *Quickly! Change the
subject...distract him...*

Smiling, she laid a hand on his arm, his eyes followed the movement. 'William, there is something
you might do for me...'

He gave her one of his teasing smiles. 'I don't
get the impression that you are about to ask for another lesson in courting rituals...'

'You are correct.'

He gave a dramatic sigh. 'Pity.'

'William, I would like to know how you came
to be enslaved.'

His smile faded, he shook his head.

'You must tell me.'

'Must I?'

'Please, William.'

'Very well. In brief, I was betrayed. I was out on
patrol near Melfi with a couple of squires when
we were ambushed.'

'Are such attacks common in Apulia?'

'They are common enough except there was
something odd about this one...' His mouth

twisted. 'As you may imagine, I have given this thought in the months since then. It was no random attack by thieves, it was well prepared and well executed, and it took place in an area that was relatively peaceful. We were vastly outmanned. Our assailants were quick to separate me from my squires, so quick that I do not know what happened to them. I can only pray my squires were not killed, I fear at least one of them might have been.'

'You think you were singled out deliberately.'

'I am sure of it.'

'So you have enemies in the Duchy?'

'I didn't think so, but clearly I was wrong.'

William's responses were brief, he was trying to discourage more questions. Nothing daunted, Anna pressed on. 'What happened after you were separated from your squires?'

'The wrangling began among my captors.'

'Wrangling?'

'Much of what they said was unintelligible, but broadly they divided into two camps. Some wanted me killed, others wanted me sold into slavery.'

'I don't understand.'

William's expression was bleak. 'My assailants had been paid to kill me, a group of them got greedy—if they sold me into slavery, they would

be paid twice over. The greedy faction won—that
is how I found myself on the slave block.'

Thoughtfully, Anna bit her lip. 'William, you
must have some idea who would want you killed,
such an enemy must be known to you.'

'All I have is part of a name.'

Anna leaned forwards. 'And...?'

'Gwion—my attackers mentioned a man named
Gwion. Once home, I intend to discover his full
name.'

'You want blood.'

'I want to find that my squires are whole. And I
want justice, not blood.' He looked at her, mouth
grim. 'I shall not fail.'

'I don't doubt it.'

His mouth softened. Lifting her hand from his
sleeve, he raised it to his lips. 'My luck had been
bad for months, but it surely turned the moment I
set eyes on you in the slave market.'

Anna stared at his downbent head. His hair was
slightly rumpled, its blond colour fascinated her.
So fair, it is so fair. He turned her hand and as his
mouth pressed gently against her palm, another
seductive tingle ran up her arm. It made her long
for the impossible, that William might be accepted
as her most favoured suitor. *That day will never*

dawn, my father will never accept a Frankish knight.

*Unless...unless...*guilt warred with longing...*unless I take matters into my own hands, by forcing William to marry me. Father would have to accept it then.*

And what about William? Would he ever be able to accept a marriage that was forced upon him? Or would he, as I fear, feel I have betrayed him?

The scent of jasmine was weakening William's resolve to keep his hands off her. He was—rather successfully, given what he felt was extreme provocation—resisting the urge to push Anna's sleeve out of the way and nibble his way up her arm.

Just then, voices broke in on them. 'No, no need to bring them in. You may leave them out here.'

Mindful of Anna's concern for the proprieties, William dropped her hand and came swiftly to his feet. He managed to be at least three feet away from her by the time the rusty hinges screeched and the door opened.

'William?' Lord Constantine leaped lightly down from the rubble heaped about the entrance and dropped a bundle onto the floor. 'Brought you supplies.'

'Good man!' William went to examine the bundle. It was bedding—woollen blankets wrapped round a rolled-up mattress. Anna was watching him, she had not moved from the couch. Her cheeks were pink and she was making several self-conscious little gestures, tidying her hair, straightening her cloak.

Constantine leaned back through the door and spoke to someone outside. 'My thanks, I shall take it from here. Symeon, wait for me outside.'

Another bundle came flying through the doorway. Sackcloth this time. William thought he could smell bread and cheese, but that was likely wishful thinking on his part. Since coming to the Palace, he seemed to be permanently hungry. Constantine vanished for a moment and returned with a clay amphora in either hand.

'Good God, Constantine, are we laying in for a siege?'

Constantine laughed. 'If you could see the kitchens, you would not mock—they are in an uproar. In truth, the whole Palace is being turned upside down by preparations for the General's enthronement. Matters will only get worse, so I thought I would sneak out what I could.'

'Because of the enthronement on Easter Day?' Anna asked, leaving the couch and coming towards them.

William frowned. 'That's only a couple of days away. Isn't that short notice for those who don't live in the City?'

'General Alexios has taken the throne by force—speed is of the essence.'

'I thought he was a popular choice?'

'He is, but his accession could be questioned. Once he has been enthroned, his position will be more secure. Heralds have been sent out to all corners with invitations, but as you say, given the time, that is largely a formality. They will not get far. However, you may rest assured that the General's allies will be attending.'

'The Doukas family,' Anna murmured. 'I expect they will be present in force.'

Anna was staring at the floor in a manner that could only be described as abstracted and when she lifted her gaze to look at Constantine, cold fingers trailed down William's back. *She is afraid. And her fear is centred on the Doukas family. Why won't she confide in me?*

'I wouldn't be so sure,' Constantine said, propping the amphorae up in a corner.

'Why do you say that?' Anna's voice was casual, but her tone did not match the intensity in her eyes.

'One moment.' Constantine scrambled over the rubble and reappeared with another sack, which he tossed onto the growing heap. 'There, that's the last of it.'

'Constantine...' Anna bit her lip. 'You had something to add about the Doukas family... I think you had better tell me, it may affect the Princess.'

'Don't fret, Anna, this is nothing to do with Princess Theodora, and in any case, I can scarcely credit what I was told.'

Anna's foot tapped. 'What? What were you told?'

'That General Alexios is so besotted with his adopted mother, he is considering setting his wife aside.'

When Anna's face went completely blank, William realised how shocked she was. He had no idea what she had been expecting Constantine to say, but this had caught her completely off guard.

Constantine gave a short laugh. 'It would appear that the battle for the throne is not yet over. The men have done their part, now it is the women's turn.'

'Whatever can you mean?'

'The prize this time is Alexios himself.' Constantine put his hands on his hips. 'Some rather surprising negotiations seem to be going on behind the scenes, it would seem that Irene's accession is by no means assured. It is possible that the General has his own reasons for allowing this idea to circulate, but there do not seem to be plans to have Irene enthroned beside him. She has not even been given an apartment in the Boukoleon, instead, Irene Doukaina and her entourage have been allocated space in one of the lesser palaces. And in the meantime, the General's adopted mother is ensconced in the Boukoleon, within earshot of his chambers. The Doukas family are outraged.'

'I am not surprised,' she said. 'At the least it is a grave insult.'

William kept his gaze on Anna, but her face was inscrutable, he was unable to tell whether this new intelligence concerned or relieved her.

'The General's wife is very young,' she went on, thoughtfully. 'If it comes to a battle between his wife and his adopted mother, whom do you think will win?'

'It's too soon to say,' Constantine said, 'but they are making wagers in every guardhouse and tavern in the City.' He crouched down beside one of the sacks and rooted through it. 'Speaking of taverns, there should be a couple of drinking horns in here. I don't suppose either of you would care to try out the wine they're going to serve after the enthronement?'

'Not for me, thank you,' Anna said. 'I shall

join you shortly. First, I have to return to the Boukoleon—I have been neglecting my duties. Constantine, is all the Palace in uproar?'

'It's buzzing like a hornet's nest,' Constantine said, flourishing a drinking horn. With its rim of chased silver, it would not have looked amiss in the hand of a Norse god. He tossed it to William.

'I shall be as quick as I can. Save some wine, I should like to try it.' Giving them a strained smile, Anna started for the door.

William watched Anna prepare to leave, guessing that she was going to search for his documents. He wanted to go with her, he didn't know what was troubling her, but it was possible she might need his help.

'Here, Constantine, I shall escort her.' William lobbed the drinking horn back.

'No, William, that will not be necessary.' Anna's voice was firm. 'I shall not be long.'

William searched her face and received an unconvincing smile. She was worried. 'Are you sure, my lady?'

'Quite sure.' Her smile was strained, her voice cool. 'I thank you for the offer of your escort, but it is not necessary.'

'Get Symeon to accompany you, he's waiting outside,' Constantine said. 'I want to talk to William.'

* * *

Constantine had not lied when he had said the Palace was buzzing like a hornet's nest, the marble corridors and stairways of the Boukoleon were crowded to the point of impassability. Anna was glad of Symeon's escort. Shouts and curses bounced off the walls as slaves laden with packing cases were elbowed into plaster frescoes. In one of the narrower passages, Anna saw the ear of a deer in a bucolic hunting scene flake off as it was knocked from the wall. Ladies in rich brocades jostled and jabbed their way along, tripping over trailing hems and shawls in the race to beat the others to the best sleeping spaces.

Breathing in a pungent mix of scent and unwashed bodies, Anna fought her way through the sea of bodies until at last she and Symeon succeeded in gaining the landing outside the Princess's apartment.

'My thanks, Symeon,' she said, as he rapped on the door. 'I did not appreciate quite how necessary your escort would be. It would seem the entire Empire is set on witnessing the General's enthronement. You may return to Constantine now.'

'Thank you, my lady.'

A Varangian Guard—it was young Kari— opened one of the double doors and Anna was

whisked inside. Kari resumed his post inside the
entrance.

Peace. Compared to the noise and desperate
scrabbling of the courtiers, the apartment was an
oasis of peace.

'Kari, are there any messages?'

'No, my lady, you have no messages.'

'Has anyone been to visit the Princess? Perhaps
her family…?'

'No, my lady, the apartment has been quiet since
you left.' The Varangian rolled his eyes. 'Unlike
out there.'

Anna went straight to the Princess's bedchamber
to hunt out William's document. She was not sure
what she was going to do with it when she found
it. *I should free him without question.* Katerina
would, she was sure, have placed it in her jewel
box. This was kept in a small dressing room off her
bedchamber, beneath the table with the icon on it.

The icon stood in place, but as for the jewel
box…it was not there. Anna's guts tightened and
she fell to her knees, feeling along the floor. Her
hand slid over smooth cool marble. It really was
not there. She leaned back on her haunches.

*Everything Katerina owns is in that jewel box,
she must have taken it with her when she left with
Commander Ashfirth. There is nothing for it, I*

shall have to go to Commander Ashfirth's house in the City. It would be good to see for myself that Katerina and the children are safe and well, and Katerina can give me that document...

It was a setback not to have laid her hands on the document at once, but it was a small one. Katerina would surely have it with her.

Anna returned to the main reception chamber. Several of the windows opened onto balconies overlooking the Sea of Marmara. Anna went over to one, silken window hangings brushed her shoulders as she went outside. The chill on the balcony was sharp enough to make her wrap her cloak more tightly about her. Easter was almost upon them, but the wind was wintry. The sea looked like beaten lead.

Anna gripped the edges of the cloak together and stared at a passing ship that was little more than a dot on the horizon. Yes, it was irritating not to have found William's document, even though she knew that Katerina would keep it safe.

Loud knocking broke into her thoughts. Her heart lifted. Might Katerina have returned?

She stuck her head through the curtain as Kari opened one of the doors, but it was not Katerina who walked in, it was Anna's father.

Saints, Father will want to know about my meeting with Lord Michael—what am I to say to him?

Pushing past the curtain, Anna unclasped her cloak and dropped it on a chair. 'Father! I did not expect to see you again so soon.'

Taking her arm, Lord Isaac drew her down the chamber, away from the door. His eyes were brighter than Anna had seen in years and he was smiling at her in the old way, as he had done when she was a child.

'Anna, I have news for you, great news!' He patted her hand, his voice became confidential. 'You have another suitor!'

'*Another* suitor, Father?' Anna fought to keep the surprise from her voice. 'I thought you favoured Lord Michael.'

Her father grunted. 'Forget Lord Michael. On reflection I thought you might look more favourably on a man of more…mature years. So when I received another approach, I realised I must tell you at once, before you committed yourself to Lord Michael. This man has served several Emperors, his record is impeccable.'

'He is a soldier, too?'

'No, no. It's the Lord Chamberlain, Basil.'

'Lord Basil?' Anna felt her face fall. 'He's twice my age!'

'As I said, he is a man of mature years. He is someone you can look up to, someone you can respect. Lord Basil has the advantage of owning lands close to ours. Which means that, in the fullness of time, when your brother inherits, you will be nearby. I find that thought pleases me.'

Anna didn't know what to say. She had been dreading telling her father that she did not want to marry Lord Michael, but this was far worse— Lord Basil was old enough to be her grandfather! 'Father, I think I prefer Lord Michael to Lord Basil.'

Face darkening, her father took his hand from hers. 'Anna, you will meet Lord Basil. He is my choice.'

He is not my choice, I want William! 'Father, only this morning you favoured Lord Michael.'

'Anna, I hope we are not going to see a repetition of the behaviour we saw two years ago...'

Anna bowed her head to shield her expression. She remembered Lord Basil as a fussy Court official whose enormous girth testified to his love of food. 'Lord Basil has already had two wives,' she muttered.

'His first wife died, you can hardly blame that on the man,' her father said coldly.

'And the second wife? Didn't she enter a nunnery?' Anna felt her hands begin to shake, she gripped them together. 'Please, Father, I have never liked the look of Lord Basil.' *I refuse to marry Lord Basil! Heavens, there's nothing for it, I shall have to tell William that his freedom comes at a price...*

'Don't be difficult. Anna, it is my wish that you meet Lord Basil as soon as possible. It is a great honour that he is prepared to consider you. He is the Chamberlain, you know.'

'A man of great influence,' Anna murmured.

'Exactly.' Her father cleared his throat. 'Lord Basil has made it clear that should you come to an agreement, he does not consider a long betrothal will be necessary.'

Anna's thoughts raced. *There must be some way I can delay this meeting, at least until I have spoken to William. I shall have to tell him that I have changed my mind about the conditions upon which I am prepared to give him his freedom.* She felt shaky and panicky, but she had some time. Marriages during Holy Week were unheard of, she couldn't marry anyone, until after Easter Day. 'Yes, Father. Perhaps...' inspiration struck and she looked into her father's eyes '...after the enthronement? I am sure Lord Basil has his hands full dealing with the demands of the new Emperor and all that entails.'

Her father smiled and patted her hand. 'Very good, Anna, that's more like it. It is most gratifying to hear you voice an understanding of Lord Basil's concerns. I shall convey your response to him and arrange for introductions to be made after the enthronement.'

'Thank you, Father.' Anna managed a smile. It hid the fact that, inside, she was fretting over what William's response would be. *He will hate me! Will I have to force him? How does one force a man like William?*

When Anna returned to the Hall of the Nineteen Couches, she swept in like a queen with an armed guard at each elbow. One glance at her set face warned William that tasting the wine was the last thing on her mind. The guards at her side were Varangians, fully armed Varangians.

The hairs rose on the back of William's neck. Exchanging glances with Constantine, he set the drinking horn aside. *What is she up to? I thought she had gone to look for my document of manumission, but I see no document...*

'Anna?' Constantine climbed slowly to his feet. 'There are difficulties in the Palace?'

The blue veil rippled as she shook her head. 'No difficulties, I thank you, Constantine.'

William nodded at the Varangians, smiling to cover the unease roiling in his gut. 'Why the guards, my lady? Are you expecting trouble?'

Anna gave him a look he had never expected to see her direct at him—it was hard, it was determined, it was implacable. 'They have come to ensure that if there is trouble, it will be...short-lived.'

Holding William's gaze, she came closer, the hem of her skirts dragging across the mosaic floor. 'Leave us, Constantine,' she said.

'Anna? What is going on?'

'If you please...leave us.'

Constantine's hand went to his sword hilt as his gaze shifted from the Varangians to William and finally to Anna. 'Anna, if something is wrong, you know I will always help you.'

'Nothing is wrong. Leave us.' Anna held William's gaze until Constantine had left the hall, then she turned to the guards. 'You too,' she said, with an imperious wave. 'Wait outside with the others. Watch the door. I shall call you if I need you—otherwise, wait outside.'

'Yes, my lady.' Bowing, the Varangians withdrew.

William's heart was cold as stone. *Wait outside with the others?* 'Anna, what is going on?'

She was standing very straight, head erect, shoulders rigid. Her nostrils flared. 'I have come to confirm the terms upon which you shall be give your freedom.'

William stopped breathing. 'You said that you would free me..."unconditionally" was the word you used.'

'I have changed my mind.'

William bunched his hands into fists and jerked his head towards the door. 'And that is why you brought guards?' *She cannot change her mind! I trusted her!*

Her chin lifted. 'You have already tried to escape. I thought it possible you might try again.'

He gave a snort of laughter. He couldn't believe it—after what had passed between them, for her to treat him like this—it was unthinkable. And yet... something about the set of her face, the stubborn lift to her chin, told him she meant what she said. *She says she has changed her mind, but was she lying all along?*

'You were never going to free me in the first place! That is why you were so quick to disarm me when we got back to the Palace.'

'No.' Her smile appeared sad, but William didn't think he could trust it. 'I was intending to free you but…but…' her voice broke '…circumstances have changed.'

'You are a liar, my lady. And I am a fool. I trusted you and you have merely been biding your time, waiting for the right moment.'

'No.' She clasped her hands, twisting her fingers together so tightly her knuckles went white. 'I was going to free you, and I swear I shall do so. But not until you have performed a simple task for me. It should not…' flushing, she gestured vaguely at one of the alcoves '…given the talents you have already demonstrated, be a task that is beyond you.'

'What is it that you want me to do?'

'I want you to marry me.'

William felt his jaw drop. 'I beg your pardon?'

'I want you to marry me.'

William groped behind him for the lopsided couch and sat down heavily. 'You must have lost your wits, I cannot marry you! I told you I have to get back to Apulia. And…and…what about your suitors? Good God, woman, surely you have enough men to choose from—why involve me?' He narrowed his eyes. 'This is part of some scheme to spite your father—you cannot mean to go through with it.'

She shook her head and her veil quivered. 'No, I want to marry you.' Her colour was heightened, her eyes would not meet his.

'And when I have married you, then you shall free me?'

'Not quite,' she murmured.

William's nails were digging into his palms. Slowly he uncurled his fingers. *Look at me, my lady. Meet my eyes.* Slowly, he uncurled his fingers. 'When will you free me, my lady?'

Her blush deepened to two bright spots of colour. 'After the consummation, of course. As I said, it… it…' Faltering, she glanced at the Imperial couch. William had made it up into a bed using the blankets that Constantine had brought. Her chin inched up. 'It should not be a task that is beyond you. I want there to be no doubt that you have…married me in the fullest sense of the word.'

'You would marry your slave?'

'Yes.'

William rubbed his face. 'Is this permitted? Surely a lady of your standing cannot marry a slave?'

She lifted her head and finally looked straight at him. 'That used to be the case in Roman times, but it is centuries since that law was changed.' Her mouth firmed. 'William, I have come to tell you that if you want your freedom back, you will have to marry me.'

Chapter Twelve

As her ultimatum sank in, William's stunned expression was replaced with a look of weary cynicism. Anna was saddened to see it. She would rather William married her willingly, but her choices were limited. *I refuse to marry simply to satisfy my father's ambitions, I cannot marry Lord Basil!*

If thought of marriage with her made William miserable—Anna's heart squeezed—so be it. She would marry him, he would ensure that the marriage was consummated, and then…she would free him.

After that, he may do as he pleases.

She straightened her shoulders, hoping to appear confident. She even managed to lift an eyebrow as she looked meaningfully at the couch in the central alcove. 'If you agree, we shall be progressing to the lesson of the nineteenth couch more quickly than you had anticipated.' She shrugged. 'You have given me reason to believe that is one aspect of our...arrangement you will not cavil at.'

He looked blankly at her for a moment. 'Why me?'

'I beg your pardon?'

'Why not Lord Constantine? He would have you in a heartbeat—a blind man can see he adores you.'

Anna sighed. 'That is exactly why I cannot marry him.'

'Your reasoning escapes me.'

'William, I can never love Constantine in the way he deserves to be loved. It would not be...fair.'

He took a step towards her. 'And it's fair to marry me? Why? Because you bought me?'

She lifted her chin. A muscle was twitching in William's jaw. Shock was being replaced by anger and he was barely managing to contain it. 'You are my slave, I bought you with this thought in mind.'

'You said nothing of this earlier. All that time... in the Palace, in the cistern...I knew there was something you wanted from me, but you said nothing. Why wait so long to tell me?'

Never had his green eyes looked so intently at her. She looked away. It was easier to look at the wall behind him. 'I...I was uncertain of you.'

'Uncertain of me? Jesu, woman, you bought me! By the laws of this land I am compelled to obey you. Particularly since...' a baleful glance was directed at the door '...you have set the Guard over me. But I am not a slave, I am a knight!'

She forced her eyes back to his. 'In the City you are my slave and, as you pointed out, I have both might and law on my side.' Men had most of the power in this world. It was ironic that all her life Anna had wanted the power that men enjoyed and now she had it, she did not want to use it. She was fond of this man, she wanted to keep his good will. She made her voice soft. 'William, I am offering you your freedom. I am sorry that I have to ask you to earn it, but that is how matters stand. I need your help.'

He gave a calculated glance at the windows. With a slight smile, she shook her head. 'That might have worked in the bathhouse, but it will not work here. Varangians are posted outside each window.'

In a blur of movement, he was on his feet, striding for the door.

'That is no good either, William. The guards are armed, while you...'

'You seem to have thought of everything.'

'I hope so.'

Swearing, William began heaving at a fallen

chunk of stone, shifting it until it was positioned in front of the door. His movements were jerky. Whirling round, he stalked back, his eyes were bleak.

Anna's heart thudded like the battle drums in the Augustaion. Edging away from him, she pointed at the stone. 'What did you move that for?'

'Can't you guess?' Strong hands reached for her. She was pulled hard against that powerful body, and he walked her—half towing, half dragging—towards the central alcove.

Towards the Imperial couch.

'We will be needing privacy for what I am about to do to you. My lady.'

Anna heard herself make an embarrassing squeaking sound, she seemed to have lost the power of speech. Her pulse was racing, there was a strange trembling sensation in her belly and her legs could scarcely hold her up.

He will not hurt me. This is William. William, who put himself in harm's way to save me from the German mercenaries, William, who was kind to me in the Basilica cistern...

'Will—'

'Those are your final terms?'

'T-terms?' His eyes were hard and cold as

Venetian glass. If only he would not hold her so tightly, she was starting to feel quite dizzy.

'If I marry you, you swear to free me, that is our agreement. I take it our marriage will be annulled later?'

'If that is your wish.'

'Lord…' he shook his head '…there was a woman in the slave market, a grand lady in cherry-coloured silks, she was bidding for me, too.'

Anna was beginning to feel quite ill. *Holy Virgin, I knew this would be hard, but I did not think he would be quite so…hurt. Is hurt the right word? I believe it is. I have disappointed him.*

'That woman looked like a degenerate with her painted face. I did not want her to buy me, she looked as though she wanted to eat me.'

Anna hung her head. 'She wanted you as a plaything.' *He is saying that what I am doing to him is far worse than whatever his painted lady had in mind. Will he ever forgive me?* 'William—'

'I was actually pleased when your princess won the bidding. Lord, if I had known what was coming….' He shoved his hand through his hair and gave a bitter laugh. 'I thought it would be easier to escape you.'

'William, try to trust me, I swear I shall free you.'

'God knows if I can trust you again. However,

if this is what you want…' William lowered his head, his grip was like iron.

Anna put her hands on his arms, trying and failing to make him loosen his hold. Instead the strong muscles shifted and his hold tightened.

'Keep still.'

'I can't breathe, you are making me dizzy.'

The grip eased, the dizziness remained.

His mouth hovered over hers. 'Swear you will not change your mind.'

'William, I shall not change my mind. In the name of the Virgin, I swear it. After we have… married, you will be given your document of manumission.'

His mouth relaxed enough to twist up at one corner. 'You may find this very strange, my lady, but I like to know where I stand. When we first met, I took you for someone else. Someone who doesn't exist.'

'William?'

'I took you for a woman whose word was her bond.' He snorted. 'I should have known better, women have no sense of honour as I learned to my cost some while ago. But you…' he shook his head at Anna's involuntary movement of dissent '…you made me forget what I had learned. But now you have reminded me—I find it hard to believe anything you might say.'

'Please—'

'Enough. Just keep your oath and when this is done, give me my document of manumission.'

'You shall have it.'

'I shall be free to leave Constantinople?'

'You will be free to leave.' She swallowed. 'I would not dream of keeping you from your beloved Duchy a moment longer than I have to.'

'Would you not?' When she shook her head, his lips softened. 'My lady, it is odd how convincing you are when you set your mind to it.'

Anna gripped the sleeves of his tunic. It was suddenly vital that he believe her. 'I shall free you!'

He gave her a maddening smile. 'Setting the Varangian Guard over me to bend me to your will is not the best way to convince me of your integrity. However, I have thought of a way to make you keep your word.'

Her pulse skittered. 'Yes?'

'We shall consummate our marriage. Today.'

Anna's mouth went dry, it took a moment to frame a denial. 'No, you are still my slave and I say it is too soon.'

He tightened his hold. 'I regret, my lady, but in this I will have my way. If you want my compliance in the matter of our marriage, you will give me your body. I take it that even this Godforsaken place when a slave marries his mistress, there must be some form of agreement on both sides. *Mon Dieu*, to think you Greeks call us barbarians!'

Keeping an arm firmly about her, he reached for the cover on the Imperial couch and whisked it aside. Constantine had equipped him well, there was a mattress…sheets…blankets…cushions…

Anna swallowed. 'Today?'

'Yes, my lady, today.' William nudged her up against the Imperial couch. 'Please, be seated.'

Anna's legs gave way and she sat, staring blindly at a leaf on the floor while William took his place next to her. *He means to consummate the marriage at once!* 'You mean this?' His eyes were no longer cold and glassy—was the bitterness leaving him?

'I mean this,' he said, softly.

A large hand reached for her, tugging her close so he could drop a gentle kiss on her mouth. He nipped her lower lip and pulled back, green eyes watchful. 'If you are to impose your will over me in the matter of our marriage, I shall have my way over this.'

'Surely, it…it does not have to be quite yet.' *I am not ready! It is too soon!* 'It would be wrong to anticipate our vows.'

'Unless you plan on using those guards to drag me before a priest, we will consummate our inconvenient marriage now.'

Our inconvenient marriage. A chilling thought occurred to her. Stricken, she looked at him. 'There is someone waiting for you in Apulia?'

His hands were at her veil, searching for pins, dropping them heedlessly onto the floor. 'My lady, there is no one. So for the moment, I accept this marriage.' Another pin tinkled onto the mosaic tiles and he tugged her veil aside. 'I had hoped for better, but...' he shrugged '...at least there is a... spark between us. And thank God I will no longer have to watch you tiptoeing around your suitors in that ridiculous manner.'

He fell silent, he was staring at her hair. That morning, before she had put on her veil, Juliana had twisted it into a coronet. He cleared his throat. 'Loosen it.'

Anna drew a shaky breath. 'It...it is a complicated style, I am not sure I can replicate it afterwards.'

Afterwards. Sweet Mother, help her, William was not going to change his mind, he was intent on consummation.

'I don't care how complicated it is, loosen it.'

She put her hand on his shoulder. Undoubtedly

William must feel some bitterness against her, but they had kissed several times and he had never hidden the fact that he had taken as much pleasure in it as she. *He is not a cruel man, I will hold to that thought...*

'William, I know you are disappointed, but can you not set that aside? I will do as you ask, only, please, let us not do this if you feel dislike in your heart.'

'Dislike?' His eyes were startled. Large fingers ran over her hair, they hesitated as he puzzled out how to unfasten the complicated braiding. 'Dislike is not what I feel for you, my lady. I want to see your hair undone, but I am afraid of hurting you.'

Reassured, Anna reached up and pushed his hand aside. 'Start here,' she murmured. 'See? There is a hairpin here...'

He leaned close, so close her breasts brushed his chest. Anna's nipples tightened. *He has put disappointment behind him.* His face was as intent as it had been a moment ago, but he was no longer driven by bitterness. *Thank God.*

'And here?' The fingers paused in her hair. 'This one next?'

She felt his fingers with hers. 'Yes.'

Several more hairpins were tossed onto the tiny tiles. Anna kept her hand on his shoulder and watched his face. *Intent, yes, but not bitter. However, he moved that block in front of the door to ensure our privacy, he will not be deterred.*

'There!' A twisted skein of hair fell heavy down her back. He grinned. 'Turn a little, my lady.'

Anna obeyed, she felt a small tug and her hair swung free.

He sighed, turned her back to face him again and pulled her hair forwards, arranging it so it flowed over her shoulder and breasts. 'I longed to see you like this...' his voice was husky '...when we took refuge in the cistern.'

Anna's breasts felt heavy, she was taken with the most scandalous impulse to press herself against him and urge the hand that was carefully arranging her hair to shift slightly, ever so slightly, and cup her breast.

Green eyes found hers, her belly lurched with anticipation. His pupils were large and dark, his eyes seemed almost black, there was a slash of colour on his cheeks. She was aching so much, she hurt. *Is this longing? It must be.* William's breathing sounded constricted, hers certainly was. *If only I did not have to force him to this, if only he were a suitor who had my father's approval...* Anna's throat closed, she swallowed convulsively.

'William.' Shyly smiling, she touched his cheek

and boldly slid her fingers into his hair, that beautiful, golden hair. William's hair fascinated her as much as hers seemed to fascinate him. 'You must accord me the same privileges that I grant you, you cannot object.'

'Do you hear me objecting?'

His hair felt like silk. Anna's fingers tingled as she combed through it. *So soft.* The light from one of the windows was falling on him, a trick of the light that created an odd effect. 'You have a halo— you look like an angel.'

He caught her to him, stopping her words with a warm kiss. Anna heard him groan. As his lips moved over hers, as his tongue entered her mouth, she groaned herself. He explored her mouth slowly and with great thoroughness, and when she touched her tongue to his, he gave another groan.

There was a delicious trembling in Anna's belly. She was conscious that her hand, as it threaded through the yellow silk of his hair, was shaking. And his—she watched as he drew back to take hold of her skirts—his hand was shaking, too.

We are equal in this desire for each other.

A pang of foreboding went through her. Anna was entering this contract to prove to her father that she was not to be dictated to, but that did not alter the fact that she was dreading the time when she must bid William farewell. *I want William to stay. I want William to remain here as my husband. I shall never want another man.*

She pushed the thought away even as William pushed her back against the cushions.

Enjoy this time with him—it will not last. Once you have proved your point with your father, you will have to release William. He is not for you.

William leaned on an elbow as he looked at her, his breath warmed her cheek. 'So lovely,' he murmured. She saw hunger in his eyes.

Somehow he had got Anna's skirts up about her knees. His hand hovered over her girdle, he scowled at it, and a moment later the buckle clattered on the tiles.

'Your belt, too,' Anna said, fumbling at the fastening with fingers that were clumsy with need. 'Off, take it off.'

His belt flew aside. She tugged at his tunic and hesitated, recalling how cold he had been in the cistern. She wanted to see him, to touch his skin, but...

'The hypocaust in here hasn't worked for years. Will you be warm enough?'

His mouth curved. Leaning over her, he put his lips to her ear and kissed it. 'You will warm me.'

William was reducing her to a writhing mass of

needs, she felt like a wild thing. She wanted to lick him, to taste him. She wanted to bite. Lord. A lady-in-waiting should not be having these thoughts. When she felt his tongue in her ear, she gasped. 'That feels…'

'Good?'

'Yes, very…animal.'

He gave a choked laugh. 'Never fear, we shall be more…animal yet.'

Anna's cheeks burned, her mind reeled. She was a virgin, but she knew what went on between men and women. In Rascia, when Princess Theodora had anticipated her marriage vows with Prince Peter, Anna had guarded the bedchamber door for them. The noises she had heard had told her that pleasure was involved, much pleasure. But this knowledge, even when added together with the knowledge she had gleaned of the actual physical act of love, had none the less left her woefully unprepared for the reality of surrendering to William. He was, quite simply, laying siege to her every sense.

'More animal?' *Saints.*

The palm of his hand was on her skin, he had found his way under her gown and—*yes!*—his hand closed firmly over a breast. Shockingly, she found herself wriggling to allow him fuller access.

'More animal,' he murmured. 'Much more.'

Anna's heart thudded. She was hot from head to toe, she ached with want.

Lifting his head, he frowned down at her.

'William?'

'What about you? Will you be cold without your gown?'

The question seemed to break the sensual spell he had cast over her. Anna glanced down the length of the hall. Yes, he had blocked the door, yes, she herself had posted the Guard outside with orders not to disturb her unless she called for them, but… 'Imagine what we would look like if anyone should chance to enter,' she muttered, flushing even more hotly.

William was sprawled alongside her, gut-wrenchingly handsome in a cream-silk undershirt. The ties at his neck were undone, revealing a sprinkling of hairs at his throat. She could smell that masculine scent that was him, William.

And as for me…

Anna's skirts were bunched up under her, her feet and legs were quite bare.

William leaned in, smiling. 'We would look like lovers.'

The hall stretched away from the Imperial couch, alcove after alcove after alcove. It seemed ridiculous, but the size and emptiness of it—*there is no one here but us*—made her absurdly self-conscious.

William's smile drew her back to him, and he placed the palm of his hand against her cheek. 'Are we lovers?'

'I…I don't know.'

'Be my lover, Anna.'

Anna nodded. Her mouth was dry, she moistened her lips and pulled at the fabric of his undershirt. 'This next,' she said.

Smiling, William dragged it over his head.

His chest is magnificent, there is no other word for it. William is magnificent.

Bruises had left faint shadows on his skin, but since coming to the Palace he was already filling out. Muscles were forming where before there had been hollows, his flesh was firming. In a daze of desire, Anna stroked his flank and heard a slight catch in his breath. She explored the muscles on his shoulders, and as she did so she warmed inside—it felt as though she were melting.

Magnificent. And, for a time, mine.

'Anna…' He tugged at her skirts.

Lifting her hips, she allowed him to draw away her gown. Goosebumps whispered over her skin as he untied his chausses. She struggled to keep her breathing even, and if William's flurried breaths were anything to go by, he was having similar difficulties. She took comfort in that.

Smiling, she shifted under the sheet, and held it open for him.

The mattress rustled. Hard, toned flesh met hers. Warm and very male.

Taken by shyness, she reached for those wide shoulders and pulled him to her, burying her face in his neck so she could breathe him in. *William.* It made her less nervous when she was breathing him in, his scent was strangely reassuring. *William.*

He was stroking her side, kissing her neck, making ripples of delight curl in her belly. She moved closer, pressing her breasts against his chest, the better to enjoy the slight abrasion of his chest hair.

A warm hand cupped her breast, two warm hands cupped her breasts. While they busied themselves stroking her into a frenzy, his mouth was working its way down the side of her neck. He kissed her collarbone and her breast, he planted kisses all over her front. His mouth, hot and wet, brushed a nipple, his tongue flicked lightly back and forth, back and forth. Making her want, want...

Animal indeed.

'William, *please.*' She heard a shaky laugh, his tongue flickered tantalisingly across her breast and then he closed his lips firmly on her and began to suckle. Fire streaked through her, breast to loins.

Anna's eyes widened. *Like a baby? He is suckling me like a baby?* She moaned. *Did the Princess and Prince Peter...?* But whatever Prince Peter and Princess Theodora had done together was fast becoming irrelevant. What was relevant was the increasing ache in Anna's belly. And the discovery that, William's mouth having freed one of his hands, that hand was free to explore the rest of her...

Careful fingertips wandered down her side, tracing circles on her ribs. The sunlight was gilding his hair to gold, it was gleaming in tiny flecks in his eyes, eyes that were dark and hungry and fixed only on her.

Strong legs nudged hers apart. She brought his head back for another kiss, heard his husky whisper as he eased back. 'Touch me, my lady. Touch me here.' He leaned over her breast, guiding her hand. 'Gently.'

Her fingers closed over him, he was hard and felt very large. Her eyes widened.

'What?'

'You feel so...'

'Animal?' His lips twitched.

She smiled back. 'Yes. And large.' Her smile faded. 'Surely it is not possible?' *It will hurt!*

His smile was complacent. He shook his head. 'It is very possible, trust me. As long as you receive the proper…stimulation, we shall do very well. Here.'

The proper stimulation?

His hand moved over hers, guiding her, showing her how he liked to be touched.

His head pressed into her neck, his groan warmed her ear. Her toes curled. He was nuzzling the side of her breasts and her nipples were begging for his attention. When she moaned, he used his tongue on her.

'Enough,' he gasped, lifting his head and looking deep into her eyes. 'It is my turn to pleasure you.'

Anna nodded as though she understood what he meant, but of course, never having had any personal experience of what went on in the bedchamber between a man and a woman, she had only a hazy idea of what to expect.

What she didn't expect was for William's fingers to slide between her legs and gently push inside. Feeling. Caressing. Making her even hotter than she had been a moment before. Of course, had she thought about it, she should have expected it. *Animal. Barbarian.*

A memory flashed in on her. Of someone telling her that barbarian lovers, once tamed, made the best lovers in Christendom. The men of the Varangian Guard, for example, were said to have more stamina than most. *Whatever that means.*

Anna had an idea that her barbarian knight from Apulia was about to prove that he was as good a lover as any Varangian.

'There is no need to worry that the hypocaust is broken,' she heard herself saying. *I am babbling.*

Green eyes watched her, they crinkled at the corners. 'No, indeed.'

'No…*oh!*…no need for a b-brazier either.'

What is he doing? William had kissed his way down to her stomach, light touches of his tongue feathered over her belly.

Hot all over, Anna shifted and writhed. 'William?'

'Patience, *chérie.*'

He placed a row of kisses lower. Lower. His finger moved in and over her, her body had become an instrument and he was playing her.

'Relax, *chérie*, that's it. Trust me. Relax and know that I will not hurt you.'

A chain of kisses was trailed down one thigh and up the other. He kissed the flat of her belly. Keeping her legs open, he shifted down.

'William?' She raised herself on her elbows, caught between pleasure and shock. That blond head had settled between her legs. He was kissing her in her most secret of places... 'William, *no!*'

He took no notice, his tongue was too busy exploring. *His tongue!*

Anna gave a shuddering breath. *He is a barbarian. Only a barbarian would do such a thing. And I am going to die of delight.* 'William...?'

His head lifted, warm fingers smoothed over her, playing, teasing. 'Mmm?'

She collapsed back against the pillows. He had stopped kissing her intimate places and, shamelessly, she wanted him to continue. 'Is that allowed?' Never had she heard of such a thing.

His eyes danced. 'We are going to be married, are we not?'

'Yes,' she managed, wishing she had the nerve to push his head back to where it had been only moments ago.

'You like it?'

'Mmm.'

His head lowered. Anna sighed. She was powerless to prevent the moan of relief when his mouth found her. She gasped. She writhed. There was something, something else...only she could not name it and it lay just beyond her reach. *If only he will do that for a moment or two more...perhaps then...perhaps then...*

Rising on his forearms, he kissed his way back to her mouth. She held him close, stroking that large male body. She licked his ear and was nibbling his neck when she felt him nudging into her.

After a moment he stopped, leaning on his elbows to watch her. *He is keeping his weight off me.* Anna was not sure she wanted him to keep his weight off her. His cheeks were flushed. The pressure increased. She felt a tight, heavy fullness pressing into her, and then he rocked back and the pressure eased. 'Too tight?' he asked, voice breathless.

'A little.'

He nodded and then he was kissing his way back down her body—breast, nipples, navel, thighs—until his lips found the core of her. Making her writhe, the barbarian. Making her want...want...

The ache of want remained when he licked his way back and took her lips in the sweetest kiss. Again that heavy fullness nudged into her, a little farther this time.

He pulled back. 'Better?'

'Mmm. William, please...!' Grasping him firmly by the hips, sensing that only this would give her the satisfaction she was craving, Anna pulled him onto her. There was a slight resistance and then he was fully inside, hard and firm and warm.

'All right, Anna? No pain?' He was gently biting her ear, his breath harsh and laboured.

'No pain.' She kissed his cheek. 'No pain, only...'

'Only...?'

She frowned. 'I hoped there would be...more.'

'Oh, there will be.' Mouth curving, he eased away and rocked back in. Eased and rocked. Her belly swooped. 'Anna. *Chérie.*' He reached between them. Ease, rock, ease, rock. 'Still no pain? I am not too large?'

When she shook her head, her hair flew out across the pillow. 'Mmm.'

The rhythm William set was a joy to follow. As they moved together, the sensations built with every stroke and every kiss.

Barbarian. Animal.

William's eyes were dark and intense, his hair gleamed gold in a slanting shaft of light, his breathing was flurried. *He has entered a place beyond speech.* He pushed, she pulled, the sensations built and built...

A dazzle of sensation took her, like a starburst.

William cried out. He muttered something intelligible, but already he was coming back from the place beyond words, because she thought she heard her name.

'Anna.'

She was struggling to form words herself—it would seem her barbarian lover had lifted her far out of herself. The man had done the most unspeakable things to her body and she had loved it. Loved it.

I love him! I loved it because I love him.

Gripped by a languor that Anna realised must be the languor of love, she cupped that blond head with her hands and held him to her. His heart thumped against hers.

He is catching his breath, in a moment he will move.

Anna shivered. The bright starburst was fading and trailing in its wake came a realisation that was cold and dark. *William does not love me. I forced him to this. He took my body because he wants his freedom, he took my body to prove that I do not have all the power.*

He lifted his head and groaned. Rolling on to his back, he drew the sheet over them. 'There is no going back now, my lady.'

'No, there is no going back.' Her heart was a lump of ice.

I love him, I loved him from the first moment

I saw him. How did I not realise? Sweet Virgin, I should never have forced him to this. No man, particularly a Frankish knight, likes to be forced. Have I lost him?

Chapter Thirteen

William rose from the Imperial couch and began to dress, he was all consideration. 'Wine, my lady?' he asked, pulling on his chausses.

'Please.'

He filled a silver-rimmed drinking horn. Despite her distress, Anna could not but admire the way his wide shoulders tapered down to that narrow waist. The play of muscles in his arms and the fall of his hair were equally intriguing. *For a time this man is mine. But only for a time...*

Pensively, she took the wine. A heap of cushions was piled behind her, a sheet was tucked demurely over her breasts. She hoped she looked calmer than she felt.

I trust him. William is a Frank, yet of all the men in the Palace he is the only man I could rely on to marry me after he had taken my virginity. He is a man of honour, deep honour.

Once we are married I do not want to lose him, but he is so determined to return to Apulia. There must be something I can do to convince him to stay, there must be something...

Yet it seemed impossible. Anna had sworn to release him and release him she must, he would come to hate her if she even thought about trying to bind him here. And what would be the point in keeping him as her husband if all he felt was hate? *Can you learn to trust me, William? Can you learn to love?* Love and trust, Anna was coming to realise, were inextricably entwined. From what William had revealed about his past, he didn't seem to have been given much reason to trust others. His father had denied his existence, his mother had secreted herself behind a convent wall.

William is a noble and honourable man, I know he is capable of becoming a loving man. If I prove that I trust him, can he learn to love me?

She refused to let him go without a fight.

William could not help but smile. Anna looked like an Empress back in the decadent days of the Roman Empire. The way she was reclining on that couch, mouth pink from kissing, hair tumbling about her naked shoulders, breasts almost, but not quite, peeping out from under that sheet...

Something about the set of her mouth, however—it was turned down at the corners—made his smile fall away. She had enjoyed the act of love, so what was the matter?

The generous way Anna had given herself completely to him, without holding back, had pleased him beyond words. She had relished their joining as much as he had done.

For his part, the act of love with Anna had moved him beyond anything in his experience. It had not been all pleasure though, he was surprised to find their union had left him with a tightness in his chest that he could not account for. Most likely it could be explained away as the pain of desire—he wanted her again.

Continuing desire had better be the cause of the tightness, because if it was not desire, what in hell was it? Conflicting thoughts were tugging him this way and that—it was most irritating. There was no point chasing rainbows, no point longing for something that did not exist. Impatient with himself, he thrust the thoughts aside. This discomfort was minor, just a moment of confusion which, like his desire for her, would soon pass.

What was important was Anna, and whatever was causing her to purse her lips in that way. She had been a virgin but he knew she had found her pleasure. What was she worrying about? Was she regretting giving her virginity to a Frank? A slave? Did she feel that he had demeaned her?

'William?'

'My lady?' When her mouth eased into a smile, the sense of discomfort eased.

'I think, since we are to be married, you must call me Anna.'

He nodded. *I want her again—what is she thinking?* The sheet was slipping, revealing the delightful curve of her breasts. A pulse throbbed in his loins.

'Anna, you are…most desirable.' Finding himself back at the couch, William sat and dropped a light kiss on her nose. One of his hands, without conscious thought, pulled the sheet clear of her body and took possession of a breast. Instantly, the nipple hardened. '*Chérie*, what were you thinking about a moment ago?'

A tiny crease appeared in her brow. 'I forget.' She shrugged, and that quiet smile appeared. 'I know what I am thinking now…'

'What's that?' Leaning in, William nuzzled her neck, he needed to breathe her in. Spring. Jasmine. *Anna.*

'Men in the Varangian Guard are said to have great…staying power.' Her voice was breathy, her eyes speculative. 'I was wondering if that is the same with all barbarians.'

Startled, William lifted his head. A delicate hand was at the fastening of his chausses, she was reaching for the part of him that was straining most eagerly towards her. It was as though she wanted... as though she was feeling the pain of renewed desire as much as he. 'Anna?'

'Well? Are you able to prove that all barbarians are made that way?'

Grinning, William whisked the silver-rimmed beaker from her fingers and dragged the sheet clear of the couch. 'Now that, *chérie*, is a challenge I cannot resist.'

By the time they had risen from the couch and had dressed, shadows were emerging from the corners of the hall. Anna found candles among the supplies that Constantine had brought and set them up everywhere.

Small constellations flickered in each of the alcoves, light flared from the rusting wall sconces, candles glowed on the floor where they had been placed directly on the mosaics in a pool of their own wax. In the dusk, with the glitter of light in every cranny, the Hall of the Nineteen Couches had regained something of its lost grandeur.

'There!' she said, lighting the last candle.

'Candles on the floor are dangerous,' William said. 'Your skirts…'

She looked across. 'There is plenty of room, I shall keep well clear of the flames. In any case, I shall not be staying.'

Her hair had been drawn back in a simple style, her veil was neatly back in place. Idly, William wondered what her maid would say when she saw the havoc he had wrought on the beautiful hair beneath the veil. Anna had tried, and failed, to replicate the complicated arrangement. 'William, I have to return to the Palace tonight.'

'I know.' William was satisfied physically, in truth, he felt utterly sated. He was also more than a little stunned by the joy they had taken in each other. Anna had been innocent before they had come together on the Imperial couch and yet she had met him, kiss for kiss, caress for caress. He had never thought to find a woman like her. *She is my match.*

Shaking his head at the unwonted sentimentality, he went on watching her. He was physically satisfied and yet…that sense of discomfort lingered. Never had he felt so conflicted.

Why did he feel this way?

Anna was moving towards the door. With an

elegant court slipper, she nudged the block of stone he had placed in front of it. 'William, please could you move this?'

William went to do as she asked. The night air was cool. Torches had been set up near the portico, yellow flames curled and waved.

'My thanks, William.'

She pressed his hand and gave him one of her subtle, beguiling smiles. Silently, he watched as she went out, picking her way across the rubble near the threshold.

'Sergeant?'

'My lady?'

'I thank you for your assistance. I have a further task for you.'

'My lady?'

That elegantly shod foot touched the heap of masonry. 'Clear this from the doorway, if you please. Then you and your men may return to your quarters. I no longer require your…escort.'

The Varangian sergeant looked doubtfully at William. 'You are certain, my lady?'

'Quite certain, Sergeant. And thank you for your help.'

'You are welcome, Lady Anna.'

While the sergeant turned to direct his men in

shifting the rubble, William caught her hand and pulled her back into the hall.

'You have dismissed the Guard?' He stared at her, not understanding.

'You heard me.'

'Why? I thought you were afraid I might attempt to escape?' That quiet smile was back—William could not think what it meant. He caught her arm. 'Are you saying you trust me?'

'Yes, of course. Particularly now we have... known...each other in the fullest sense. You are entirely trustworthy. I know you will not attempt to leave the City until after we have married.'

William found himself struggling with a mix of emotions that for a moment had him feeling dazed. It was as though he had been floored in a fight and had completely lost his bearings. From the midst of this confusion a warm glow emerged. She trusted him! *Mon Dieu*, he must take care, there was a danger that this woman would turn him into a sentimental fool.

'It was clear from the start that you are a man of honour,' she was saying, calmly. 'You have taken my body, you will honour our agreement.'

It was strangely humbling to be trusted in so large a matter—they had had carnal knowledge of each other, there could be a child. Anna was taking a great risk by trusting him in this. His throat ached. It was a pity they had to part.

Her head had tipped to one side and her smile eased a knot of tension deep inside. Anna had such a beautiful smile, it would ease the tension in anyone.

'William, if I invite you to escort me to Commander Ashfirth's house, so that we might discover that document, will you accompany me?'

It took a moment for William to answer, he was transfixed by Anna's mouth. That smile, that subtle, beguiling smile...

'At this hour?'

'Why not? With you as my escort, I shall be perfectly safe. And this is important. Also, you will be able to satisfy yourself that Daphne and Paula are happy.'

The desire to drag her to him and kiss her senseless hit him in his gut, but she had spent so long trying to dress her hair...he wouldn't be able to kiss her as he wanted to without wrecking her efforts.

William didn't give a fig for the document of manumission. In his mind it was worthless—he should never have been enslaved in the first place—but if Anna wanted him to have it, he would accept. Besides, now that he had made her his, he had questions…

'Thank you. Anna?'

'Mmm?'

'I should have asked this earlier had I not been so eager to…seal our agreement, but what happened to make you change your mind? You said circumstances had changed.'

She jerked her face away.

He put his fingers under her chin to make her meet his eyes. 'You saw your father when you went back to the apartment.'

'Yes.'

'Don't tell me, he was bullying you again.'

She blinked. 'Bullying me? It is just that Father found another suitor.'

'Another suitor? What about Lord Michael?'

'Lord Michael is already out of favour.'

William's stomach cramped. He didn't want Anna to have any suitors except him. The thought was unnerving—he did not care to examine why. 'You don't have to marry any of the men your father chooses. You are marrying me.'

'Yes.' Her smoky eyes gleamed and what looked suspiciously like a tear formed at the end of her lashes. Sight of it caused more pain than a dagger in his gut. Anna had come to him, not because she had wanted to, but because she could no longer stand her father's bullying.

'Lord Isaac *is* a bully, he does not deserve you,' he muttered.

Anna should be protected. Anna should be cherished. If their marriage was to have been a real one, he would be honoured to protect her for the rest of his life, he would be honoured to cherish her. Anna was a woman worth cherishing—the image of her lying in abandonment on the Imperial couch would be with him for ever. It was not, however, merely her sensuality that appealed. She was kind and thoughtful, she was beautiful and generous and gentle and... His breath froze. Was he in love with her? That could not be. It must not be. He must remember, she had bought him to thwart her bullying father.

And yet, that image of her lying on the couch amid a tangle of blankets and sheets was so bright. Her expression as she had looked at him, the loving way she had touched him...if he lived for a thousand years, he would never forget it.

This must stop, his thoughts were running away with him. What he felt for Anna was not love, it was desire, and it was akin to what he had felt for Claire at Melfi. There was no escaping the fact that what he felt for Anna was stronger than what he had felt for Claire, but it could not be love. Love was...

Baffled, William shook his head. He would be the first to confess that he had no idea what people meant when they spoke of love. Love was a word used by women and poets. A landless knight, an enslaved and landless knight, had little use for it. He did *not* love her.

'William, whatever's the matter?'

'Nothing.' He crooked his arm at her. 'Come along, let us take you back to the Boukoleon.' They were halfway to the door when someone rapped on it.

'Anna? William? Are you still in there?'

'Constantine,' William said, exchanging glances with her.

Anna snatched her hand from his sleeve. 'Come in.'

Constantine came into the hall, breaking step as his eyes fell on Anna. 'Everything is well, Anna?' he asked, eyes lingering thoughtfully on her hair and veil. 'I see you have dismissed the guards.'

Anna went pink. 'Thank you, Constantine, all is well.'

'Good, good.' His eyes shifted to William. 'I have a message for you.'

'A message? No one knows I am here.'

'Not so. A deputation of Frankish knights has arrived at the Palace. They are enquiring after Sir William Bradfer.'

William went very still. 'Frankish knights? Did you get their names?'

Constantine grinned. 'Naturally. There is one Sir Bruno of Melfi—'

'Sir Bruno!' William could not help but grin back. 'Sir Bruno is in the Palace? Are you certain you got the name correctly?'

'Of course. Sir Bruno of Melfi is here, along with Sir Louis La Roche-Guyon and a party of squires whose names, I confess, escaped me.'

William rubbed his chin. 'Sir Louis La Roche-Guyon? Never heard of him.'

'That's odd, he is claiming to be your cousin.'

Even in the fitful candlelight, Anna could see that William had lost colour.

'My cousin? You must have misunderstood, I was not aware I had a cousin.'

'William, I did not misunderstand. My Norman French is likely better than you realise, I only need your help with certain...' Constantine winked at Anna '...refinements. Sir Louis definitely said he was your cousin.'

William was already moving to the door. 'Where are they?'

'Stabling their horses. No need to rush off, man, I left Symeon with them. He has orders to direct them here when they have finished at the stables.'

William clasped Constantine's hand. 'My thanks.'

'In the meantime, since you are to have guests, I have ordered the servants to bring you a brazier. It's freezing in here.'

'Freezing?' William murmured and Anna felt his gaze on her. 'Can't say that I noticed.'

Anna's world rocked. *A cousin—William has a cousin he did not know about! And Sir Bruno has come to find him. What will this mean for him? For us?*

While they waited for the Franks to arrive, servants brought more candles to the Hall of the Nineteen Couches. The wall sconces glowed and the mosaic floor was rimmed with golden pools of light. A brazier was carried to the centre of the room and piled high with coals, a red reflection danced in every window. Even the ancient gilding on the Imperial couch had a dull gleam to it.

The Franks marched into the hall not long afterwards. Their boots rang loud on the floor tiles, the gemstones in their brooches and rings winked in

the candlelight, the jewelled pommel of a barbarian sword-hilt flashed.

They are wearing swords! Anna felt her jaw
drop. Somehow, these Franks had persuaded the
Palace Guard to admit them with their weapons.
It would be another matter, of course, if they were
to enter the presence of the Emperor, but it said
much for their credentials that they had been allowed through the Palace gate wearing swords.

There was an older, stocky man whose face was
crumpled with lines—Anna realised he must be
Sir Bruno. He was missing part of an ear. She
knew she was right when William strode towards
him, wreathed in smiles. The two embraced and as
they drew apart, the lines eased on the older man's
face. There was a revealing gleam in Sir Bruno's
eyes, a matching gleam in William's, and a hearty
clearing of throats all round.

When William clapped one of the younger men
on the back, briefly gripping his arm, Anna realised this was William's squire.

*There is warmth here, and deep affection.
William is fond of his squire, and Sir Bruno and
William love each other.* Anna could not but warm
towards Sir Bruno, the man who had taken the
young William into his household and fostered
him. It was he, she was sure, who had formed

William's character, giving him his sense of honour and surety of purpose.

As William and Sir Bruno began speaking rapidly in that foreign tongue of theirs, Anna tugged the hem of Constantine's tunic. 'What are they saying?'

Constantine grimaced. 'Give me a moment, the dialect is not easy.'

While Anna waited, she studied the Franks, now warming their hands at the brazier. There were six of them. It was clear from their clothing which were knights and which were squires. Sir Bruno and the other knight—William's cousin if Constantine had it correctly—were wearing short wool tunics skilfully embroidered in colours that matched the colours of their cross-gartering. The tunics of the four younger men bore less intricate designs—all were well dressed, all were clean shaven.

'I have it now, roughly speaking,' Constantine murmured. 'Sir Bruno has just told William that he thought he had seen the last of him when his horse came back without him...

'And William is saying, no such luck. He is asking Sir Bruno if he has come for the enthronement. Sir Bruno...' Constantine's lips twitched '...

Sir Bruno just swore. What he said is not fit for a lady's ears, so I shall not translate.'

'Go on, Constantine, what else are they saying?'

'Sir Bruno and Sir Louis have been following the slave routes for months, trying to find William. There was no news of any enthronement when they set out.'

Anna watched William's throat work. *His friends have been looking for him and he is moved beyond words to hear this.*

'Sir Bruno just called William "boy", he is introducing him to Sir Louis.' Constantine touched Anna's arm. 'Anna, perhaps we should leave?'

'Leave?'

'Give them time to exchange their greetings in private.'

Anna shook her head vehemently, she was not going to leave. She wanted, no, she *needed* to hear what was said. After all, William had agreed to marry her, she had a right to know. *Except that... our marriage is not going to be a real marriage. As far as William is concerned it is intended to ward off my suitors and make Father think twice about marrying me to the man with the largest purse in the Palace.*

'Here, boy,' Sir Bruno said, 'this is Sir Louis La

Roche-Guyon.' He gestured at William. 'Louis, this is Sir William Bradfer.'

William smiled and held out his hand.

Constantine looked at Anna. 'William is saying that he is glad to meet Sir Louis, Sir Louis is glad to meet William. Anna, I really think we should bow out...'

'*No!* Get on with it, Constantine, you're missing bits!'

Sighing, Constantine continued. 'Sir Bruno discovered William and Louis were kin after William had vanished. When the squires returned to Melfi without him and they could find no body, Sir Bruno says he knew William was alive. He tore Apulia apart looking for him.'

William's cousin, Sir Louis, murmured something.

Anna's foot tapped. 'Constantine...?'

'Sir Louis says that his uncle had been also enquiring after William.'

William looked puzzled.

'The name of this uncle is Count Jean La Roche-Guyon and...' Constantine caught his breath.

Anna plucked at his sleeve. 'What? What is he saying?'

'If I have it aright, Count Jean La Roche-Guyon is William's father.'

William went white. Anna stopped breathing.

'My father?' William said, in a dazed voice. 'My *father?*'

Across the brazier, green eyes found hers.

Anna took an involuntary step towards him. 'There is no need to translate that, Constantine.'

Sir Louis withdrew a small parchment from his tunic and passed it to William.

'Here, cousin,' Constantine muttered, resuming his translation of what Sir Louis was saying. 'Your father's letter explains everything.'

William broke the seal with a snap. He turned to the light of a wall sconce and, as he read, his finger marked his place.

William's father has found him. William shall at last know his father!

Anna felt her lips curve. She knew how much this would mean to him and was pleased for him. But how strange it must be to meet your father after a lifetime of neglect. For herself, Anna felt a pang of dismay. *This news will strengthen William's determination to leave the City, it will eradicate any chance I might have of persuading him to remain as my husband.*

But why should his father contact him now, after years of silence?

'My lady.' William stood before her, parchment

in hand. Anna had never seen a man look quite so stunned. 'My father is acknowledging me as his son.'

Anna nodded, touched that, in what must be a moment of the greatest importance to him, he wanted her to know what was happening. 'And so he should.'

On the other side of the brazier, Sir Bruno proved he understood a little Greek by giving her an approving nod.

William took her hand, eyes serious. 'No, you do not understand. Count Jean is going to name me his heir. His heir.'

Anna's heart jumped, she fought to keep her smile in place. 'You will be a count?'

'God willing, so it would seem.' Swinging back to face his fellow countrymen, William muttered something to Sir Louis.

He will never stay, he is heir to a count! I have lost him. He will uphold our agreement because he is an honourable man, but he will never stay, never. He will insist on an annulment.

Constantine stirred. 'Apparently, the Count searched for William's mother for years. She hid herself away in some convent under a different name and Count Jean never could discover where she had gone.'

Sir Louis, Sir Bruno and William then engaged
in a fast and lengthy conversation which must have
been too complex for Constantine to follow because when Anna looked to him for a translation,
he merely shrugged.

For the next few minutes, Anna had to content
herself with watching while they talked. The mood
was friendly, easy. Sir Louis handed William a
purse she gathered was a gift from his father. It
struck her, as she watched William accept it, that
she was catching a glimpse of his future. *There
he stands, tall and proud amid his peers...this is
what he will look like in Apulia, when he inherits
his father's county—a barbarian lord entertaining others in his hall.* Her eyes misted, and for a
moment she saw nothing but a blur of candlelight.

Blinking rapidly, she recovered herself to see
Constantine opening the door and gesturing for
a servant.

'More wine, if you please, Demetrios!'

The wine came quickly. William acted as host,
ensuring every guest had the wine of his choice.
*Yes, this is how he will be in his own hall, this is
how he will be in his castle. William is naturally
gracious. When the time comes he will make a fit-
ting count.* Her throat ached. *This man does not
belong to me, he never did.*

Trays of refreshments appeared, cakes sweetened with honey and almonds, stuffed dates, bowls of olives. She and Constantine were also brought wine and a chair was unearthed for Sir Bruno. As the older knight eased into it with a sigh, Anna noticed he had a slight stiffness in one leg. *Sir Bruno is no longer young, the search for William has exhausted him. He knows William's worth—he must think the world of him to have embarked on such an enterprise.*

Unexpectedly, the mood in the hall shifted. In a heartbeat it moved from friendly to distinctly edgy.

William's brow darkened. He snapped at his cousin, and Anna caught the words 'Lady Felisa Venafro'.

Lady Felisa Venafro?

A shiver ran down her spine. From a purely selfish point of view, she could hardly imagine how matters could worsen. But watching William's face flood with angry colour as he glanced her way, she feared they were about to.

He led her to one side. 'Lady Anna, I think you should know that Lady Felisa Venafro has indicated to my father that she is prepared to accept my hand in marriage.' His mouth twisted. 'It seems that since I may one day become a count, she now approves of me. My father urges me to agree, he reminds me that she is an heiress and it would be a good match.'

Anna stared at him, heart in her mouth. Her mind raced. *Lady Felisa Venafro? Does he want this woman? If so, marriage to me will be an impediment, I will be an impediment.*

William held his hand out to her, an eyebrow lifted. 'Do you care to walk outside for a time, my lady?'

Putting her hand in his, Anna stared at the strong fingers closing over hers and let him lead her from the hall. She was dizzy with dread. The world she had hoped to build—a world in which Lady Anna of Heraklea and Sir William Bradfer might find happiness together—was collapsing about her.

He is going to tell me that he must break our agreement. I love him and I want him to be my husband, but why should William choose me over an heiress in Apulia? I have no lands. I live in a place that is foreign to him and far away from his inheritance. And, most damning of all, why should William choose me when he knows I bought him with the intention of thwarting my father?

Anna recalled the sudden sheen in his eyes as he and Sir Bruno had embraced. *William wants to be loved. Likely, he is unaware of it, but ever since he was a small boy in that convent, he has wanted to be loved. My one hope, my only hope, is to confess my feelings for him and pray he can forgive me. I should never have bought him. I should never have tried to use him for my own ends. I will confess as much and pray that he believes me.*

Chapter Fourteen

William escorted Anna away from the glowing hall and into the night. The moon was rising in a sky that was full of stars. The air was cool and salty, the ground wet with dew. They followed the winding path into the copse until they came to a shadowy bench positioned snugly in a curve of the sea wall.

'Please, my lady, be seated, if you are not too cold out here?'

'I am not too cold.'

William's mind was in chaos, this news had thrown him. *How much has Anna understood? How much of what we said did Constantine manage to translate for her?*

The bench creaked as William took his place next to her. In front of them, the roofline of the Hall of the Nineteen Couches was clearly outlined against a dark, starry backdrop. With candle-glow leaking from every window, the hall looked like a giant lantern that had been tilted on its side.

'My lady, do you understand what this means?' William could not blame her if she did not. He was himself struggling to absorb the implications of what he had learned.

'I have not grasped the whole, but I do understand that you are the son of a count.' Slender fingers rested briefly on his arm. 'I am pleased for you, William, it is very gratifying to learn that your father has long wanted to acknowledge you.'

William nodded. 'I confess, it is not easy to digest these revelations. For years, I thought my father uncaring, but Louis tells me that he moved heaven and earth trying to find my mother. She hid herself away and would have none of it. I am told that eventually, my father lost hope of finding her and made a marriage of convenience with an Apulian heiress. They had no children.'

'And your father needed an heir.'

'He named Louis his heir. Louis is the son of my father's younger brother, Robert.'

'So your uncle's name must be Robert La Roche-Guyon?'

The moonlight was full on Anna's face, she was looking very pensive, a deep crease was etched on her forehead. Reaching up, William smoothed the crease away with his thumb. 'It is—what of it?'

She caught his wrist. 'William, you said that in Apulia after you were ambushed, you heard a name you believed to be linked with the name of your unknown enemy—Gwion. I am not familiar with your Frankish names, but it strikes me that *Gwion* and La Roche-*Guyon* have a similar ring to them.'

Smiling, he leaned back. 'You are perceptive, *chérie*, they do sound similar. My cousin has confessed that it was his father—my uncle Robert— who planned for me to be attacked. He wanted me out of the way because—'

'He feared your father would find you and he wanted Louis to inherit!' Her fingers tightened on his wrist. 'William, how dreadful. You are united with your family only to discover that your uncle tried to arrange for your murder!'

Gently, William touched her cheek. *Anna has the softest skin. I love touching her.* Reluctantly, he pulled his hand back. Why was it so hard to re-member that since they were in a public place, he must not touch her? *We are not yet married. We may never be married.*

'On balance, I judge myself fortunate,' he said. 'I have a father who has named me his heir and a cousin who has proved himself the most honourable of men. When Sir Louis discovered Sir Robert's perfidy, he spoke out against him in the name of justice—against his own interests.'

'That is honour indeed,' she murmured.

'I am proud to be related to Sir Louis.'

There was a thoughtful silence before she spoke again. 'William, have you learned why your mother would not marry your father?'

He lifted his shoulders. 'My guess is that she felt she could not compete with the Apulian heiress in terms of wealth, but we shall probably never know.'

Anna lowered her gaze. 'I see.'

He took her hand. It was cold, absently, he began to chafe it. 'Anna, do you still wish for me to honour our agreement?'

Her chin lifted. 'I do, but I would not force you.' She gave a strange laugh. 'Who am I to force a knight who will one day become a count? You will have lands, wealth, everything you ever wanted.'

'Yes.'

'This Lady Felisa Venafro—do you want her, too?'

'At one time I thought I did,' William said, carefully.

'Lady Felisa will not like it if you return with an unwanted Greek bride.'

'If I return with a Greek bride, she must accept

it,' William heard himself saying. He leaned towards her, close enough for her scent to make his gut clench—jasmine and that tantalising hint of spring. 'Anna, I don't have to leave immediately.'

'You don't?'

'No. I should like to stand as your good friend. I should like to remain in the City until you have chosen the husband you want.'

'The husband I want,' she murmured, giving him a mysterious glance from under her lashes.

'As opposed to someone your father foists upon you. I do not wish to leave knowing you are...unsettled. Also...I shall not leave until we know for certain whether we have made a child.' When she shook her head, he ploughed on. 'Anna, you trusted me with your body and we must consider that there may be a child. I shall not turn my back on my responsibilities, I shall stay in Constantinople until we know the outcome.'

Her face was milky in the moonlight. 'Yes. I see. My goodness, circumstances have changed.'

There was a flatness in her tone that William could not read, some nuance of feeling she was concealing from him. Sadness? Regret? It was most likely regret. She had surrendered her virginity to a Frank and her father would never forgive her. Lord, she could end up blaming him for ruining her.

'If there is a child, I will stand by you,' he said.

'I…I…thank you. Like your cousin, you are an honourable man. William, there is something I must tell you—'

She broke off, staring silently into the night for so long that William squeezed her hand to prompt her. 'Yes?'

She took a deep breath. 'When I first saw you at the slave market, I saw a resemblance to someone I knew. But I also saw the most handsome man I had ever seen.'

He snorted, ruefully rubbing his chin and ribs. 'You exaggerate, the bruises still ache. I was filthy…half-starved.'

'I am not referring to your looks, William, but to other qualities.'

'You saw qualities in a man on the slave block?'

'I saw them,' she insisted softly. 'I confess that when I bought you my motives were mixed. I did not trust what I saw either. But the outcome is the same. I love you, William. I would be honoured if you chose me for your wife, your true wife. I love you.'

William stared—this sudden declaration made him uneasy. 'You cannot mean this. You loved

Erling and saw him in me, you are confusing me
with Erling.'

'It was not Erling who helped those children, it
was not Erling who fought off that mercenary. Nor
was it Erling who kept me company in the Basilica
Cistern.' She smiled and lowered her voice. 'And it
certainly wasn't he who made love to me so beautifully. You made love to me with more than your
body, I know it or I would not be so bold. William,
I love you.'

William was dumbfounded. Of all the things
Anna could have said to him, this was the last
thing that he had expected. She loved him? She had
loved him from that first moment? That could not
be true. The suspicions began to pile up and the
sense of euphoria that had held him since leaving
the hall began to fade.

'You do not consider I have ruined you?' he
asked.

'*No!*'

'You love me?'

'Yes, William, I do.' Her voice was almost inau-
dible. 'I did from that first moment.'

'If this is true, why did you not tell me earlier?'

'I did not think you would believe me, I scarcely
believed it myself. In truth, it took time for me to

accept the feeling as a true one.' Her chest heaved. 'You do not believe me.'

'You are right, I don't. I can't. Anna, if you had told me when we took our joy of each other on the Imperial couch, then I might have believed you. But to wait until you hear that I am the heir to Count Jean La Roche-Guyon?' He shook his head. 'It pains me to say this, but I cannot believe you. You love the thought of the lands I will one day inherit.'

She sat very straight. 'Do you really think that?'

'Women want land, women want security. Lady Felisa is just the same, using me for her own ends.'

'What do you mean?'

'Some time ago, I offered for Lady Felisa's hand and she accepted me. What I didn't realise was that she had only accepted me in order to force another knight, a *landed* knight, into declaring himself. Once he had done so, I was forgotten.'

'She broke your betrothal?'

William nodded.

'And now?'

Weary, he rubbed his face. The moon was trapped behind the branches of a tree, a white globe caught in a black claw. He wanted Anna, not Lady Felisa. Furthermore, he wanted her to want him for himself, not because he resembled Erling or because he might one day inherit a county…

'What do you see when you look at me, *chérie*?'

'I…I beg your pardon?'

'Do you see Erling? My inheritance? What do you see?'

'I see the man I love.'

'I cannot believe you.'

'Then we have no more to say.' Rising, she shook out her skirts. 'William, it is very late. Think about what I have said. I am speaking the truth, I love you. In the meantime, I would be grateful if you could ask one of Constantine's servants to accompany me back to the Boukoleon. In any case, tonight is probably not the best time to make to any decisions—we both have much to digest. And…' smiling, she gestured towards the hall '…you have loyal friends who have come a long way to see you.'

Mind reeling with this last revelation in an evening of revelations—Anna had said that she loved him, could it be true?—William rose and offered her his arm.

He was at last to meet his father, he was heir to a county, Anna would have him, Lady Felisa would have him…

William had never felt more miserable in his life.

* * *

From the steps by the hall portico, William watched as Anna and her escort made their way up the path. When the shadows swallowed them, he made no move to go inside. He had plans to make with Sir Bruno and his cousin, but he was in no hurry, too much in his mind was unresolved.

Above him, the moon had broken free of the black claw that had snared it, high above the tree-line, it was sailing serenely through the midnight sky.

Anna claimed to have loved him from the first moment—if she had told him earlier, he might have believed her. The ache in William's chest told him that he wanted to believe her, he wanted to believe her more than he had wanted anything in his life. Except perhaps—a reminiscent grin touched his mouth—that irresistible body of hers.

Lady Felisa Venafro meant nothing to him. Once, William had longed for Lady Felisa's hand in marriage. He had, quite simply, coveted her lands. Now his longings were more complicated. Lady Anna of Heraklea's smoky grey eyes were ever in his mind. He longed for the touch of her hands, that delicate touch that wreaked havoc with his peace of mind. He would never forget her generous love-making, nor the way her head tipped back when she looked up at him.

Once William had thought Lady Felisa pretty, now he must struggle to recall what she looked like.

William was torn. Was he honour-bound to accept Lady Felisa? She had rejected him before, but he had never actually rescinded his offer. Was he bound to accept her?

He was certainly honour-bound to marry Anna, he had unquestionably agreed to her terms. Terms she made purely to thwart her father.

Mon Dieu, as he read it, he was honour-bound to two women! What was he to do?

As the moon drifted on through the constellations, it seemed that Anna's grey eyes had blanked out the stars. Never had he met anyone with such long black eyelashes, eyelashes that she hid behind when she wished to conceal her thoughts.

Ought he to consider Anna's father? For all that Anna and Lord Isaac disagreed over the question of her marriage, she obviously loved her father and wanted him to think well of her. If William was to marry Anna, and their marriage was not annulled, would Lord Isaac forgive her?

When the night breeze played over his face, and all he could feel was the whisper of Anna's skin against his, his mind cleared. *I want to marry Anna of Heraklea.* He wanted Anna to come back to the Duchy with him, he wanted her to meet his father even though it meant uprooting her from everything she knew—her own father, the Princess...

He rolled his shoulders. Lord, he had forgotten about the Princess! Anna was in some difficulties there, he was certain of it. If only she would allow him to help. Just before Sir Bruno had arrived, Anna had asked him to go with her to Commander Ashfirth's house. If only they had got away. She had said that she trusted him—surely she had been about to open up to him?

Mon Dieu, William would never regret Sir Bruno's appearance, but from the point of view of finally uncovering the mystery surrounding Anna and Princess Theodora, the timing of Sir Bruno's arrival could not have been worse. William wanted to help Anna. He wanted her as his wife.

Light from the hall windows was spilling out, making oddly shaped patches of brightness on the grass. William stared broodingly at them. He wanted Anna, but he was promised to Lady Felisa, that was the sum of it. His thoughts had led him to a dead end. There was little use in knowing what he wanted, when he was still honour-bound to two women.

For the present, it looked as though his best course would be to stand his ground. His father might have summoned him home, but he could not leave, not yet. He would tell Sir Bruno that commitments would keep him here for a few weeks—that should be long enough for him to learn whether Anna was bearing his child.

Heart lighter than it had been all evening, William reached for the door.

Back at the Princess's apartment, Anna could find no sign of Katerina. On being pressed, the young guard, Kari, confirmed that Katerina was still at his commander's house.

Yes, Kari knew the whereabouts of the house and, yes, it was close, just off the Mese. And, yes, Kari would escort Lady Anna there, if she so desired.

Thus it was that, shortly after breaking her fast the next day, Anna left the apartment with Kari as her escort. Not only did she need to set her mind at rest about Katerina—whom she had not seen since the German mercenaries had chased her into Hagia Irene—but also she needed that document. She must sign William's manumission, so that he would legally be free.

Commander Ashfirth's house turned out to be a gracious three-storied building set behind a wall in one of the more prosperous streets. There was an airy courtyard with cypresses and a plane tree to give shade in the summer, there was a grand portico, a stable…in truth, there was every luxury a woman could want.

In any event, Anna need not have worried about Katerina—one look told her that her friend was thriving. And deeply in love.

'The Commander asked you to marry him?' Anna asked as she and Katerina sat on a cushioned bench in an inner courtyard that was open to the sky. The courtyard had a fountain and was as grand as any in the Imperial Palace. Outside, sparrows were chirping. 'You accepted, of course?'

Katerina laughed. 'Of course.'

Leaning forward, Anna pressed Katerina's hand. 'I am glad. The Commander is a good man and you deserve a good man.'

'I am happy you approve, my lady. Some would say that a barbarian is a poor choice of husband.'

'Not I,' Anna said softly, even as she noticed some of the light went out of her friend's expression. 'Katerina, what is it?'

Katerina bit her lip. 'There is one difficulty, and try as I might I cannot think how to overcome it.'

'Oh?'

'The Commander will not permit me to return to the Palace,' Katerina confessed, grimacing. 'He is adamant I may not leave the house until…until… the Princess herself returns. There is no arguing with him, I am afraid.'

'He fears what may happen to you if it comes to light that you are not the Princess—he wants to protect you.'

Nodding, Katerina began pleating the skirt of her gown into folds. 'Ashfirth tells me that Duke Nikolaos is one of the new Emperor's closest allies, his regiment is camped outside the City.'

'So close?' Anna's heart fell. 'I thought he was in Larissa.'

'As did I. Anna, the Duke is expected in the Palace any day—he is bound to want to meet the Princess. What shall we do? I can take her place no longer. It is one thing to pull the wool over the eyes of a handful of courtiers who have not seen the Princess in years—it is quite another to attempt to do the same to the man to whom she is betrothed.'

Anna leaned back. 'Oh, Lord, I see what you mean.' She and Katerina had agreed to this deception because they loved the Princess and knew that these might be the last few weeks she could spend with her daughter. At the time, everyone had believed Duke Nikolaos to be safely in Larissa with his ailing mother. But this coup had obviously changed all that. 'The Duke is actually outside the City?'

'Camped outside the very walls.'

Anna thought swiftly and came to a decision. 'Commander Ashfirth is quite right—you have done your part, you must stay here.'

'But the Princess…!'

Anna patted Katerina's hand. 'Leave it me. I notice the Commander has not withdrawn his men from the apartment.'

'No, it was in Ashfirth's mind that by leaving the Guard in place, there would some semblance of normality. He hopes to keep suspicions at bay for as long as possible.'

'It's a good thought. My dear, I do believe the Princess is about to come down with a sickness. It is possible she has eaten something that does not agree with her.'

A slow smile spread across Katerina's face. 'Perhaps she picked up a fever on the voyage from Dyrrachion.'

'It may be that—yes, it may be that. Poor thing.

At any rate, Princess Theodora will not be receiving visitors until she is quite recovered. I take it that the Commander will not object if I enlist his men to back me up in this?'

'He will be pleased to help. Oh, thank you, my lady, I have been worrying and worrying!'

'You may stop worrying, Katerina, you have done your part.'

Soon afterwards, Anna and Kari returned to the apartment in the Boukoleon, whereupon Anna briefed the young man that should anyone come to enquire after the Princess, they were to be told that she was ailing. The Varangians could take messages for her, but the Princess was simply not well enough to leave the apartment or to receive visitors.

Then, William's document firmly in hand, Anna went to a table in the reception chamber that overlooked the sea. She stared at the signature on the document, already she had signed it. William was now officially, legally free.

For some reason, she was reluctant to send it to him. She was half-afraid that even though he had promised to stay for a while, if he had his manumission, he might change his mind and leave. *No, no, William would not do that, he is an honour-able man.* But the fear remained.

It might be best to avoid his company for a time, even though it would feel as though she had cut off her arm. It was hard to believe she had known him for so brief a time. Of course, they had been flung together much in these last few days. In truth, because of the way unmarried men and women were segregated in the Palace, she and William had spent more time together than many who had known each other for years.

Time apart might bring William to recognise a truth Anna had known when she had first set eyes on him. *We are made for each other.* If he were not angered by her attempt to force him into mar-riage, if he were not reeling from the message his father had sent him, he would surely realise this, too. *He loves me. William is an honourable man, a truthful man. He would not have made me his so beautifully unless he loved me. He needs time to realise this. If he does not see me, perhaps he might miss me. Perhaps he will come to realise that I was telling him the truth, and that I really do love him. Perhaps...*

Over a week of seclusion in Princess Theodora's apartment went by, it had been put about that she was nursing the Princess. Only she was allowed in the Princess's bedchamber. Time dragged. Day after day, Anna returned to the table and gazed at the sea and the flocks of gulls. A green scarf she was embroidering rested idle in her lap.

Anna's thoughts started veering down darker paths, they twisted and turned...

Of course, it was possible that she was mistaken, she must not be arrogant—not everyone who fell in love had their love requited. *He loves me, I know he does.*

She had put aside all thought of making William marry her purely to thwart her father. From the beginning it had been the most foolish of impulses. *I loved him from that first moment, that is why that impulse was born in me.* Sadly, Anna was coming to see that whilst she might have fallen in love with William at first sight, her feelings might not be reciprocated.

Yet.

I cannot force him. I shall give him time and then...if I make it clear I will not force him...

William had offered her friendship. He liked her. He had been the most breathtaking of lovers, not once but twice. It was not as much as she had hoped for—Anna wanted a lifetime of such loving. William was the only man she could imagine giving herself to in such a way, but she wanted him to marry her with a light heart, freely, of his own volition.

What is he doing? What if he has already returned to Apulia?

Despite William's promise to remain in the City until they knew whether she had quickened with his child, the morning came when Anna was gripped by the fear that she might never see him again.

In a rush of panic, she called for her maidservant. 'Juliana!'

'Yes, my lady?'

'I should like you to enquire what is happening at the Hall of the Nineteen Couches. Try to discover whether Sir William Bradfer is still there. Be discreet. I do not want him to know I am asking about him.'

'The Hall of the Nineteen Couches? I thought it was disused.'

'Not any longer…a party of Franks are using it to lodge in. Find out what is happening there.'

'Very good, my lady.'

With a curtsy, Juliana let herself out of the apartment.

Anna picked up the green scarf and scowled at

her clumsy stitching. *I can do better, that whole row will have to be reworked.* Sighing, she reached for the scissors.

It was painful, not seeing William. She had lost her appetite. It was hard to sleep. It was impossible to think. *Does he miss me, as I miss him?*

'My lady?'

Anna started. She had fallen into a daydream, her sewing sat untouched on the table. 'Juliana! I didn't hear you come back.'

'Sir William is still at the hall, my lady. And as you said, several other foreigners appear to be lodged there.'

'And did you…?' Anna was about to ask Juliana if she had actually seen William herself, when she felt an all-too-familiar twinge in her belly and the quiet throbbing of backache. The time of her monthly courses was upon her. She bundled the green scarf into her sewing basket and put her hand on her stomach.

No baby, there will be no baby.

'My lady? Is something wrong?'

Anna forced her lips to smile, inside, she was weeping. *No baby. I must tell him at once.*

The moment of truth was upon her. If William chose to leave, this was the moment when she must face the fact that she had lost him. 'Nothing's wrong, Juliana. It is my time again, I fear. Are the cloths in the bedchamber?'

'Yes, my lady.'

'Is it cold outside?'

'The breeze is rather brisk.'

'Please bring me my cloak, I shall be going out shortly.'

'Yes, my lady.'

'So, Sir William...' Anna concluded brightly '...there is nothing to keep you here.'

They were walking past a fountain in the Palace gardens. Anna's hand lay formally on William's arm, his head was turned politely towards hers and the guard she had remembered to bring with her waited with great tact by a latticed gate a few yards away. She had given him his document of manumission, which he had tucked off-handedly into his belt. As confirmation that he had never accepted his enslavement, the off-handed gesture was telling.

Green eyes bored into her. 'My lady, you are certain?' He lowered his voice, Anna had to strain to hear him over the sound of water hissing into the pond from the mouth of a bronze fish. 'You are certain there will be no child?'

'Quite certain. There is no need for us to marry. As of this moment, there is nothing to keep you here.'

William rested a boot on the edge of the fountain. His expression was so wooden, it was unreadable. *He is very distant. How is it that we have become strangers in only a few days? It is as though that flare of passion we shared in the Hall of the Nineteen Couches was but a dream.*

I will not beg. I have told him that I love him and I will not beg. Why does he not believe me? Wildly, Anna wondered what the difference was between insisting you loved someone long enough to make them believe you, and begging.

Surely his expression was too carefully blank to be natural? Hope flared as she waited for his response. *I know William loves me, there must be some way I can convince him that we belong together.*

She swallowed. The pity was that she had tried to force him—that had been a grave error. It was not, she prayed, an irredeemable one. *I made a mistake, but William has a generous heart. He must come to forgive me.*

Not all of her felt so confident. *William has had little experience of love in his life. He was hardened by his early years and then there was Lady*

Felisa. She is much to blame—she rejected him when he was a poor knight, now that she thinks him rich and powerful, she wants him. Lady Felisa's change of heart has soured him. It will be hard, if not impossible, to win his trust. William is not capable of love.

No, he is capable of love! Look at the way he cared for Daphne and Paula, look at his reaction when he saw Sir Bruno. Sir Bruno knows his worth—Sir Bruno would never have come all this way for a knight who cared for no one.

'My lady, are you content to marry one of your suitors?'

Bracing herself—she would *not* beg—Anna forced the lie past her teeth. 'I am content.'

'What of your revulsion for…your father's choice—I forget the name, Lord…?'

'Lord Basil.'

'I received the impression you loathed the man.'

'Your…' cheeks on fire, Anna gave him what she hoped would pass for a coquettish smile '…tuition of me was most thorough, Sir William. You have made me realise that I have nothing to fear from marriage. I confess it was the…' she leaned confidentially towards him '…physical side of marriage that concerned me, but you have allayed my fears.'

'I have?'

'Yes.' She glanced at him from under her lashes. The wooden expression had gone. If anything, he looked slightly stunned. He was also gazing at her mouth and his eyes were dark.

'You are no longer repulsed by the thought of Lord Basil?'

'Indeed, no.'

'Have you met Lord Basil yet?'

'I have not seen anyone this past week.'

'Not even your father?'

'No, much has been happening, as I am sure you are aware. The Emperor's enthronement, the coronation. My father will have been busy.'

'You did not attend the coronation yourself?' William asked.

She shook her head.

'When will you meet Lord Basil?'

'When my father arranges it.'

'Where will you meet him? Will he come to the apartment?' His voice was casual, as though he were indifferent to her response.

'Oh, no, Lord Basil will not meet me there, even though he is the Palace Chamberlain, it would be most unorthodox. The apartment is reserved for ladies of the Imperial household and their immediate family.'

He frowned. 'What about the guards?'

'Varangians are utterly trustworthy, they answer only to Commander Ashfirth and the Emperor. Those exceptions aside, only women are allowed in the apartment.'

'What about Lord Constantine?'

Anna smiled. 'If you recall, Constantine had my father's permission.'

'And what about me—why was I allowed in?'

'You were a slave, William. Slaves don't count.'

As soon as the words had left her lips, Anna wished them unsaid. *You were a slave, William. Slaves don't count.* As he recoiled, a band tightened round her heart. She closed her eyes. If she had been trying to alienate him, she could hardly have said anything worse. She had reminded him that she had bought him.

She forced herself to look at him. He was staring fixedly at the water spout, his profile so hard and unyielding, it might have been carved in stone. *All warmth has left him, it is as though my words have robbed him of his humanity.*

'William?' Anna started to reach for his arm, but remembered the watching guard and thought better of it. Her nails dug into her palms.

'My lady?' His head turned, his eyes had that glassy gleam to them. It was as though he had already returned to Apulia and was looking at her from afar.

My words did that. I hurt him.

'William, a thousand apologies, I spoke carelessly.'

He looked down at her for a long moment. 'You spoke from your heart.'

'No, no, my words were unguarded, you misunderstand…'

He folded his arms. 'Sir Bruno maintains that the truth is often to be found in unguarded words. It is rather the same when someone has drunk too much wine. *In vino veritas.*'

'That may be true, but in this case—'

He gave a swift headshake. 'You meant it. I was your slave. Likely you will think of me as such until your dying day.'

This is dreadful! Shivering, the breeze coming over the sea wall was raising goosebumps on her arms. Anna hugged her cloak to her. 'No. *No.* All my life I have seen slaves around me. But I do not think of *you* in those terms.' *I want you for my husband. I love you. But I will not beg.*

William's gaze returned to the water spraying into the pond. 'So, in sum, there is not to be a child.'

'No.'

He shoved his hand through his hair. 'I thank you for telling me so promptly.'

'I would hardly dissemble on so important a matter!'

William smiled. It might be wishful thinking on Anna's part, but the smile seemed full of regret. 'No, you would not.' Again, he raked through his hair. Rather than tidying it, he was disordering it, blond locks were lying every which way. 'Anna, I find myself in an awkward position.'

'The lady in Apulia,' she murmured.

'As you know, my father has given his blessing to my union with Lady Felisa Venafro.'

Anna's eyes stung, she jerked her head away. The bronze fish was lost behind a glitter of tears. 'I remember.' *William needs to be loved, he does not want marriage to a cold woman who has only accepted him because he has been named heir to a count... William loves me, I know it.*

Why, oh, why did I try to constrain him? A Frankish knight cannot be constrained. I must not beg. I will not beg.

William's sigh was loud enough to be heard over the hiss of the fountain. 'It seems I must honour my commitments in Apulia.' He gave her a bow that was heartbreaking in its formality. In its finality. 'My lady, since you have made it clear there is nothing to bind us, I shall book my passage home.'

Chapter Fifteen

'So,' Sir Bruno said, in a stomach-twisting echo of Anna's words, 'there is nothing to keep you here?'

Apart from William and Sir Bruno, the Hall of the Nineteen Couches was deserted. Sir Louis was out riding with Constantine, who had offered to give William's cousin and the squires a tour of the City.

'No, sir,' William said. The thought of separation from Anna, particularly permanent separation, made him ache in every fibre of his being. He loved her, but what future could he have with someone who would always think of him as the Frankish slave she had bought at the market? There was no sense in prolonging the agony, and leaving Anna in Constantinople when he left to meet his father was, William was rapidly learning, a particularly excruciating form of agony.

I love her. He was no longer in any doubt of that, but she had said, with devastating plainness, 'there is nothing to keep you here'. She had reminded him he was once her slave. If there had been a child, he would have insisted on marriage, he would have refused an annulment. *She thinks of me as a slave.*

'There is nothing to keep me here,' he said.

Sir Bruno lifted a grizzled eyebrow. 'You certain of that, boy?'

'Quite certain.'

'Very well. When Louis gets back, the pair of you can get down to the docks by the Gate of the Drungarii, there should be time before dark. I am sure Lord Constantine will loan you a horse.'

'Good idea, I shall do just that.'

'A ride might clear away the cobwebs, boy.'

William grimaced. Sir Bruno was right on target, his head did need clearing. He couldn't shake the memory of Anna telling him that she was ready to accept her father's choice. Furthermore she—he ground his teeth together—she had actually had the gall to offer him thanks for relieving her of her concerns about the physical aspects of marriage.

'There are plenty of merchantmen in the docks along the Golden Horn,' Sir Bruno added, watching him speculatively. 'You should be able to find one willing to give us passage home.'

William grunted and turned away. He picked up the costly pattern-welded sword he had bought from an armourer in the City and was testing the edge of the blade when Sir Bruno spoke again.

'Pretty girl, Lady Anna, it's a wonder she's not wed. Become a good friend, has she, boy?'

William lifted his gaze from the shining blade of his sword. 'Sir?'

'Couldn't help but notice the way she watches you. Seemed very affected by the news that your father is to recognise you.'

'Lady Anna is a good friend.'

'It will be hard to bid her farewell, I expect.'

'Drop it, Bruno.' William spoke so curtly that his former mentor fell silent, leaving him to think in peace.

Lord Isaac fixed his daughter with a look. 'Anna, you will be pleased to hear that I have arranged for formal introductions to take place here the day after tomorrow. It is a great honour that Lord Basil has arranged to meet you in this room.'

Anna's father had brought her to one of the Emperor's minor reception chambers on the ground floor of the Boukoleon. She had never been allowed in before. Although her father referred to it as a minor reception chamber, it was almost as large as the whole of the Princess's apartment. The walls were encrusted with gold mosaic, the Imperial standard hung like a canopy behind a couch that was gilded and upholstered in purple velvet.

Anna scowled at the double-headed eagle on the Imperial standard. *A great honour? There must be some way of getting out of this. I cannot do this! If I cannot marry William, I will not marry anyone.*

'The day after tomorrow? I am to meet Lord Basil so soon?'

'Of course.' Her father nodded. 'There is no reason for further delay. With the enthronement and coronation behind us, and the Empire safely in the hands of the Komneni, Lord Basil has time to see you. He is eager to do so. Now, when you enter— do remember to wear your most formal gown and the most modest of veils—Lord Basil will be standing here, in front of the throne. Doubtless, he will have his attendants with him. Make sure you greet him with humility. Lord Basil expects—'

Anna took a deep breath. 'Father, before you continue, there is something important I must tell you.'

Lord Isaac took her hand, shaking his head. 'Anna, I know what you are going to say, and I am sorry, but—'

'You know? How can you possibly—?'

'You favour Lord Constantine and have done since your return home.' Her father's expression softened. 'I am sorry, Anna, but Constantine is not acceptable. Lord Basil will be your husband.'

'No, Father, he will not.'

Lord Isaac flinched and drew himself to his full height. 'Anna, it is Lord Basil or it is no one.'

He wasn't listening! It was as though her father was playing the part of kindly father when in truth he wasn't really listening at all. Taking another deep breath, Anna tried again. 'Father, I regret this deeply, but I cannot and will not marry Lord Basil.'

'Yes, yes, I see you are upset. I am sorry about Constantine, indeed I am. My dear, you must understand how much better it would be if the family had close ties to someone with the ear of the Emperor.'

'Father—' Anna held his gaze and made her voice hard '—I will *not* marry Lord Basil! I will not come here to meet him the day after tomorrow, and if you try to force me, I shall not hesitate to embarrass you. Publicly.'

Lord Isaac shifted back, mouth slightly open. At last it appeared he had heard her.

'You would humiliate me in public? *Again?*'

He narrowed his gaze. His fists were clenched, his beard quivered. Anna knew the signs, he was working himself into a frenzy. 'I can't believe you would do this again! Running off to Rascia was bad enough, but now…if you knew the trouble I had gone to to arrange such a prestigious marriage for you.'

'Father, you might have asked me first. You did say you would give me a choice.'

'You ungrateful girl, God knows why I was cursed with such a daughter. After all the effort that has gone into making this alliance!' Abruptly, her father's shoulders seemed to slump, a wheedling tone entered his voice. 'You cannot mean this, you will meet Lord Basil.'

'I will not. Furthermore, Father, I also have to tell you that I do not want Constantine either—we are simply friends as we have always been.' Her throat was dry, she swallowed hard. 'Lord Michael is also unsuitable. I will marry a man of my choosing or I will remain unwed.'

Her father looked at her as though she, like the double-headed eagle on the Imperial standard, had grown an extra head.

'Lord Basil is a kind man, Anna,' he said. 'I know you are nervous, he has been married before, but there is no need for you to worry. I am sure he will learn to love you.'

'It is not enough, Father, I will not marry Lord Basil. It is not enough to be kind, and love…' her voice cracked on a blinding flash of insight '…love must be freely given, it cannot be commanded. I refuse to marry Lord Basil.'

Her father tugged at his beard. 'That is your final word on the matter?'

'Yes, Father, it is.'

'Very well. You drive me to take other measures.' His hand fell from his beard. 'Since you will not obey your father, you will be leaving the Palace. You have until tomorrow morning to pack your belongings.'

Anna's stomach lurched. 'You are sending me away?'

'A retreat, yes, that is what I shall say. You, my dear daughter, are going into retreat. Bishop Maurice is an old friend, he will be delighted to take you under his wing until you come to your senses.'

For a moment it seemed as if the golden room was swirling around her, dazzling in its opulence. Dizzying. Finally Anna found her voice. 'But, Father, what about my duty to the Princess?'

How am I to pretend to be nursing the Princess, if I am sent away?

Her father's face was dark, he was weaving his fingers into his beard. 'Your first duty is to me, girl. The Princess has had you to herself for two years, she will understand you need time near your family. A retreat at Saint Michael's in Heraklea will refresh you. Bishop Maurice will remind you of the importance of doing your duty, and you will emerge a new woman. Be ready at daybreak. And, Anna…'

'Father?'

'Do not be alarmed if you notice extra guards have been posted to Princess Theodora's apartment—they will be there to protect you.' Lord Isaac turned on his heel, and a heartbeat later, Anna heard him outside. 'Sergeant!'

'Lord Isaac?'

'When my daughter comes out, be so good as to see her safely back to the Princess's chambers. She has announced her intention of going on a silent retreat and will speak to no one. Understand?'

'Yes, sir.'

Anna stood amid the glories of the Emperor's throne room, dazed by her father's pronouncement. He was making a prisoner of her, he thought by doing so he could bend her to his will, he thought he could break her. If he had stayed a moment longer, she could have told him that he would only succeed in alienating her, some things could not be forced.

Her eyes misted and the room became a blur of gold. She had not been able to force William to love her, no more would her father force her into obedience.

It was the sound of the hall door being flung back on its hinges that woke him. Groping for his sword, Willliam pushed aside the sheet that held Anna's scent and sat up. A light flared in the dark, falling on a face he knew.

'Constantine! It's past midnight—what brings you here at this hour?'

'Anna,' Constantine said, coming to perch on the edge of the couch. 'I came as soon as I knew.'

William went cold. 'She is in trouble?'

'Yes.'

'What's happened? She's not hurt?' William should not care. Anna had told him she was content to marry Lord Basil, and William was leaving the City in a couple of days. He was meant to be going home to renew his acquaintance with the woman his father had approved as his wife. Despite this, he had been toying with the idea of asking to see Anna. Just once more. As an excuse, he had being going to say that now he had his father's purse he was in a position to repay her. At the very least he owed her a bracelet. 'Constantine, *what's happened*?'

'Anna is leaving the City in the morning.'

'What!' William swung his legs off the couch. 'I have to see her.'

'You can't. Her father forbids it—she is not allowed to see or speak to anyone. I only found out because Juliana managed to get word out. Lord Isaac has Anna sealed up in that apartment as though it were her tomb.'

'*Mon Dieu.* Why is her father doing this?' William ran his hand round the back of his neck. 'Do you know?'

'Anna has refused to marry Lord Basil. She is to stay in retreat until she comes round to her father's way of thinking.'

'She told me she was ready to accept Lord Basil,' William said, slowly.

Constantine lifted a brow. 'And you believed her?'

'Fool that I am, I did.' Swearing, William reached for his tunic. 'Something she said had angered me, I was blind to anything else. Where is she being sent, do you know?'

'To the Bishop in Heraklea—he's a friend of Lord Isaac's. Poor Anna, they won't let her out until she agrees.' Constantine smothered a yawn. 'Anyhow, thought you would want to know. Her ship leaves shortly after dawn.'

'My thanks, Constantine.' William dragged his tunic over his head and watched Constantine give another yawn. 'Come on, Constantine, you can't fall asleep, there's too much to do. You can start by waking the others.'

Constantine gave him an ironic salute. 'Yes, *sir*!'

The sun was lighting the eastern sky as Lady Anna of Heraklea boarded the vessel her father had booked for her. She took but one maidservant with her, as befitted a lady about to go into a serious retreat. Her ship was a merchantman that had been moored in the docks along the Golden Horn, it was bound for Venice with a cargo of priceless silks. After some hasty negotiations with Lord Isaac, the captain had agreed to stop off at the port of Heraklea. Lady Anna and her maidservant would disembark there, as would the handful of foot soldiers Lord Isaac had so thoughtfully provided for his daughter's protection.

Anna stood alone at the handrail as the ship nosed down the Golden Horn. The wind was pulling her veil, the smell of brine was sharp in her nostrils. Her heart was so full of pain, she thought it must burst. She had hoped that the message she had sent out via Juliana might have reached William, that he might realise how much she regretted trying to force him into marriage, that he might...well, she would never have expected rescue, but she would have liked to bid him farewell.

Obviously, it was too late for that. *I will never see him again.*

The sun rose higher, a dazzling ball of fire. The City walls glided by, strong and solid. They were sailing so close to them, Anna could see the red lines of brick that ran like veins through the stonework. Soldiers were stationed on every tower and turret. Soon, they would round the point and enter the Bosphoros and shortly after that, they would reach the Sea of Marmara. Soon, she would get her last glimpse of the Great Palace.

What is he doing? Will he marry this Lady Felisa? Will he do so willingly, or simply to please his father?

Her nerves were raw with misery. *Sir William Bradfer will do as he chooses. It is not my concern. I should be planning my future, not thinking about him. I should be pondering whether it will be possible to win my father round. I cannot marry Lord Basil!*

It was irritating the way her mind kept coming back to William when she should be thinking of other things, such as how she would pass the time on her enforced retreat. She was like a woman bewitched and had been since the moment she had seen him.

I can't get him out of my mind. Sweet Virgin, am I going to feel this way for ever?

The sunrise had gilded the sea ahead of their ship, the far horizon was a swirl of pink and gold, as bright as the mosaics in the Emperor's throne room. Anna was so intent on the sunrise and her thoughts, that she did not notice the other ship edge into the Golden Horn.

This second ship had been moored in one of the wharves reserved for Varangian vessels. It was a warship. The row of painted shields mounted along the guardrail were immediately recognisable as Varangian—a black wolf snarled on one, a green serpent writhed on another. There was a dragon, an eagle, a white bull...

The crew leaned on their oars and the warship entered the main channel, following the path of the trader.

Given that the second ship was a Varangian warship, it carried a strange cargo. The man standing in the prow with his hand on his sword hilt was no Varangian, he was Sir William Bradfer, heir of Count Jean La Roche-Guyon. The wind ruffled his blond hair.

A party of Frankish knights had boarded with Sir William, they had squires and horses with them. The horses were tethered in a makeshift stall by the mast, with the squires close by, lest the horses need soothing.

William kept his eyes pinned on the trader ahead. Timbers creaked as the warship's hull flexed and settled into the current. Anna had told him that she was content to marry Lord Basil and now, now that her lie was revealed, he could not abandon her. The thought of Anna being immured until she gave in to her father was appalling.

As the walls of Constantinople slid past, William thought he recognised the small harbour they were passing. He couldn't see the Boukoleon, but perhaps the angle was not right…there were two towers…

He gestured at a sailor. 'Is that the Imperial harbour?'

'No, sir. That's the Gate of the Forerunner. You

won't see the Palace until we are further out. We
haven't got past the chain yet.'

'The chain?'

Sir Bruno came to stand at this elbow, his cloak
snapped in the breeze. 'The chain is part of the
City's defences. See the watch points built into the
fortifications on either side of the estuary?'

William looked, but he was only half-listen-
ing. Anxiety curled inside him. Thank God
for Constantine, he thought. It was doubtful he
could have enlisted the Varangians without him.
Constantine was surely the only man in the Palace
to know that not all of the Guard had pledged their
oath to Emperor Alexios and were thus free to take
other commissions. For a fee, naturally. Men who
had been in the Guard did not come cheap. They
were efficient though, damned efficient, once they
realised he was serious about hiring them.

Nevertheless, it would be a close race—the
trader ahead was making a fair speed. If it came
to a chase, would they be outrun?

'There is a massive chain that reaches from one
side to the other,' Sir Bruno was saying. 'It is raised
when there is a need to stop vessels entering or
leaving the ports in the Golden Horn.'

William stared with renewed interest at the fortifications on either side of the water. 'A chain that

stretches across the Golden Horn? I heard a tale about a chain being used to try to stop a Norse king from leaving the City. Thought it was just a myth.'

A gull hurtled past them. Sir Bruno grunted. 'It was no myth, the Norse king's name was Harald. He got away, but the chain broke the back of one of his ships.'

William studied the great towers. 'They must have powerful winches.'

'And a pretty large chain.' Sir Bruno grinned.

For a moment, William grinned back. Then his grin faded whilst what Sir Bruno had told him about the chain sank in. They didn't have much time. The trader would shortly be entering the Bosphoros, when they reached the main channel, boarding would become tricky. He didn't want anyone killed.

He gave the two towers another careful look and touched Sir Bruno's arm. 'Sir, about that chain? Do you reckon the men in those towers would see if we signalled them?'

Sir Bruno leaned on the guardrail. 'Bound to.' He paused. 'They will use flags, I expect.'

'Very well,' William said, smiling. *'Captain!'*
'Sir?'

'Signal the towers, if you please, I should like the chain raised.'

The captain opened his mouth to protest, but William fixed him with a look and he shut it again. The order was given and moments later several flags raced up a halliard.

A movement in the mouth of the Golden Horn caught Anna's eye, the sun appeared to be bouncing off a silvery line that lay on the water directly in front of the ship. She gestured for her maid. 'Juliana, come here a moment.'

'My lady?'

Anna pointed. 'What's that?'

'Holy Mother, it's the chain! My lady, they are raising the chain!'

The lookout yelled. Sailors hurtled across the deck. Ropes were hauled, the steersman put the tiller hard over, the oars were raised. Slowly, the ship began to turn.

Anna focused on the thread of light—it stretched right across the mouth of the estuary. The chain had indeed been raised, thousands of water droplets were sparkling as they fell back into the river. Their ship was the only vessel on this section of the waterway—someone had decreed it would not be permitted to leave.

The lookout let out another cry, he was pointing frantically upriver. Anna's pulse quickened.

Juliana glanced back at the docks and clutched Anna's arm. 'Someone of importance is determined to hold us. Look, my lady, a Varangian galley is on its way.'

'A Varangian galley?' With hope and despair battling it out inside her, Anna turned to see. Juliana was right, a few hundred yards away, a Varangian warship was indeed bearing down on them. Anna could see the row of shields, she could see the crew, rowing towards them as though their lives depended on it. Water dripped from the blades of their oars.

'Sweet Mother, they are coming right at us!' She gripped the guard-rail.

The trader heeled sharply to one side as it tried to evade the warship. Ropes groaned, men swore.

'No chance,' Juliana muttered. 'The channel is too narrow. My lady, with the chain blocking our way, and the warship bearing down on us, we are not going anywhere.'

'The Varangians are not wearing mail,' Anna observed, thoughtfully. 'I can see battleaxes, but where are their helmets?'

William, I can see William! The warship was almost on them, water frothed at its prow, its oars were raised…and there was William standing by the prow. She forgot to breathe. *William!*

Ropes snaked into the air, men strained at the helm. The captain of the trader ran this way and that, his words snatched away by the wind.

'They intend to board, my lady.'

'So I see,' Anna said, feeling a smile creep over her face. *He came! William came!* She watched the warship draw steadily closer, grappling hooks appeared, shields were whipped out of the way. They were determined to board.

William searched the deck of the merchantman. *Where is she?*

A drift of blue flickered at the edge of his vision. *There!* She was standing by the handrail, veil rippling out like a banner. Once he had seen her, he could see nothing else. Blindly, he fumbled for Bruno's sword arm. 'There's no need for violence when we board, but I shall not go on to Apulia without her.'

'Of course not.'

For a moment William was rooted to the deck, unable to take his eyes off her. What a mystery life was. *I love that woman. She saw me chained like a dog at the market and she bought me, yet I love her.*

Bruno inhaled sharply. 'We shall have to be

wary, though. It looks as though her father has sent his guards. Look, boy, they have her surrounded.'

'We outnumber them,' William said.

The Varangian galley drew alongside the trader. Their ship shuddered as two sets of timbers met and grappling hooks flew over the side. The warship's captain shouted, the captain of the merchantman shouted back, and for a few minutes there was a chaos of bellowing and confusion. Finally, the ships were secured so tightly there was not an inch between them.

Anna filled his vision. Moments later, a party of erstwhile Varangians had boarded the trading ship. William was quick to follow.

It was soon over. A swift exchange of words took place between the former Varangians and Isaac of Heraklea's guards, and Lord Isaac's men set down their arms.

And then Anna was standing before him. Her cheeks were aglow, dark tendrils of hair had been teased from her veil by the wind. With rare tact, Sir Bruno effaced himself.

'Lady Anna.' William bowed, they were alone by the guard-rail.

'You got my message,' Anna said, smiling up at him.

He caught her hands in his. 'A little late, perhaps.' He grimaced. 'I should have realised earlier. Anna, my apologies, but I have to know, is it true you have refused Lord Basil?'

'I have refused all my suitors.'

William tightened his grip on her. 'You told me you were going to accept him. May I know why you changed your mind?'

Anna tipped her head on one side, she knew she was flushing. 'I...I thought I could marry Lord Basil, but when it came to it I found I could not.'

'Why?'

Anna swallowed. 'I told you the reason before, but you would not listen. William, I love you. I could not marry anyone else.'

Green eyes looked steadily at her, warm hands went to her waist and pulled her close. 'Anna, you can't let your father immure you in some convent. Come back to Apulia with me. Meet my father.'

She gave him a hesitant smile and bit her lip, a small nervous gesture that made William's gaze drop to her mouth.

He grinned. 'What do you suppose they will do if I kiss you?'

She gave a startled frown. 'Who?'

He waved at the Varangians and the two sets of crew. With a lurch, Anna realised their every move was being watched. 'You are going to kiss me?'

'Perhaps.' Leaning on the guard-rail, twining his fingers with hers, he stared at the City walls and the church dome behind it. 'Anna, I will not let your father bully you. Come back with me.'

'Are you sure?'

'Anna, I want you, I want no one else.'

Anna, I want you. As a declaration of love, it was less than she longed for, nor had he mentioned marriage, but she could not blame him. She had some apologising to do.

'William, I want to say how sorry I am. Love is a gift, it cannot be commanded. I should never have attempted to constrain you.'

'That no longer matters.'

'It *does* matter! Hear me out. After we left the Basilica Cistern I truly did intend to free you. But then I realised that my father was not going to give me my choice. By then I had come to know you and to l-like you.' She gave him one of her slanting glances. 'I thought that you liked me, too.'

'I did like you,' William said. 'I do.'

'Well, after I met Lord Michael, and you started teasing me about courting techniques, I thought you might like me a little.' Her lips curved. 'I certainly hoped so. I didn't think you would mind a… temporary contract with me as long as it meant you would have your freedom at the end of it.'

'I do mind.'

She looked swiftly away. Out at sea, a porpoise was diving in and out of the waves. 'I am sorry.'

William gripped her hand. 'I don't want a temporary contract, Anna, I want a permanent one. Marry me.'

Anna felt as though the wind had snatched the breath from her lungs. William was such a tease, but this time he did not look as though he was teasing—those green eyes were serious.

'Marry you?' His grip on her was unyielding, he was crushing her fingers to the bone.

He nodded as his throat worked. And then a large arm was heavy about her shoulders. He turned her gently so they were no longer facing the men. Anna saw the porpoise again, it looked as though it was dancing. '*Chérie*, I would be honoured if you would marry me.'

Her pulse began to race. 'Your father wants you to marry Lady Felisa.'

'When my father meets me, he will have to learn that there are some matters I must decide for myself.'

'William…' Anna reached for his shoulders, hope blooming inside '…I have no lands.'

'I do not care. Marry me, Anna. As I said, I want no one else.'

'Why? Why marry a woman with no lands when you might have an heiress?' Anna scarcely dared breathe. *I told him I loved him and he did not respond. Is he ready to respond now?*

He grinned. 'Because I ruined her and no one else would have her?'

Shaking her head, Anna curled her fingers into the fabric of his tunic. 'Why? Why marry a woman who has no lands?'

He tipped his head to one side, hair tousled by the wind. 'Because…she is lady-in-waiting to a princess?'

Anna shook her head. 'That is not a good enough reason.'

'Because…she is the most beautiful woman in the Empire? Lord, woman, what do you want me to say?'

Anna smiled. He loved her, it was there in the softness of his gaze. 'William, what does *chérie* mean?'

'*Mon Dieu*, you want blood, don't you?' When she nodded, a faint flush ran over his cheekbones. Putting his lips to her ear, he said softly, '*Chérie* is a barbaric Frankish word, you don't need to know its meaning.'

'*William…!*'

'It means, "beloved", "dear one". It means I am

for ever enslaved. Of course I love you, Anna of Heraklea. There is no other reason on earth that could induce me to marry a woman who bought me so that I might give her tuition in courting. I love you.' He pulled back and smiled deep into her eyes. 'Well? Will you have me, *chérie*?'

Anna reached up, pulled that fair head down and gave her acceptance in the form of a kiss, a long and greedy kiss.

A ragged cheer went up, a series of catcalls followed. Anna's cheeks burned, her stomach swooped and she wished, for a moment, that they were on their own in the derelict hall in the Palace, and the Imperial couch was at their disposal. After an ear-splitting whistle from one of the sailors, and a lewd comment that was intriguingly inventive, she tore her lips from his.

'You will tell me your secrets,' he murmured.

'Will I?'

'Yes, every last one. I want to hear most particularly about Commander Ashfirth and Princess Theodora.'

'Commander Ashfirth barely knows the Princess,' Anna murmured, playing with his fingers.

'How can that be possible when she hid herself away in his house in the City?' He frowned.

'Although lately I heard she had taken sick and had returned to the Palace.'

Anna's lips curved. She was going to enjoy telling William the full story, but now was not the time. 'The Princess never went to Commander Ashfirth's house. My friend Katerina, however, did.'

His frown deepened. 'Katerina?' His gaze was penetrating. '*Mon Dieu*, Anna, don't tell me your friend has been impersonating the Princess?'

Anna nodded.

'And you have been colluding with her?'

Anna nodded. 'We have been acting on Princess Theodora's orders.'

'*Chérie*, that sounds like a very dangerous game.'

She looked out over the waves and shrugged. The porpoise had vanished.

'Anna, where is she now?'

'Katerina? She's with the Commander.'

He was shaking his head. 'No, no, I meant the Princess—where is the Princess?'

'I wish I knew—she must be somewhere en route from Dyrrachion. But as far as the Palace knows, she is recovering from a brief illness in her chambers.'

'What will happen now you are no longer at the Palace to back up this tale?'

'I asked Kari—the young Varangian guard—to let Commander Ashfirth know that my father was sending me away. The Commander will ensure that the Varangian Guard cover up the Princess's absence until she returns.'

William let out a slow whistle. 'A dangerous game, indeed. Well, that settles it, I cannot possibly let you go back to all that. You will come with me to Apulia,' he said, taking her face in his hands.

'Will I?'

'You will. My father must meet my bride.'

'Your father…' Her smile faded.

'What is it?'

'I was thinking about *my* father.'

'Undoubtedly he will be angry—'

'Angry?' Anna bit her lip. 'He will be beside himself with rage!'

'My hope is that when we return—'

'We will return?'

'Of course. I have relations here, relations I should like to meet, but my father must come first. By the time we return to Constantinople as man and wife, Princess Theodora will have returned and your involvement in this deception will have become irrelevant. I am also hopeful that your father will be mollified by the thought that his daughter may one day be a countess.' Reaching up, he captured a windblown twist of hair, winding it slowly round his finger before releasing it to the wind again.

'A barbarian countess...heavens!'

He laughed. 'A Frankish countess.' He took her shoulders in a firm grip. 'Anna, I shall not let you go.'

Sliding her hand round his neck, she gave him quick nod and brought his lips to hers. 'When do we leave?'

William gestured at the warship. 'Today. I have hired these men and their galley is at our disposal. If my lady is agreeable, of course.'

'Today?' She looked across at the warship with a frown. 'Where will we sleep? It doesn't look as though there's any shelter below that deck.'

William shrugged. 'I hadn't thought that far, I expect something can be arranged.'

'When I sailed from Dyrrachion, Commander Ashfirth put a pavilion up on deck. I rather liked the pavilion.'

'A pavilion, eh?' William pulled her to him and pressed a warm kiss on her neck. 'Do we need a pavilion, *chérie*?'

'I was thinking...' cheeks warming, Anna stared at the pulse in William's throat '...that since the voyage to Apulia could take several weeks, you might be able to teach me more of your barbarian courting practices.'

Their lips met in a passionate kiss, eliciting more raucous cheering from the sailors. Only this time, neither of them noticed…

* * * * *